# The Magician

# Magician

## a novel by SOL STEIN

AN AUTHORS GUILD BACKINPRINT.COM EDITION

*The Magician*

AN AUTHORS GUILD BACKINPRINT.COM EDITION

Published by iUniverse.com, Inc.

For information address:
iUniverse.com, Inc.
620 North 48th Street, Suite 201
Lincoln, NE 68504-3467
www.iuniverse.com

Originally published by Delacorte Press

ISBN: 0-595-09316-7

Printed in the United States of America

## Acknowledgments

I am grateful to Renni Browne, Patricia Day, and the Hon. Charles L. Brieant, Chief Judge of the Southern District of New York, for reading the manuscript of this book and making literally hundreds of useful suggestions. I am also indebted for valuable help to Judge Harold Dittelman, Sandford Astarita, my editors Manon Tingue and Ross Claiborne, and Peter Van Ness, Kevin and Jeffrey Stein, and Leslie A. Fiedler, a friend whose trial gave me firsthand evidence of the disparity between the practice of law and the administration of justice.

NOVELS by Sol Stein

*The Husband*
*The Magician*
*Living Room*
*The Childkeeper*
*Other People*
*The Resort*
*The Touch of Treason*
*A Deniable Man*
*The Best Revenge*

PLAYS

*Napoleon (The Illegitimist)*
(New York and California, 1953)

*A Shadow of My Enemy*
(Broadway, 1957)

For Henry Schwarzschild

*inimicus curiae*

*That man is an aggressive creature will hardly be disputed. With the exception of certain rodents, no other vertebrate habitually destroys members of his own species. No other animal takes positive pleasure in the exercise of cruelty upon another of his own kind. We generally describe the most repulsive examples of man's cruelty as brutal or bestial, implying by these adjectives that such behavior is characteristic of less highly developed animals than ourselves. In truth, however, the extremes of "brutal" behaviour are confined to man; and there is no parallel in nature to our savage treatment of each other. The sombre fact is that we are the cruellest and most ruthless species that has ever walked the earth; and that, although we may recoil in horror when we read in newspaper or history book of the atrocities committed by man upon man, we know in our hearts that each one of us harbours within himself those same savage impulses which lead to murder, to torture and to war.*

—ANTHONY STORR,
*Human Aggression*

*There is no crime of which I do not deem myself capable.*

—GOETHE

The characters and situations in this work are wholly fictional and imaginary, and do not portray and are not intended to portray any actual persons or parties.

—FRANZ KAFKA,
*The Trial*

# You Are Reading a Banned Book
## Foreword to the Twentieth Anniversary Edition

I became a novelist by accident. Over the years, I'd written plays, essays, poetry, reviews, but not fiction. In the late 60s, a play of mine called "Of Love or Marriage" was performed at the Actors Studio in New York, with Darren McGavin in the lead, and was then licensed by Bernard Delfont (later Lord Delfont) for production in London. Peter Coe was signed to direct and Kenneth More was to play the lead.

Play production, like the film business, is fraught with uncertainty. (During an earlier production of another play, I was warned that neither the director nor I should stand close to an open window.) In London, a squabble between producer, director, and star turned into a melee, while the production hung from the rafters, unnoticed and soon quite dead. The book publishing world I inhabited then was a quieter place. I retreated to my study and in seventeen nonstop days rewrote the play as a novel. Not knowing whether this first attempt at fiction was worth a farthing, I arranged to have the manuscript sent to six publishers without revealing the author's name. To my astonishment, five of the six were interested in publishing it, and one particularly perceptive editor, Marc

Jaffe, guessed that I was the author because a character in the book loved L.P. Hartley's *The Go-Between* and he knew I did.

The book, now entitled *The Husband*, was published by Coward-McCann in 1969 and by Pocket Books the following year. I found the world of fiction hospitable.

Roger Stevens, a brave man who had lost a bundle on a play of mine, entreated me to return to the theater. I didn't for two reasons. First, Broadway had begun a long period of avoiding new plays in favor of musicals and revivals. The odds against having a new drama produced successfully seemed as great as winning at Lotto seems today. Second, putting on a play is a communal enterprise involving an impromptu family of actors, director, producer, and investors, with all of a family's tensions elevated to a pitch because of the billowing sums at stake.

I had tasted the solitary regimen of a novelist, who is his own cast and director, and I relished being solely responsible for whatever merits and flaws the final work might have. Moreover, a playwright then had a decisive audience of six on Broadway, the newspaper critics. In truth, the audience was really one, for if *The New York Times*'s critic didn't bless a production, it could easily vanish forever before the next Sunday. A book, I had learned, has many critics and audiences, and is less dependent for life on the predisposition or gastronomy of one man sitting in an aisle seat on a particularly tense night. And so I opted for "deserting" (Roger Stevens's word) the theater in order to write what I thought of as a real novel—that is, a work conceived as a novel from the beginning, and written not in seventeen days of anger but taking whatever time it needed for completion. That book was *The Magician*.

Delacorte published *The Magician* in 1971. It was selected by the Book-of-the-Month Club and published in many countries. Though the central character of the book is George Thomassy, a lawyer who has persisted through four of my novels, the action centers on a group of teenagers involved in an extortion racket that in one form or another seems to be universal in high schools. As evidence I cite an incident on the David Frost Show when I was promoting the book. Early in the interview, I turned to the studio audience—mainly visitors to New York who had come from all over the country—and asked whether any knew of a high school extortion racket in their home community. The camera swung to catch an army of raised hands.

The film rights were sold to Twentieth Century Fox. Imagine my happiness! Frank McCarthy, who had just produced *Patton*, assigned to produce *The Magician*, proclaiming it was the best novel he had read in the six years he'd been working on *Patton*. McCarthy journeyed to my home in Scarborough, just north of New York City, to discuss the script, which, as a former playwright, I was eager to do.

However, within weeks, the management of Twentieth Century Fox changed and, as is not unusual in Hollywood, the new regime decided to shelve every project initiated by the previous management. Though the script was later characterized by a writer for the American Film Institute's magazine as "one of the great unproduced screenplays of all time," Fox refused to let others produce the movie, which, as an accountant's asset, was left to atrophy.

Life abounds with countervailing forces. Dell's paperback edition of *The Magician* was being adopted in high schools from Phoenix to Poughkeepsie, often, I was told, in place of *The Catcher in the Rye*. Apparently teenagers were taking to *The Magician* because it seemed to reflect their life as it was rather than the way it was perceived by most adults. Sales mounted and eventually passed the million-copy milestone.

However—it is the "howevers" that tangle our feet wherever we go—in 1981 *The Magician* suffered a midlife crisis when the School Board in Montello, Wisconsin, banned three books: Scott Fitzgerald's *The Great Gatsby*, *The Diary of Anne Frank*, and *The Magician*. It was mind-rattling to imagine what the three books might have in common, but as the only author of the three still alive, I decided to do something about the ban.

I persuaded the powers at Dell to join me in a proposal to the citizens of Montello. We offered a free copy of *The Magician* to every head of household in the school district so that each could judge whether the School Board had made the right decision in banning the book. The offer made headlines in Wisconsin, of course, and reverberated in the news elsewhere. I was informed that people in Wisconsin were driving as far as three hundred miles to try to get a copy of the banned book because, to the dismay of the book banners, it had sold out everywhere within reach.

I received some nine hundred letters from people in the school district, almost all opposed to the idea of having the youngsters' reading censored. According to a large number of the letters I received from the parents of teenagers, the teacher who put *The Magician* on the reading list had in the previous generation been their teacher, a remarkable woman who had imbued these parents with an appreciation of literature. In their letters, the parents said they wanted their children to have the same advantage, and if that particular teacher picked *The Magician*, they didn't want anyone else dictating what their older teenagers could or could not read.

The American Library Association's *Newsletter on Intellectual Freedom*[1] reported both the reason for the banning and the outcome:

> After a lengthy debate marked by shouting, catcalls and Bible-reading from members of the audience, the Montello School Board voted 6–1 February 9 not to remove *The Magician*, a novel by Sol Stein, from the high school curriculum. Several parents had objected to the book on the grounds that it contains explicit sexual scenes and profanity, and that it allegedly presents a pessimistic view of the U.S. judicial system.

Before one leaps to the pleasure of vindication and the defeat of censorship, hear this: The *Newsletter on Intellectual*

---

1. May, 1981, Volume 30, No. 3, p. 73.

*Freedom* reported that Montello's School District Administrator told the seventeen and eighteen-year-old students they had to have their parents' permission in writing to take the dangerous "English novels" class in which *The Magician* was being taught! And, the report stated, exactly one week after the decision to reinstate *The Magician,* a group of "Concerned Citizens" removed thirty-three "objectionable" books from Montello school libraries and declared their intention not to return them. If you can't ban books, steal them.

I later learned that the one member of the School Board who voted against restoring *The Magician* to the curriculum was the only member not re-elected. I was tempted, echoing E. M. Forster, to give two cheers for democracy.

*The Magician* thrived as a Dell paperback for fourteen years. In 1985 I reacquired the rights and licensed them to Stein and Day, the publishing company I headed for a quarter of a century. Sales of the reissue surged (as many as a hundred thousand at a time were printed), but within two years, I discovered that in a democracy there are ways other than censorship and stealing to remove books from public view. In my book *A Feast for Lawyers*[1] I described how *The Magician* was one of some twelve hundred books whose continued publication was stopped by two descendants of Gutenberg and Caxton, R. R. Donnelley, the largest printer in the United States, and BookCrafters, U.S.A., whose actions, detailed in *A Feast for Lawyers,* hurt some seven hundred authors who did no wrong. Once the mercenaries of our society—the hired guns of the law—took over, Stein and Day was never permitted to publish another book. Fewer than a dozen books escaped the judicial net woven around the company. Judge Howard Schwartzberg sentenced nearly thirteen hundred books—the backlist and the ones about to be published—to a deep freeze from which some never emerged alive. In effect, the inept judicial system bears a major part of the blame for causing what may have been the biggest long-term suppression of books in the history of the United States.

---

1. Published by M. Evans, distributed by Little Brown, 1989.

One result of the new interdiction was that for the first time in its then sixteen-year history *The Magician* could not be reprinted or sold on pain of imprisonment. The demand continued, even in the form of large, prepaid orders from school wholesalers. But the aberrant legal system was adamant: Reprint *The Magician*, it said, and you are committing a criminal act. And so schools throughout the country, not just an isolated school district in Wisconsin, were compelled to remove *The Magician* from their curricula because copies were unavailable at any price. Apparently my view of the U.S. judicial system twenty years ago was not pessimistic enough.

In any event, like a cat with multiple lives, here is the twice-embattled book once again.

Sol Stein
Scarborough, New York
December, 1990

# The Magician

# Chapter 1

IT HAD BEEN SNOWING OFF and on since Christmas. For nearly a month now, while the men of the town were at work, boys would come out in twos or threes with shovels to clear a pathway on their neighbors' sidewalks. An occasional older man, impoverished or proud, could be seen daring death with a shovel in hand, clearing steps so that one could get in and out of the house, or using a small snowblower on a driveway in the hope of getting his wife to the supermarket and back before the next snow fell.

At night mostly, when the traffic had thinned, the town's orange snowplows would come scraping down the roads, their headlamps casting funnels of still-falling snow. Alongside these thoroughfares, the snow lay in hillocks, some ten or fifteen feet high, thawing a bit each day in bright sun, then refreezing, forming the crust on which it would soon snow again. It seemed impossible that spring might come, and that these humped gray masses would eventually vanish as water into the heel-hard ground.

Of course, it was beautiful to those who looked up at the huge evergreens dusted with snow, and above them the bare

webs of leafless silver maples reflecting sunlight. In the
fields at the outskirts of town, one could see, after twenty-
nine days of snow, half-mile stretches of the untrampled
season's glory.

Young children enjoyed the marvelous fluff to tramp in or
throw, but to their elders in the village of Ossining, the
snow was nature's trick, daily defeating the salt spreaders,
snowplows, calcium chloride, studded tires, and the hopeless attempts to get rid of the garbage stuffed into cans
outside the back door. The food scraps and containers
crammed into huge plastic bags and other makeshifts alongside the overstuffed cans testified that through a month of
relentless snowfall, human consumption continued day after
day.

Unlike the neighboring village of Briarcliff Manor, which
was almost entirely middle-class, and the small section
called Scarborough, which was upper-middle-class, Ossining also had working-class neighborhoods, and a large black
slum.

Located in the richest county in the United States,
Ossining itself was not at all rich. Though Ossining had the
highest tax rate in the county, the center of the village had
numerous empty storefronts; nearby homes were run down,
fled from. The biggest drain on taxes was, of course, the
schools, in which violence was not unknown. Working-class
family cars, like gunboats, displayed the flag. Parents
suffered their children who succumbed to long hair. It was
not an unusual town in a country on the decline after only
two centuries.

Ossining had originally been named Sing Sing, after the
Sinq Sinq Indians who inhabited the area from the Pocan-
tico River to the Croton. But long before Hollywood made
Sing Sing prison known throughout the world, the local in-
habitants divorced themselves nominally from the men behind the walls and changed the name of their village to
Ossining. The state eventually caused the prison to be re-

named the Ossining Correctional Facility, but the towns-people did not have the will for a further change of name. They accepted it as they did all-numeral telephones, the inefficiency of public servants, the dearth of honest crafts-men, and the lack of a place you could take a car to be repaired by a good mechanic. It wasn't the end of the world.

In Ossining this January day, an extraordinary young man of sixteen named Edward Japhet was practicing magic tricks in front of a large mirror in his parents' bedroom. He had been performing tricks for three years. At thirteen he had started with the usual cards and thimbles and sponge-rubber balls, working his way up through black boxes and gadgets to stage-size illusions. At sixteen, because of his skill at legerdemain, a lightness of hand, and his ability to dis-tract even sophisticated adults with amusing patter while his hands did their covert work, he could be fairly called an accomplished magician.

Ed's touch with an audience was apparent also in the classroom. His social-studies teacher, Mr. Wincor, tradi-tionally provided his students with a list of fifty subjects from which they were to choose one to talk about for five minutes in front of the class. Ed Japhet was the first ever to choose "The Difference Between a Republic and a Democ-racy," and delivered such a precise, clear, and even witty comparison that Mr. Wincor found himself joining the stu-dents in spontaneous applause at the end. It was only later that he began to wonder if Ed had not cribbed his speech from some source unknown to Mr. Wincor, and at a suitable moment after class that week he called Ed aside when the others had left the room.

"How did you go about preparing your subject?" he asked.

"Well, I browsed."

"What do you mean?"

"I looked up 'republic,' 'democracy,' 'Jefferson,' and 'Jack-son' in the encyclopedia, read the Constitution, looked at

my notes on *The Federalist* papers, and started de Tocque-
ville's *Democracy in America*, but I couldn't finish it because I had a date last weekend."

"You said some funny things."

"That was for the kids. I hope you didn't mind. The hard
part was keeping it under five minutes. I timed it okay at
home, but it ran over in class, because they laughed."

"Did you get any help from your father?"

"My father and I have never discussed democracy or
republics," said Ed with a straight face. He didn't tell Mr.
Wincor that in his pursuit of perfection he had rehearsed his
speech, as was his custom, before both his mother and father.

Mr. Wincor, who prided himself on giving *A*'s rarely, gave
one to Ed.

The fact that Ed's father taught at the high school was a
source of embarrassment to them both. Terence Japhet was
respected but not liked by the other teachers. He didn't
fraternize much with his colleagues, in part because he felt
himself a captive in his vocation. A child of the depression,
he had learned by the age of ten that teachers were
secure in their jobs, and though he later realized that his
interest was in research, and perhaps not even in biology,
the subject he had elected to teach, he stuck to the job. He
told himself that he was a prisoner of economic necessity,
which was a lie. The fact is that Terence Japhet did not find
in himself those qualities of initiative and leadership he so
much admired. And so, like many men, he tried to encourage his son to be what he was not.

When Ed was just a little over a year old and had begun
to walk, Mr. Japhet had watched him toddle across the
room right up to the wall, but he could not as yet turn
around without falling. And so Eddie would plop down,
turn in a sitting position, then get up again and walk to the
opposite wall, where he would repeat the performance.

"Isn't he agile?" Mrs. Japhet had said. Her husband corrected her, "It's not his physical agility, it's his mind. He's just figured out how to overcome a problem."

It was nearly a year later that Mr. Japhet began to notice a small piece of ragged cardboard stuck from time to time between the back door and the jamb. It was the Japhets' practice not to lock the back door leading out to the yard except at night, but Eddie, whose hands would later be so dexterous, had difficulty turning its tight knob. And so when Mr. Japhet went out to the garage each morning that winter to warm up the car, he'd come back in to find Eddie at the back door, shivering a bit but ready to catch the door on its return swing and let it close on the piece of cardboard. Then, having breakfasted, he could run out to play simply by pulling the knob. Mr. Japhet, who believed children could be taught courtesy by being courteous to them, was careful to reinsert the piece of cardboard whenever he had to use the door, until Eddie learned to manage the knob some months later.

Such seemingly ordinary occurrences were to Terence Japhet momentous events in the life of his only child, noted with quiet pride.

Terence Japhet didn't need to encourage Eddie to ask questions; all children do. But Mr. Japhet never sloughed off his answers. When Eddie, at four, asked, "Why does it snow?" he explained about rain freezing. And when Eddie went on to ask, "Why does it rain?" Mr. Japhet took the time to explain until Eddie seemed to understand.

It wasn't easy. When Eddie entered kindergarten, Mr. Japhet, with Josephine Japhet's help, taught him to read simple books and then to write sentences, not because he wanted to give his son a head start, but because it seemed necessary. It also turned out to be convenient, because Eddie wrote his questions down in his jagged stick writing, each letter its own size. This way the questions could be dealt with before dinner, carefully, instead of on the run.

Eddie was six when he wrote, "Why is my peenee big when I wake up?"

That evening Mr. Japhet tried to explain how urine accumulates during the night. It stored up in the bag called a bladder, he said, showing Eddie where it was, and said the full bladder caused a pressure that made the boy's penis stiffen. He then tried a simplified explanation of Harvey's conception of the circulation of the blood, relating that to the pressure of the bladder that dammed up the blood in the boy's organ. It took a lot of careful repetition before Eddie understood and seemed satisfied.

By the time Ed was fifteen, he had the run of his father's library as well as the libraries at school and in town, and questions were directed to Mr. Japhet much less frequently. Ed at that age was pursuing answers that couldn't be looked up easily, and formulating school reports on such subjects as why were families necessary, were Americans too dependent on electricity, was patriotism useful, what was the difference between law and justice—questions that in the Japhet household usually resulted in a contretemps over dinner from which the parents learned as much as the son they were guiding.

"I have a feeling," Mrs. Japhet said to her husband one night as they decided to go up to bed, "that Ed is headed for a fascinating career."

Mr. Japhet, after a moment's reflection, said, "I have a feeling we have provided him with the capability of getting into trouble."

He proved right, of course.


COMMENT BY HIS FATHER
*(Terence Japhet, age 46, teacher)*

I've been teaching at Ossining High for fourteen years. It's awkward having your son a student in the same school.

The rule is he can't be in my class. We sometimes pass each other in the halls in the morning, and I say, "Hello, Ed," even though I may have seen him over breakfast, and he usually waves, but he doesn't say, "Hi, Dad," even though the friends he's with know who I am, of course.

When this thing happened at the prom, I mean the show itself, I wasn't there and heard about it secondhand, from teachers, students, Ed himself; and not all the versions jibe. People always ask me how he does his tricks. I don't have anything to do with his magic; he just started it as a kind of hobby when he was about twelve, bought a few mail-order tricks, built some equipment in my downstairs workshop, then started attending these magicians' meetings in New York and getting better at it. The hobby seems to have had a constructive effect. A central interest is what I mean, something he fusses with every day, especially weekends.

But I can't believe that the danger he found himself in was an accident. In a world that affects egalitarianism, the cardinal sin is to make yourself conspicuous.


## COMMENT BY HIS GIRL FRIEND
(*Lila Hurst, age 16, student*)

People think a girl notices first how a fellow looks. Well, Ed looks, you know, tall, blondish hair and all that, his face is okay even if his right ear sticks out a little, but lots of fellows have okay looks. I guess what I first liked about Ed was his manner. Most boys his age are elbows and knees, they don't stand up right, but Ed stands and walks like he was somebody great, and I don't mean pompous-ass, though I know inside he's not that secure. Except when he's doing his magic tricks.

We started dating, nothing special. We liked each other's company more than we liked hanging around with the others. The grown-ups think we go off and bang all the time because we're alone. Of course, everything has changed since the prom. I wish it had never happened.

## COMMENT BY DR. GUNTHER KOCH
*(Manhattan psychiatrist, age 57)*

Since my wife died, it is my habit to go to the kitchen in my bathrobe, pour myself a large glass of orange juice, which I sip slowly instead of gulp down as the Americans do, and read *The New York Times* until the water comes to a boil and I can have my coffee. Then I take the cup into the living room and sit in my comfortable chair, as I did in the days when Marta was still alive, and finish the newspaper.

To read the newspaper thoroughly every morning is essentially a boring habit because you can get the full information of the news by skimming the headlines and maybe a first paragraph here and there. But what attracts me to the process of looking up and down the columns of each page is the little stories about people one occasionally finds: a mother who left four young children to go only to the corner and found the apartment burning when she came back; a taxi driver mugged for the second time in a month, who broke the mugger's arm with a jack handle and then proceeded to kill him with the same jack handle; a colorless doctor I met once at a medical meeting who is accused of having performed more than two thousand abortions. All of this, which seems like little gossip of the world, enables me to go upstairs, shave, dress, and sit in a chair behind patients from eleven o'clock until seven listening to their troubles.

The Monday morning after I read about this boy Edward Japhet in the *Times*, I cut the item out of the paper and, in thinking about it, forgot to shave and went through the entire day with a stubble for the first time in my life. From the facts, it doesn't seem like the boy needs analysis, and I have therefore been analyzing my own interest in the case. Is it my own interest in magic that leads me to this young magician? I have now been tempted for the first time in my career to do something considered unethical, that is, to solicit a patient. But I wonder whether the facts, if known, would really clear things up. Certainly his father must be as upset by the boy's fame as by what happened after the show. I wonder what his relationship with his mother is like.

I have caught myself wondering if there isn't a way of looking into this case. Perhaps I could do a research paper on the psychology of children who take up magic as a hobby; then I could arrange, through the society, of course, to approach . . .

# Chapter 2

THE ROOM WAS DARK except for the thin sheets of moonlight coming between the slats of the venetian blind. Ed Japhet lay atop the bedspread, his eyes closed, fully dressed in the tuxedo that had been rented for the occasion. One hour more and he'd be onstage. His arms at his sides, he had bade his muscles go limp, one limb at a time, the way some of the great magicians were reported to have done before every performance.

His body felt relaxed now, but the circus of his mind resounded with the orchestrations of rehearsal. Each trick had had its turn before the mirror in his parents' bedroom, again and again. Much of the patter he was planning to use had fixed in his memory, though there was always the hazard of being in front of people with a suddenly blank mind. He ticked off the crucial gestures, the misdirections he would use to deflect the attention of the audience at each critical time.

Ed thought of himself as a part of a tradition he had come to know during the course of his thirteenth year; while browsing in the public library at the beginning of a ten-day Easter recess, he had found a shelfful of books he had not known existed. He discovered that the term "magi" went back to Babylon and Media, that it then meant "august" and "reverend" and was the word the learned priests used to describe themselves. Among the Persians, Ed found, the magis were the keepers of the sacred objects, and from these they divined the future, not through hanky-panky, but largely because these ancient magicians had a knowledge of the powers of nature superior to that of the people around them. They were the wise men, and their influence was unbounded.

Ed read of the struggle of knowledge and ignorance, light and darkness, good and evil, and how the ministers of old became in time the wandering fortune-tellers and quacks, the sleight-of-hand artists and conjurers who, instead of advising kings and princes about their most important transactions, entertained or merely fooled.

He pleaded successfully with the librarian to let him take the best of these books home, though they were only for reference, and he gorged himself the way a glutton consumes the meal of his dreams. He neglected the history paper he was supposed to complete because he kept thinking of Thomas Jefferson as a magus and the politicians of today as tired vaudeville performers, doing their thing for the thousandth time. Ed had hated the magicians he had seen at school and in shows. Having lost their sense of surprise, their hands darted gracelessly, their chatter became mechanical. A magician, Ed felt, needed to believe anew that each trick really worked, just as the audience did. Like life, in magic there was always the unpredictable.

His father, seeing no light under the door, came in on tiptoe. He turned on the small desk light rather than the overhead in order not to startle him.

"I thought you might have fallen asleep."

"No," said Ed, "just resting."

"I feel awkward about this."

"About what?" said Ed, raising himself from the bed.

"Well," said Mr. Japhet, "I'd like to see the show."

"You've seen all these tricks."

"It's just that it's different in front of an audience." Mr. Japhet examined his fingernails. "I mean, if you were playing football, you wouldn't mind my coming to the games."

"That's different."

"How?"

"All a player sees is the crowd. When I do a show, I see people's faces. In fact, I fix on one or two and talk to them. If you were there, I'd see yours, and it'd make me nervous."

"Doesn't Lila's being there make you nervous?"

"She's going to sit way in the back."

"I could sit back there, too."

"Oh, Dad, the prom isn't for parents."

Mr. Japhet touched the inside corners of his eyes, then rubbed the bridge of his nose as if he had been wearing uncomfortable glasses. "Well," he said, wanting to try again but not able to, "I'll drive you down and pick you up afterward."

Parents shouldn't have feelings like that, thought Ed; they have a job to do.

Rescue came in the form of his mother, moving briskly through the door, saying, "Your tux'll get all wrinkled."

Ed got up from the bed and slowly turned around for her inspection. He had thought of the possibility of wrinkles and had lain down in a way that he thought would do no damage.

"I guess it's all right," said Mrs. Japhet. "I'm sorry I won't be there to see your act. Are you going along, Terence?"

"They only need a few teachers as chaperons, and they're all assigned," said Mr. Japhet.

"You'll drive him, won't you?"

"I've been chauffeuring him for sixteen years," said Mr. Japhet, leaving the room. "It's too late to stop," his voice trailed after him.

"*He's* in a good mood," said Mrs. Japhet thinly. "Never mind, are you all packed?"

Ed nodded, and glanced at his watch. Better get cracking.

It had snowed in Westchester that morning and all day long the day before. The main roads had been cleared, but the side streets were car traps, and now it was snowing again. Better allow plenty of time in case they got stuck. The school hired a professional orchestra for the prom every year, and two years ago had even had a professional magician, who was clumsy. This was the first time the main act would be performed by a student. He didn't want to goof it. Or be late. There were two suitcases full of apparatus to unpack backstage, and he didn't want any help from anyone who might see something he wasn't supposed to see.

His father helped him get the heavy suitcases into the car. Ed himself carried the brown one, which had the big pitcher in it, the only thing that could break easily. He was glad he had thought to put his tux pants inside his boots because the snow was high.

The starter didn't catch at first. It took a half-minute till it turned over in the cold. The waiting seconds brought back the stomach jump he had lain down to get rid of. His mouth felt dust-rag dry. He took the tiny breath sprayer out of his pocket and shot twice into his mouth.

"What's that?" asked his father, now easing the car out of the driveway, which had not been shoveled out too well.

"Nothing," said Ed, pocketing the spray.

Once they got on Route 9, everything was okay. He reminded his father to turn off to Holbrook Road so he could pick up Lila.

She was standing just inside the front door of her house, her face visible in the pane of glass. Ed got out of the car as she came down her walk, her dress buffeted by the swirling wind.

As she slid into the front seat next to his father, she said, "Hi, Mr. Japhet. I appreciate your picking me up."

His father just nodded. It wouldn't have killed him to say something.

Ed got in. It was a tight squeeze. Lila seemed anxious not to sit too close to Ed's father, as if she was afraid their legs might touch.

She and Ed therefore sat very close, but didn't talk. The windshield wipers swept two half-moons out of the fast-falling snow. Through them they peered at the road and the white lawns on either side. The wind whistled through the right-front vent window, which had never once closed airtight since they bought the damn Dodge. He wished his father would hurry some.

The grade leading to the lit-up school stretched for a quarter of a mile ahead of them, the road an almost continuous chain of cars moving slowly, each afraid to come to a complete stop in case it had trouble getting started uphill again in the hard-packed snow. The last quarter-mile of inching along seemed so slow. Ed kept glancing at his watch, hoping he'd have enough time to prepare.

"You're making me nervous," said his father.

It was hopeless to get out and walk the distance with the heavy suitcases. Now, however, the cars started moving at a somewhat faster pace, and they could see the tiny figure of the policeman at the head of the line, trying to keep the unloading cars moving. That was the bottleneck. Though their windows were raised, they could hear the good-byeing and helloing.

"We could get out here," Ed said.

"It'll only be a couple of minutes more," said his father. "The suitcases are heavy. I'll help you backstage with them."

"No, it's okay, I'll manage. You can't leave the car here, it'll just block traffic."

*He could pull off the road right there and not tie up anything, and he'd have the satisfaction of helping you, you are a shit, Ed Japhet.*

When the car stopped, there was some honking, as if it weren't the star of the show but just some kid getting out. Lila ran for the doorway alone.

Mr. Japhet helped Ed get the suitcases out as fast as possible, the cop yelling at them to hurry-up-you're-holding-up-traffic, and then Mr. Japhet was back behind the wheel waving good-bye, which Ed didn't see because he was already lumbering toward the door, one suitcase in each hand, feeling the sweat in his armpits and hoping he wouldn't look a mess for the show. Where the hell was Lila?

A kid he didn't know held the door open for him, obviously wondering what the suitcases were all about. Well, he'd know once the show got started.

Around the corner in the hallway Ed put the cases down, looked at his hands as if he expected instant calluses instead of just redness, then dusted the snow bits off his shoulders, like dandruff, except wet.

Lila, suddenly standing close in front of him, gave him a quick kiss on the lips. Nobody noticed.

"Good luck," she said, showing her crossed fingers to him.

He abandoned her there, telling her to get a good seat not too much on the side, and headed for the back of the gym, one suitcase in each hand, like Willie Loman. He didn't *feel* like the star of the show, that was for sure.

Backstage, he was greeted by Thin Lips, Mr. Fredericks, the faculty adviser.

"Mr. Fredericks," he said, trying to make his voice sound like one professional talking to another instead of a student to a teacher, "it'll help a lot if I can set up in private, I mean, none of the students around, okay?"

"Understood," said Mr. Fredericks. He showed Ed the two tables he had asked for.

"Just before I'm supposed to go on, this here, the first table, needs to be put out on the left side of the platform, with no jiggling, because there'll be a pitcher of milk on it, in addition to other things. It wouldn't be too good for me to do that myself—I mean, carry it on. They shouldn't see me until I appear."

Mr. Fredericks smiled that shitty smile of his.

"The second table," Ed said, "should go toward the back, against the curtain, so I have to turn around with my back to the audience to take anything off it. That's very important."

"Sure," said Mr. Fredericks. "I'll put them out there myself."

"Oh, I didn't mean for you to carry—"

"Quite all right. Pleasure to help."

Maybe he wasn't so bad.

Ed had left himself barely enough time to arrange his things from the suitcases onto the two tables. On the first was a quart-size pitcher of milk, a folded tabloid newspaper, a piece of soft clothesline, his mother's good scissors, and a brown paper bag.

On the back table he carefully arranged the material he needed for his pièce de résistance. Then he took his three-by-five cue card out of his pocket and went over the items one by one. He turned the card over, closed his eyes, and repeated the cues from memory. It wasn't like doing a magic show for a little kid's birthday party for five dollars.

Mr. Fredericks came over to say that the lights in the gym were being lowered. He could hear the scraping of the folding chairs, which would be gotten out of the way later for the dance.

"Are you ready?" asked Mr. Fredericks. "Roberta's number takes three and a half minutes."

Roberta Cardick was the ice-breaker. She would take the

head off the mike, as usual, and sing as if she were making love to it. Roberta, a senior, was good, but she was no Janis Joplin, and the kids had all heard her lots of times. Still, she'd put them in a good mood for him.

"I'm going to introduce her," said Mr. Fredericks. "All set?"

Ed wanted to say, "Anytime," casually, but what came out was a dry, barely audible, "Yes."

He watched Roberta. Sideways, her tits seemed even bigger than from the front. She was singing something new, and they loved it, you could tell.

Never mind. When Roberta came off to wild applause, he held up an approving thumb so she could see. Then Mr. Fredericks carried the tables on carefully.

Ready or not, thought Ed, here I come.

# Chapter 3

LILA, HER BACK STRAIGHT, sat on one of the wooden seats way in the rear of the gym, between strangers, isolating herself. When she shrugged her shoulder-length auburn hair out of her vision's way, the toss of her head and the movement of her long neck were barely perceptible, the slight sway of her beads just touching the very top of her breasts.

Other students seeing her at that moment might have thought of her as aloof, when in fact she was consciously arranging herself to be alone amidst an audience, to watch as if she were the sole spectator. If asked, she would not deny the pleasure she felt at her escort's being the star of the evening's events.

Mr. Fredericks was just then carrying the second table on. The buzz in the audience turned to a breath and then to silence as Ed appeared, looking so different. Was it the distance, or the tuxedo he wore? Or just the way he strode onstage and, with the slightest nod at Mr. Fredericks, touched his hand to his forehead in a salute to the audience that greeted and put them in their places at the same time.

"Ladies . . . gentlemen . . . anachronisms . . ." Ed said, looking directly at the cluster of teachers standing against one wall. A titter, a ripple, and, finally, restrained laughter.

"I want to thank the English teacher who taught me the meaning of 'anachronism,' " he said, and the laughter continued.

"Fellow students, future dropouts, members of the post-alcoholic generation, what lies in store for you is not rational—just pure and simple magic that we can all understand!"

All that applause, and he hadn't yet begun his first trick.

"Over here," he said, "I have a sheet of ordinary newspaper, filled with advertisements, comic strips, help-wanted ads, and half-truths."

He rolled the newspaper into a simple cornucopia, and holding it with his left hand, with his right picked up the brimful pitcher of white liquid.

"This, as all you Four-H Club members know, is full of the milk of human kindness."

Ed tilted the pitcher and let the milk pour slowly into the cornucopia. A few drops trickled out of the bottom of the paper cone, and he set the now half-full pitcher down so that with his right hand he could twist the bottom of the cone and fold the end up tight. Then he resumed pouring. There was a hush in the audience.

Ed looked up. "I learned this trick from my first milkman, Mrs. Terence Japhet."

Laughter fluttered through the gymnasium as Ed finished pouring the last drops of milk into the cornucopia, set the pitcher down, and carried the cone gingerly over to the edge of the platform.

With a sudden motion he tipped the paper cone toward the girls in the first row, who shrieked, but it was empty, and as he crushed the paper cone the foot-stomping started. He held up a hand for silence and said, "As every student knows, the milk of human kindness has completely disappeared."

As the laughter and applause became tumultuous, he noticed for the first time that Urek and three members of his gang were sitting next to the girls, up front in the first row.


## COMMENT BY FRANK TENNENT, ED'S BEST FRIEND

Urek and his gang run this school the way the Mafia runs parts of the United States. I saw a kid go over to the apple machine and let his fifteen cents show one inch before he put the money into the slot and got a whack on the wrist from Urek that'd send the dough flying. It'd be scooped up in seconds by the others. Once I saw this girl, real innocent, pick up one of the coins and try to hand it to the kid who dropped it. One of Urek's greasers took her wrist and said "Thank you" before he took the coin away.

Student gym lockers used to be free until Urek started renting them out at two bits a month for protection—you know, if you paid up, your locker was protected, and if you didn't, your combination lock got hacksawed, which cost a buck and a quarter to replace, and anything usable inside was missing. I *told* Ed it just didn't make economic sense to fool with Urek. Ed paid $5.75 for that tempered-steel lock the guy in the hardware store said couldn't be hacksawed through. It's true, it couldn't, but can you imagine how burned Urek and his friends were every time they passed Ed's locker? I pay my two bits a month; it's cheap. I tell you, Ed and I walk home together because we're on the same block, but if ever the pack came on him on the way home, I'd haul ass out of there.

I'm not his best friend. I'm a senior, and he's a junior. It's just that on our block we're the only teen-agers except for a girl. I play first-string football, and he doesn't even like sports. When I go off for a game, he says, "Oh, you're going to be an American"—some crack like that.

Ed can defy Urek all he wants to, just so he leaves me out of it. I told him, and he said, "Okay, just get to a phone and call the cops." Now, you know the cops can't do anything about people like Urek, there's always a gang like that, whether you're in school or got a business somewhere, don't you read the papers?

## COMMENT BY MR. CHADWICK, THE PRINCIPAL

Yes, I know about the locker-room business, and I don't know how to stop it. If I issued another edict, it would have the same effect as the first: nothing. We never see them taking money from the students. Not one has ever been caught sawing through a padlock, though there are always reports of these things happening. I can't let the police enter the school premises. What could they do, anyway? They haven't been able to stop the Mafia's garbage-collection activities in the area, and that's much more serious because several gang members have actually been found dead in Westchester, and there's been no fatality at the school as yet. I mean, we're a long way past the age when you could encourage boys to masturbate less and eagle-scout more. We believe more than a third of the children in school smoke pot or take amphetamines. How do you stop all that? What would you do in my place? I've got less than two years to go to retirement. That's my solution.

For his second trick, Ed Japhet held up a piece of soft clothesline that went from one outstretched hand to the other, perhaps two yards in length.

"What," he asked his audience, "would be the best way of cutting this length of rope into two equal parts?"

"Cut it in the middle!" yelled a boy from the back.

"What's the easiest way of finding the middle?" Ed asked the anonymous voice.

"Measure it!" came the voice.

"Well," said Ed, "I don't have anything with me to measure it with, and besides, that might take a long time. How about this way?"

He held the two ends together and let the middle drop straight down, then picked up the rope at midpoint, while a titter went through the audience at the obviousness of the solution.

"Now, the student who yelled from the back . . . at least I hope it was a student . . . would he please step up to the platform and with these trusty scissors cut the rope exactly in half?"

He recognized the boy when he was halfway down the aisle, a tubby, awkward kid from his gym class who was unable to chin himself up even once. Bigmouth.

The boy took the proffered scissors and cut the rope through at midpoint in one angry snap.

When Ed let the cut ends fall, it was clear that one part of the rope was at least two inches longer than the other. The audience laughed, and tubby wandered back to his seat in disgrace. Ed tied the two cut ends together into a knot, circled the scissors around the knot, then stopped. Carefully, he put the scissors down on the table, took one end of the rope, stood stock-still until there was absolute silence, then suddenly snapped the end of the rope: the knot had disappeared, and the rope was restored to one uncut piece. A beat, and then a stomping of feet and applause as Ed tossed the restored rope out to the audience for examination.

"How'd you do it, Ed?" someone yelled.

Another, standing, said, "Can you fix my broken guitar string the same way?"

Ed held up his hands for silence. "Fellows, girls, teachers," he said, surveying the tight bundle of faculty members at the side of the room, "I need an adult volunteer."

He looked at the knot of teachers, then at each of their faces in turn, knowing that all of them probably dreaded the prospect of being asked onstage.

Stretch the moment out, he told himself. It's as important as the trick.

Ed held his hand over his eyes Indian-fashion, as if it were hard for him to see the cluster of teachers he was staring at.

"Any adults here?"

The kids howled.

Still, none of the teachers stirred.

Take it slow, he said to himself.

It was at this moment that Jerry Samuelson shifted his body weight. Jerry, a senior, a journalism major, was not only editor of the school paper but a paid stringer for *The New York Times.* He had intended to file his usual two-paragraph story about the prom, expecting that none of it would be published. In fact, he had begun to feel guilty about the small checks he received from the newspaper because they had actually used only one item from him all semester. When the black students, goaded by the gang, had staged a one-day fracas in the lunchroom, an overzealous policeman called in by the principal had accidentally hurt himself while trying to wrestle an ashcan top away from one of the students. The *Times* had used his story in a roundup of similar incidents in other schools. Even then they had stolen his thunder by sending a by-line reporter up the next day to interview students and faculty and do an in-depth piece on the sociological bases of student unrest in the suburbs.

The shift of Jerry Samuelson's body weight was to get his pad out of his pocket and start writing because some intuition had made him feel that perhaps a story was developing. Jerry would go far in journalism because he had already discovered that anyone could cover an event that was obviously news but that much of every newspaper was filled with stories in which the news, if any, was made by the reporter's discernment, not the event itself. Samuelson made a quick note about the disappearing milk and the rope trick and now watched Ed trying to get a response from someone in the faculty.

"Ladies and gentlemen, please don't trample each other in the rush to volunteer," said Ed. He had expected there would be resistance. His coaxing was intended to reinforce it, because he had already selected his target.

"Mr. Fredericks," he said, "I'm so glad you decided to volunteer."

He could actually see Mr. Fredericks' face turn red. Maybe it was a dirty trick picking on him; he had tried to be helpful about setting up the tables. "Please do come right on up."

Mr. Fredericks, encouraged by his colleagues, who were relieved not to have to go themselves, minced his way to the platform, but did not step up onto it.

"Would you like me to help you?" Ed extended a hand. There was a great guffaw as he helped Fredericks up the one large step.

"Could I ask a favor, please?" said Ed. "Would you unbutton your . . . jacket?" Again a laugh, as Mr. Fredericks slowly undid all four buttons of his neo-Edwardian jacket. He dressed more stylishly, and more elegantly, than any of the other faculty members, but Edwardian jackets just weren't meant to be worn open.

"That's an awfully nice tie," said Ed, gesturing at the wide gray wool neckpiece. This was the instant when timing was so important. With his left side facing the audience, he took the tip end of Mr. Fredericks' tie in his left hand and brought his right hand around—with the scissors open—and in a flash sliced the bottom four inches off the tie before Mr. Fredericks could tell what was happening.

The roar from the crowd was immediate. Mr. Fredericks let a moment of instant fury show, then quickly covered it with a cheek-splitting grin to show that he was a good sport. His reaction caused the audience to laugh even more, and as Mr. Fredericks tried manfully to join them in laughter, Ed cut another piece off the tie.

The kids were in stitches, howling, stomping their feet, and banging their hands. Even the cluster of faculty members couldn't suppress its amusement.

"Mr. Fredericks," said Ed, his voice a shout so that he could be heard by the audience as well as by his victim, "could you take your tie off?"

Mr. Fredericks started to undo the remains of his tie.

"Let me help you," said Ed, and his scissors flashed again perilously near the knot, snipping another segment off the neckpiece.

Jerry Samuelson was busy scribbling.

In the back, Lila was recovering from laughter along with the others, as on the platform Ed took the paper bag off the table and dropped into it, one at a time, the pieces of poor Mr. Fredericks' tie. When the last piece from around Mr. Fredericks' neck was also in the bag, Ed proceeded to blow the bag up. Then, holding the inflated bag in his left hand, he brought his right fist over sharply. The bag exploded in a loud pop, and out of it tumbled Mr. Fredericks' necktie, all in one piece.

Mr. Fredericks was a perfect foil. He stooped down, picked the tie off the floor, dusted it, examined it meticulously, and shook his head. It was indeed in one piece, and he couldn't figure it out. Nor could the audience. The applause lasted for as long as it took Mr. Fredericks to turn up his collar, tie his tie carefully, and rebutton his Edwardian jacket. Ed bowed to Mr. Fredericks, and Mr. Fredericks started to step off the platform to seek refuge among his colleagues.

"One moment, sir," said Ed. "I wonder if you would be good enough to help me with my last experiment?"

The audience noised its approval. Mr. Fredericks looked at the mob of faces, then at Ed, whose remorseless stare gave him no relief, and finally at the adult minority clustered at the side of the large room. He had no face-saving alternative. He had to play along. The show must go on. With him.

On the second table, at which Ed was now officiating, stood a small-scale model of a guillotine. It was too small to take a head, but easily accommodated the apple Ed placed in the large opening beneath the blade.

Ed watched Mr. Fredericks' expression intently as he slammed the blade down, splitting the apple.

Beneath the large opening was a smaller one, and into that Ed inserted a long carrot. Again he brought the blade down sharply, and it cut the carrot in half.

It was then that Mr. Fredericks involuntarily stepped back, realizing what was to come next. What if Japhet slipped up, what if the blade actually . . . No, he avoided airplanes, he drove only when necessary, he never walked on unsanded ice, he didn't go near open windows, why should he take the chance that some ungodly error . . .

Ed led him by the arm back toward the table with the guillotine and then around behind it. He whisked a clean handkerchief out of his pocket and tied it around Mr. Fredericks' wrist, "To soak up some of the blood," he told the audience.

"Are you sure you know how to do this?" Mr. Fredericks whispered, his voice percolating.

"There is no certainty in this life," said Ed aloud, and the students roared.

"Would you be good enough . . ." he continued to Mr.

Fredericks, "would you be kind enough, would you please place your arm through the large hole in the guillotine?"

Mr. Fredericks tried desperately to remember having read about a trick like this once and how it worked.

"Please?" asked Ed, gesturing toward Mr. Fredericks' reluctant arm.

Mr. Fredericks wished he could be elsewhere. He wished there weren't so many people staring at him and laughing.

"Please," said Ed again, and guided Mr. Fredericks' arm to, and then into, the hole.

"One last handshake," said Ed, and shook Mr. Fredericks' hand on the other side of the guillotine. Then Ed placed a small wicker basket on the floor beneath Mr. Fredericks' now clenched fist. "To catch the hand," he said. He waited for the kids to stop laughing. Then he placed a whole carrot in the smaller hole beneath Mr. Fredericks' hand.

"What I am now going to do," said Ed, "is to bring the guillotine down and cut through Mr. Fredericks' arm at the wrist and through the carrot, leaving the carrot miraculously whole and Mr. Fredericks' arm in two pieces."

The audience roared.

"I didn't mean that. I meant the other way around."

Mr. Fredericks' brain had given up on the trick.

"Sir," said Ed, "since my handkerchief is tied around your wrist, I wonder if I might borrow yours?"

Mr. Fredericks looked surprised. "Don't worry," said Ed, "I won't blow my nose in it."

With his free hand Mr. Fredericks removed his elegant handkerchief from his breast pocket and handed it to Ed, who proceeded to mop Mr. Fredericks' brow. Ed again had to hold up both hands for silence.

"One," he counted.

"Two," he counted. Then he relaxed and said, "Mr. Fredericks, did I ever tell you the story about . . ." He looked at Mr. Fredericks' face. He'd better get on with it.

"One!" he began again.

"Two!"

"Then, with just a second's beat, "THREE!" And Ed brought the guillotine smashing down.

Every eye in the room was fixed on the blade as it descended through Mr. Fredericks' bandaged hand and the carrot below it. From the impact, the cut carrot's halves went hurtling one in front and one to the rear of the guillotine. Mr. Fredericks' knees sagged.

In an instant two or three students and the gym teacher were up on the platform holding Mr. Fredericks under the armpits as Ed raised the blade and freed the hand, which was entirely intact, a fact that surprised Mr. Fredericks more than anyone. He had not fainted, and now he wanted it to seem that he had merely played along to help the dramatic effect. And so he brushed off his rescuers and smiled at Ed and the thudding, stomping, applauding audience.

It was at that moment that Ed saw Urek and the three members of his gang stand up in the front row. In two swift movements Urek vaulted onto the stage, saying, "Lemme see that blade!"

*Of course you can't examine the blade,* thought Ed: *It'll give the trick away.* But he was too late—Urek had seized the guillotine and was trying to pull it apart.

"Let go of that guillotine," said Ed.

"It's not sharp," said Urek, running his hand along the blade.

"It cut the apple," said Ed in desperation. "It cut the carrot."

Mr. Fredericks, regaining his composure, touched Urek's arm. "You'd better get back to your seat."

"It's a trick!" said Urek.

"Of course it's a trick," said Ed, trying to wrest the guillotine away without breaking it.

"Tell us how you did it."

"He's not supposed to," said Mr. Fredericks. "You get back to your seat."

"I'll break it," said Urek, "unless you tell us how you did it."

In the melee, Jerry Samuelson had got himself onto the platform. Two or three years earlier, when he was a kid, he had been given a miniature guillotine, big enough for a finger or a cigarette, not an arm or a carrot. He knew the principle on which it worked, but couldn't figure out what Ed Japhet had just done.

"What did you do with the other blade?" he asked Ed.

"What other blade?" said Ed; then, thinking fast, he said to Urek, "Put your hand in the hole."

Samuelson and Mr. Fredericks were suddenly silent.

"Whadya mean?" asked Urek.

"Put your hand through the hole."

"And?"

"I'll cut it off. Like this." Ed took the guillotine out of Urek's hands and put it on the table. He bent over and picked up off the floor half of the apple he had split. He put the apple into the hole and then with a sudden slam of his hand sent the blade smashing down. The apple split, the pieces flying with force, front and back.

"Now your hand," said Ed to Urek.

The audience watched in silence.

"If it's a trick," said Ed, "you've got nothing to be afraid of."

"Who's afraid?"

"Put your hand in it."

Urek shot a glance at the audience.

"Put your hand in," Ed challenged.

He could hear Urek's breathing.

"Come on," said Ed quietly.

"Fuck you," said Urek, and jumped off the stage.

The audience howled, then stomped and applauded.

It was the gym teacher who joined Mr. Fredericks in

quieting everyone down. "I'm sure," he said, "we're all grateful to Ed Japhet for a fine magic show. It must have taken a lot of rehearsal and practice. I personally enjoyed it, and I hope you did too."

The applause, rhythmic and formal, came like waves. Ed went forward to the edge of the platform. He could just see Urek's face in the near-darkness below him. Lila must have been sitting away out back. He couldn't see her.

It took fifteen minutes for Ed to get the equipment packed away into the suitcases backstage. He could feel his shirt soaked in sweat. He didn't want to dance or anything except go home and take the damn tux off and get into the shower and then go to sleep.

He put the suitcases into the faculty room and changed into a dark blue suit. He was buttoning his shirt when he heard Lila.

"It's okay," he said, "I'm almost dressed."

"I figured out the milk, I think," Lila said. "And I got an idea about the rope trick, though I don't think the others caught on, and I know how the tie thing had to work, but the guillotine trick—are you going to tell me how you did it?"

"You're not supposed to ask."

"You can tell *me*," she said. "I won't tell anyone."

Ed thought a moment, then shook his head. "I'm sorry," he said.

# Chapter 4

IF HIERONYMUS BOSCH had painted the city room of *The New York Times* in all its cluttered detail—the scramble of desks, three jammed together, two facing each other with no space between, desks dropped into place like a child's blocks in no regular order, and everywhere on them the long sheets off the teletype machines with the day's happenings all in monotonous capital letters, the insane black telephones ringing for someone who was bound to be away from his desk and would never find the message telling him about the call he didn't want to receive—Bosch would not have overlooked the cigarette packs, the smoking plug end of newsmens' nerves, the match folders, most of which were frustratingly matchless ("Who in hell has a light?"), the chewing-gum packs and balled-up wrappers from those who were chewing more instead of smoking less, the cartons of no-longer-warm coffee, and, most important of all, the blank sheets of typing paper in small piles on every desk, and near them the men waiting for something to happen somewhere.

At this late hour, in the left center of this Boschian canvas, one would have seen Avram Gardikian, rubbing the skin of his head, which was regretfully bald at age thirty-four. Avram's eyes skimmed through the typed-up messages from student stringers. Nothing. Nothing. Nothing, nothing, nothing.

The message from Jerry Samuelson took him by surprise. He reached the sleepy stringer only after persuading an awakened adult intermediary that it was indeed *The New York Times* calling.

"What is it, kid?"

Samuelson could barely restrain his excitement. He had a standing deal with one of the girls in the emergency room at Phelps. Ten dollars for a tip, something he could get to before a regular could cover it.

Gardikian listened carefully. After half a minute, he started taking notes.

"You're in luck," he said finally. "Get down there in the morning and get all the facts straight. If you can't handle it, call and we'll send someone. Okay, okay, big man. Take this name. George Hardy. I'm off Sundays. I'll leave this for him. He'll pick up."

Gardikian thought about the time when he had hit on his first real story. "Listen, kid," he said. "I think you'll make Monday."

Jerry Samuelson's head was full of bells. He knew that first jobs, full-time jobs, were out in the sticks somewhere, but maybe now . . .

Gardikian stuck a piece of blank paper in the typewriter and zipped the carriage to the right. Headlines were written by headline writers when pages were made up. But he had to signal the rewrite man, so he typed: STUDENT MAGICIAN BEATEN UNCONSCIOUS BY CLASSMATES. He lit a cigarette. Jerry Samuelson ought to be one happy kid tonight.

Lila had gone back to the dance floor. He wouldn't have told her how a trick was done even if she was his wife, which she wasn't. She'd get over it.

He left his suitcases in the faculty room and checked the mirror in the adjacent washroom. His hair needed combing.

He used his fingers first, as always, then fished out the broken-toothed comb to finish the job, cursing himself for having forgotten to bring his brush. Combed hair looked combed, brushed hair looked brushed. Damn!

The dance floor was crowded. As he edged around the perimeter, bouncing up on his toes once in a while to see better, he noticed some of the kids stopping to look at him as he looked for Lila. The magician in street clothes, like everybody else, but they were staring; to those he knew, he waved casually. He saw five or six kids clustered around Roberta Cardick. Fan-club stuff. Then he spotted Lila dancing with the geek.

Why some of the girls thought the geek was cute was a mystery to Ed. He had red hair and freckles, but six feet, three inches was too tall for a kid with a face like a kid, and look how clumsy he was, kicking his legs and moving his elbows like the things that connected train wheels.

Ed caught Lila's eye. It would only be a minute till the number ended. When it stopped, he ambled over, letting one shoulder droop a little. The geek was snowing away a mile a minute at Lila, polysyllabic like Danny Kaye.

"Hello, Lila," Ed said, cool.

The geek ground his nonstop to a stop and looked at Ed sideways.

He'll get the message in a minute, thought Ed. Be patient.

"The magician," said the geek. "Nice show."

"Thanks."

"Hello, Ed," said Lila's soft voice.

"Hello, Lila," said Ed.

The message came through.

"This your girl?" asked the geek.

Lila, the bitch, didn't say a thing.

"Well, I brought her."

"Okay," said the geek. "No hard feelings." Then to Lila, "Remember what I said." He sauntered off.

"What'd he say?" asked Ed.

"Oh, you know, he talks a blue streak."

"I mean, what was he referring to?"

"He said I looked beautiful."

"Well," said Ed, "I guess you do."

Nothing wrong with Lila dancing while she was waiting for him; it wasn't as if he owned her. Even married women don't always dance with their husbands, do they?

"The show went off very well," said Lila.

"I guess it did," he said. There they go, some of the other kids staring again. He hoped they wouldn't when the music started up. Dancing was not his thing. He felt stupid squirming around and snapping his fingers.

Lila was leading him out by the hand to a comparatively open space on the floor when he noticed four or five greasers bunched up, chewing away, staring at him. *I should have used an American flag in a trick*, Ed thought, *that would have got to them.*

Lila noticed him noticing, and took his elbow to move him away. "Don't look for trouble."

"I'm not looking for trouble," he said, following her lead, but taking a last glance over his shoulder and seeing that there were now eight or nine of them.

# Chapter 5

As soon as the last dance was over, Ed took Lila by the hand and hurried to the faculty room to make sure no one had walked off with his two suitcases. They were untouched.

The pay phone in the hall had a line of seven or eight kids. Several nodded to him. Nobody offered to let him go to the front of the line. Why should they?

The kids cooperated with each other by keeping their calls short, but it still seemed to take forever until his turn came. Most of the kids had left. Some dutiful parents had arrived early. Some kids had their own cars; others picked up rides from friends. The school was practically deserted by the time he got his father on the phone.

"Give me fifteen minutes," said Mr. Japhet. "Snow's been steady all evening, and the roads are worse."

"Take your time," said Ed, hanging up.

Only the custodian was left, and he headed immediately for the basement "to turn the heat down," but Ed and Lila knew, as did all the kids, that it was to settle himself near the boiler with a pint of Thunderbird, having been denied his evening's comfort because of the festivities.

It was a peculiar feeling looking down the empty hallway, seeing the school suddenly desolate, as if he and Lila had been the hosts of a large party whose guests had left and now they had this huge house to themselves.

"We've got eleven minutes," he said, glancing at the school clock above Lila's head.

He shut the door of the faculty room. They stood in the center of the silent rectangle. The huge overhead bulb seemed much too bright. Ed turned the switch off at the door and found Lila's hand in the darkness. The windows were laced with snow. His heart seemed louder in the dark.

He touched her beads and lifted them, his fingers brushing for an instant the nakedness above her breasts. He let the beads drop gently back into place as he put his hands to the sides of her face and kissed her, closed lips barely touching closed lips.

She took his hands away from her face, and he thought for a moment she was stopping him, but that was not the case at all, because she had merely spread his arms apart so that she could step closer to him, and when they kissed the second time her body was touching his.

They were both out of breath and laughing about it out of embarrassment, and Ed said, "It sounds ridiculous, but that felt swoony—it's the only word."

As they kissed again, he felt the beat. A pulse was what the doctor felt in your wrist, or what you saw in someone's temple when they were agitated, but the pulse he felt now was elsewhere, and he could tell from the expression on her face that she knew.

"God," he said.

"I know," she said.

He felt her breasts against his chest and let one hand slip to her buttocks, something he had not dared before.

"We'd better stop," Lila said. "It's almost time."

And so it was. Where had the minutes gone?

Very close to her ear he said, "I love you." He meant it, and hated that it sounded so corny. And then, impulsively, he kissed her hand, and in a second's breath he was hugging her, kissing her lovely neck and then her mouth again, which was now open a little, and he could—oh, suddenly— feel her tongue on his lips and in his mouth and, at the same time, the fierce hanging ache in his testicles.

It was Lila who turned the light back on.

He let her adjust her hair in the mirror first, and then, when she was through, he combed his hair, and looked at the high color in his face. He straightened his suit a bit.

Just in time. As they went out of the faculty room, he could see the outside door at the far end of the hall open and the small figure of his father enter amidst a whirl of snow, white on his hat and overcoat shoulders, and as he came closer one could even see the snow on his eyebrows. Strange how he expected his father might have *known* what was going on inside the faculty room.

Ed waved awkwardly.

Mr. Japhet blew into his frozen hands. "Forgot my gloves. That steering wheel's cold. Where are the bags?"

Ed gestured toward the faculty room.

Mr. Japhet insisted on taking the heavier bag. "How'd it go?"

"Oh, the prom was okay. You know." He knew his father hadn't meant the prom.

"The show went beautifully," said Lila. "It was really great. You ought to have seen it."

Outside, the snow was gusting in a directionless swirl of flakes, large and dry, sticking where they fell. Mr. Japhet pointed at the car, which, though only fifty feet away, was barely visible in the wild whirl.

They trooped off single file, Mr. Japhet first, then Ed, then Lila trailing behind, trying to walk in their new footsteps. They nearly collided when Mr. Japhet stopped without warning.

There were four figures sitting inside his car.

"What the hell," said Mr. Japhet. He put the case down in the snow and slogged to the car. He opened the door on the driver's side before recognizing the greaser behind the wheel.

Mr. Japhet tried to keep his voice level. "What's up, boys?"

Ed had come up behind his father.

"That's Urek, Dad. And his friends."

The four boys let loose a gang laugh, arrogating confidence from each other.

Urek said, "That's some special kid you got."

"Yeah," said one of the others, "a magician."

Mr. Japhet saw the chain wrapped around Urek's fist.

Urek had a strange face: gnarled, it looked older than his years. It was acne-pitted, and an uneven scar marred the right cheek.

"I think you boys better be getting home," said Mr. Japhet. "It's cold out here. Out of the car, now."

"Ask nicely," said Urek.

"Come on before I lose my temper."

"That's not nice, Mr. Japhet." Urek signaled the three others with a rough gesture of his head. They got out of all four doors simultaneously. "We were just going to help the magician with the bags—right, fellas?"

Ed put both hands on the handle of his bag as Urek approached. Urek made a feint toward the bag, laughed at Ed's instinctive flinch, and then with a grunt picked up the suitcase Mr. Japhet had left standing in the snow.

"Leave that alone!" said Ed.

"Put that bag down," said Mr. Japhet. He crunched through the snow after Urek. "Give it to me."

"You don't want me to help?" said Urek.

"No," said Mr. Japhet. "Put that bag down."

"I'm gonna show you what kind of magician your son is," said Urek, lifting the bag with tremendous strength; and then, as Lila, and Ed, and Mr. Japhet watched, he smashed the case against the side of the automobile again and again and again.

Ed recognized the sound of breaking glass. The milk pitcher, he thought.

"Hey, Mr. Japhet, I bet your boy can put all the pieces back together," said Urek.

Mr. Japhet, losing control of his voice, as if he were suddenly in a world out of the grasp of his mind and conscience, said, "What satisfaction does that give you? What kind of human being are you?"

"Some magician!" screamed Urek.

"What harm did he ever do to you?"

Ed, afraid of the chain around Urek's fist, tried to take his father's arm. "Let's get out of here, Dad."

"Let's go home, Mr. Japhet." It was Lila, ten feet back, silhouetted against the light from the school building. The minute the words were out of her mouth she was sorry she had spoken, for Urek was bounding over to her, leaving new holes in the snow. "This your girl, magician?"

Mr. Japhet, who was not as slow to grasp the shifting reality of a situation as most sons think their fathers are, knew a line had just been crossed. "Come on, Lila, Ed, get in the car."

Ed, both hands still on the handle of the safe suitcase, started to drag it toward the automobile.

Lila screamed as Urek twisted her arm behind her back, and with his other hand yanked her hair.

Ed, unthinking, blind, let the case drop into the snow and rushed at Urek, grabbing at the arm that was twisting Lila's behind her back.

"Watch out!" said Mr. Japhet.

Ed punched at Urek's arm.

"Watch out!" said Mr. Japhet again, but Ed in his rage

did not see that Urek, still holding the girl's arm behind her back with his left hand, had let several loops of chain unwind from around his right fist. Suddenly Urek pushed the girl forward on her face, and letting go, swung the chain. Ed tried to hold his hands up in front of him, but not fast enough to thwart the full force of the end of the chain against his cheek, a blinding impossible pain, and blood from somewhere; then Urek was crashing into him, knocking him onto the snow, and Urek's hands, one of them still with the chain around his knuckles, were around Ed's throat, choking him.

Urek was yelling, "You think you're something, huh?" as Mr. Japhet pounded on his back, then pulled at his shoulders, trying to drag him off his son, and Lila screamed and screamed. Mr. Japhet got a grip on Urek's hair, and pulling with a strength he didn't know he had, actually tore hair out of Urek's head. Urek was now up, off Ed, yelling at the other three to get the bag. "Smash it, smash it!" Urek yelled, and they smashed the second bag against the bumper of the car, and stomped on it, though Ed was now beyond caring about the crushed contents.

It was a miracle that the school door opened and the half-soused custodian appeared with his huge flashlight, stabbing its beam at them. "What you! Stop, stop, what you do?"

"I'm Mr. Japhet. Get help! Quickly!"

He didn't seem to have gotten through to the custodian, who stood in the doorway looking out into the snow. Could he see?

Thus distracted, Mr. Japhet did not see Urek bring Ed down to the ground again until his ear caught the gurgling sound and he turned to see Urek with his hands around Ed's throat, squeezing, squeezing. Mr. Japhet pulled the back of Urek's coat collar without effect, then drummed his fists fruitlessly on Urek's hunched back, wishing he had a gun to blow the boy's head off.

Just then the old custodian at the door yelled, "I call the police!"

That did it. Though it would take the police forever to get there in the snow, Urek let go of Ed's throat and suddenly got up, knocking Mr. Japhet backward.

Urek bellowed at the other three, who circled around the car and started to lope down the road away from the school.

Mr. Japhet felt a surge of relief seeing them retreat. He got his snow-soaked body upright and stepped toward Ed, lying, it seemed, unconscious, when in the periphery of his vision he thought he saw—he did see—Urek, not yet finished, lift his chain on high and swing it against the windshield of the car, shattering the huge curving pane to smithereens.

Ed had been unconscious only for seconds. As his father raised his head from the snow, he could see the three boys off in the distance, Urek still some distance behind them, swinging the chain.

Ed could not manage on his feet, and Mr. Japhet couldn't carry his weight alone, but with Lila's help, somehow, with one of Ed's arms around each of their shoulders, they were able to get him onto the back seat of the car.

Ed gestured toward the forgotten suitcases.

"They're both smashed, son. Might as well leave them till morning."

Ed shook his head. He tried to speak, to say he didn't want people finding out how the tricks were done, but the pain in his throat was excruciating, and the words weren't clear. He gestured toward the bags again.

Mr. Japhet got the two cases into the trunk of the car. He saw Lila had gotten into the back seat, was holding Ed's head in her lap, the blood from his face where the chain had first hit him staining her dress.

Mr. Japhet put the key into the ignition, stepped down on the pedal twice, turned the key, and after a few seconds of churning, the engine caught, and he put the car into gear and headed slowly downhill toward the highway. With the windshield gone, the snow whipped through at his face. He held on to the wheel with both hands, his eyes grim against the white night as he headed the vehicle toward the hospital.

# Chapter 6

STUDENT MAGICIAN BEATEN UNCONSCIOUS BY CLASSMATES.
*The New York Times*'s story was picked up by many other
newspapers in the country.

The Washington *Post* angled its story differently: HIGH-
SCHOOL HOOLIGANS ATTACK STUDENT, WRECK TEACHER'S CAR
AFTER TERM-END PROM. SITUATION IN NEW YORK SCHOOLS
WORSENS.

In the *Post* story one learned that racial tension was not
the cause of the incident inasmuch as the attackers and the
victims were all white. "The student who was severely
beaten had just performed a magic show at a school dance.
He was attacked after refusing to explain how his magic
tricks were done."

The centerspread of the New York *Sunday News* carried a
large photo of the Japhet car seen from just in front of the
shattered windshield. The caption read. "Teacher's car
smashed by students' chains after Friday-night prom. (See
story, p. 6)." On page 6 there was no story because its nine
inches had been dropped for a late-breaking subway-station

rape that had produced no picture to substitute for the
smashed Japhet car.

The headline on the Associated Press story said: GANG
FIGHTS TEEN TRICKSTER, which, at least, had the virtue of
brevity.

Mr. Japhet drove in the night through the swirling snow,
pumping the brake carefully, sensing the inadequate trac-
tion of the snow tires on the slick patches where the snow
hadn't held. The snow streamed past the jagged edges of the
open windshield, the flakes landing on his face, eyelashes,
eyes, dissolving his vision, causing him to blink and blink to
keep seeing the road ahead until finally he swung right on
the turnoff and followed the signs to the emergency room
around the back of Phelps Memorial. Though his speed had
slowed, when he applied the brakes and held, the car
skidded somewhat, stopping at a crazy angle to the curb. He
looked back at Lila holding Ed's head in her lap. "Is he
sleeping?"

"I think he's unconscious. It must be hurting terribly."

Mr. Japhet stumbled out into the snow, and in a minute
returned with two attendants and a stretcher. They removed
Ed clumsily from the car. He was awake now, his face gray-
green, his voice a low rasp, then groaning. They got him
inside, Mr. Japhet and Lila trailing, suddenly feeling the
warmth of the indoors, and with it, now that the mad ride
was over, a jolt of fear as the intern in the emergency room
touched Ed's forehead, took his pulse, quickly looked up
and down the body, asked, "Accident?"

Mr. Japhet said, "His throat. Someone tried to strangle
him."

Immediately the doctor ordered Ed transferred from the
examining table to a morgue cart, saying something to the
taller attendant which Mr. Japhet couldn't hear, and then
Ed was being whisked away. "I'm having him put in the
intensive-care unit," said the doctor.

Mr. Japhet and Lila hurried after the morgue cart, not hearing the doctor's parting words, and got into the same large elevator, watching Ed's face in the harsh light.

They were made to wait outside. Very soon the senior resident was going through the swinging doors of the intensive-care unit, still buttoning his white coat, followed by the emergency intern, talking. Mr. Japhet made out something about the difficulty of getting the tube through Ed's nose down into the stomach because of the swelling in the throat, and that was all.

Mr. Japhet felt the hot ache in his shoulders, the stiffness of his back from the difficult drive, a sudden great tiredness and a need to sleep. When he went into the waiting room across the hall to talk to Lila, he saw her being questioned by a large policeman.

"Oh," she said, "that's his father, Mr. Japhet."

The policeman took his cap off; it seemed to Terence Japhet a sign of condolence. "The radio car at the school," he said apologetically, "they talked to the custodian, but he didn't know much. Can I ask you a few questions?"

"I have to call home," said Mr. Japhet, then thought, "Lila, you'd better call first. Here's a dime." He gestured to the phone booth just outside.

After a minute she let the receiver dangle and told Mr. Japhet her mother wanted to talk to him.

When he hung up, Mr. Japhet said, "Your father's going to get dressed and drive down for you." He searched in his pocket for another dime.

"You're allowed to use the hospital phone to call the patient's mother," said the policeman, pointing to the phone on the nurse's desk.

"Try not to tie up the line too long," the desk nurse said.

His mind went blank about his own number. He'd feel like an idiot asking Lila; she was calling them all the time. Then he remembered and dialed.

"Terence. God, I was getting worried."

He played down everything, making it seem as minor as would be plausible, emphasizing the broken windshield on the car and the fact that he'd have to get a ride home, probably from the police.

The senior resident was coming out. "Have to go now, Jo," he said and hung up.

He stopped the doctor.

"I'm his father."

"Well," he said, "I think we can get the tube down, we'll be careful. He came damn close to being strangled. Can't tell too much from the contusions. Nothing broken in the neck, but could be a fair amount of trauma on the inside, have to see. You'd probably better get home and come back in the morning. We won't know much till then anyway."

In the waiting room the policeman said, "She says it looked like the attack was planned. Would you agree with that?"

"I don't know," said Mr. Japhet without really thinking.

"It makes a difference. It's premeditated if your boy dies."

"What did you say?"

"I was just explaining the legal part." He turned to Lila. "Go on about that chain."

"I really don't remember clearly. I remember the windshield breaking."

The policeman, his notebook ready, said, "Mr. Japhet, could you start at the beginning and tell me everything you remember?"

And so Terence Japhet told what he knew, wanting to sleep, droning on, sentence after sentence, till he saw the resident and the intern returning to the intensive-care room with a small table of instruments, leaving the door open long enough for him to see the nurse at Ed's bedside taking his pulse.

"Go on," said the policeman.

Terence Japhet, who might have made a great deal more money in the outside business world, and who had stuck to teaching because it seemed so far removed from stress, went on talking a minute more until he had to stop because he realized he was crying through his spread-fingered hands.

# Chapter 7

UREK, thick-tongued from four beers, pressed the point of the opener into another sweating can top, sending a small spray into his own grin. He punctured two more triangles and passed the can to Scarlatti, who threw a quarter on the pile.

Feeney still had half a can, waved away the offer of another. Smoking, drinking, sex, made him sick. The others put up with him because of old credentials. Feeney had been booked at age seven, caught by cops prying open a parking meter on an older boy's dare.

Dillard, half-pissed like Urek, motioned for another beer. Urek pointed to the pile of change, waited till Dillard put his money in, then passed the can.

Urek hated the formality of chairs. The four squatted hump-hunched on the linoleum floor of the playroom near the fake brick fireplace Urek's father had built during one of his layoffs. A fan behind the electric log cycled a monotonous pattern against the brick wallpaper.

"Scared the shit out of 'em last night," said Urek.

"Shouldna smashed the suitcases," said Scarlatti. "He'll make trouble."

"What trouble?"

Dillard shifted weight. "Shouldna smashed the windshield."

Urek raised himself to his feet. "It's insured, ain't it?" Six eyes stared up at him. "Whatsa matter with you guys?"

He stood over Dillard.

"Okay," said Dillard, sucking at the beer can. "When's the kraut coming?"

"If you can't wait," said Urek, "whyncha go pull off?"

While they waited, Urek sold each of them, including Feeney, who wasn't really drinking, another can of beer.

The playroom walls had been papered in imitation pine board, which looked real except at the seams. At regular intervals on the main wall memorabilia hung from spikes. The centerpiece was a World War II M-1 stolen in parts by Paul Urek, who kept the ammunition upstairs in his bedroom drawer alongside the package of rubbers.

Near the M-1 hung a black-wood-framed, captioned photograph of a squad of soldiers, second platoon, C Company, 18th Regiment, 1st United States Infantry Division. A red crayon circled Urek's father's face. He was the only one in the squad, he had told Urek, who never collected a Purple Heart or a dose.

To the right hung a plaque from the Volunteer Firemen's Association, same style black frame. Then a certificate from the Croton Bowling Alley with a score of 299. At the other end of the wall was a picture of Jesus; if you caught it from the right angle, the eyes seemed to open and shut.

Scarlatti let a fart go just as the doorbell rang.

"Not now, stupid," said Urek. "You'll smell up the place."

"I couldn't help it," said Scarlatti.

They heard the shuffling of feet upstairs, the front door being opened by Mrs. Urek, who hadn't cared about anything since her right breast was removed seventeen years ago. She figured the cancer would come back. It didn't. Afterward, she figured maybe she hadn't had cancer, the stupid doctor shouldn't have taken the breast off. Her husband said she disgusted him. She had given birth to Urek with one breast, bottle-fed the baby, hating him.

Mrs. Urek let the kraut in. She didn't care.

The kraut came down the stairs into the playroom. Dillard, happy now, shut and locked the door behind her.

They all acknowledged her presence with a wave or a grunt.

"Beer?" asked Urek.

"Why not?" Unlike the boys, she got the beer free.

The kraut was built, big tits, blonde, round face, German accent. Came over with her mother five years back. They all laughed when she said her mother was a war bride.

The kraut didn't go to school dances because the other girls made her miserable, even the ones who did it, because the kraut would with anybody. They told her about the events of the night before.

"How bad you hurt Japhet?" she asked.

The question startled them because they had been talking about the suitcases and the car.

Urek laughed. "He'll live."

"Someday you're gonna kill somebody," she said. "You nearly did me."

"Shut up!" said Urek. Once, when Urek couldn't get it up, he had tried an implement on her.

Urek tried to talk in a gentler voice. "You wearing pants tonight?"

"Maybe you'll find out," said the kraut.

"Did you take it today?"

"Take what?" she said.

"Don't make like you don't know. The pill."

"Maybe."

"Don't give me smartass talk. I don't want no trouble."

"Okay," she said. "Who's first?"

# Chapter 8

TERENCE JAPHET watched the two nurses, the intern, and the resident come and go; and then, just after three A.M., the specialist arrived, still wearing an overcoat laced with snow. One of the nurses helped him out of it and into a clean smock. The nurse pointed Mr. Japhet out. The specialist acknowledged his presence with a nod of his head, then went into the intensive-care unit. For the longest time he didn't emerge. Why, thought Terence Japhet, didn't someone tell him what was going on. Was the news that bad?

He was sitting on the bench, watching the wall clock like an idiot, his muscles aching with fatigue, when the taller of the two nurses brought him a piece of paper, a hospital consent which read like an obituary.

The nurse pointed to the bottom of the page and asked him to sign.

"Why are they operating?"

"No, no, it's just authority if they have to."

His mind wandered.

"Mr. Japhet, we can't go ahead with procedures until you sign."

"What procedures?"

"Whatever the doctors decide."

"Will they tell me?"

"Yes, they'll keep you informed. Please hurry."

He signed, unaccepting and compliant, just as he had signed countless bank notes, government forms, charge-account agreements, the language of which always needed emending, and you didn't change a word unless you were ready to be thought a crank.

Where it said "Parent or Guardian" he scratched out "or Guardian" with a stroke that penetrated the paper. Then he went to the phone booth.

He counted eleven rings before he heard Josephine's voice, thickened by sleep.

"Terence, why aren't you and Ed home yet?"

*Lie,* he thought.

"Terence?"

"Yes, Jo."

"I thought you'd left the phone. Are you bringing him home?"

"Can't do that, Jo."

"What's wrong? You said it was minor."

"It may be, they just don't know yet."

"Let me talk to him."

"You can't, Jo. He's in the intensive-care unit."

"What's wrong with him?"

"They don't know. It's the throat, some internal thing."

"There's something you're not saying."

"Please, Jo, I—"

"Let me talk to the doctor."

"The doctors are all busy, Jo."

"Are you lying to me?"

What could he say?

"Terence, is he dead? Terence!"

"No, no, Jo, he was choked."

"Badly?"

"No, well, yes, his throat's swollen on the inside."

"Anything else?"

"Don't know yet. Jo, someone else wants to use the phone." That was a lie.

"Don't hang up. Terence, I'm coming down."

"It's nearly four in the morning, Jo."

"Maybe the Tarrytown taxi is running."

"Jo, there's nothing to be done here. All I've been able to do is pace the floor and sign a consent."

"A what?" It took a moment for her to realize that he was crying. "Terence, if there is nothing you can do by being there, why don't you come on home. We'll both come back in the morning, love. You need to sleep."

"There's the intern, Jo, I'll call you back."

He hung up, blew his nose again, and caught the young man as he came down the hall. "How is he, please tell me."

The intern looked at Mr. Japhet's red-splotched face. "He's had morphine twice, he's asleep, he's not feeling any pain. His breathing is okay, but we're watching him carefully. The ice reduced the swelling a bit, but if the inside of the throat swells up again, we might have to give him another access to air."

"A tracheotomy?"

This father, the intern thought, is an educated man. "Sort of," he said, and before Terence could ask him what the specialist said, the intern excused himself and vanished down the hall. Mr. Japhet sat down to watch the clock again, to keep awake, until he remembered Josephine.

This time she answered right away.

"He's had morphine."

"Is he conscious?"

"Sleeping." He didn't say anything about the tracheotomy.

After a moment she said, "I could walk it down there."

"No, Jo, it's dark, you could get hit by a car on Route 9;

by the time you'd get here in this weather, it'd be morning. Phone Elsie, she'll drive you down."

"It's the middle of the night."

"I meant in the morning."

"The morning is Sunday."

"She wouldn't mind, if you explained."

"I'll call her at seven."

"I'll be here," he said. It sounded idiotic.

"Call me if there's any change. Promise?"

"Yes."

"I love you," she said and hung up.


## COMMENT BY MR. JAPHET

People, by and large, love their children. Seeing them grow up and taking pride in their achievements makes up for the chores and expense, but is love of a child an irreversible habit? How often does one feel love for children past the age of eight or ten? Less and less. Surely from the children's side, they can't feel this kind of continuing love for their parents, certainly not in their teens.

During that vigil in the hospital I felt for the first time a kind of love for Ed quite apart from what I felt for him when he was a child. I mean, at sixteen he is such a different human being from what I had known him as a child, different from me and from Josephine, not just his interests, magic and the like, but the whole cant of his life, his interest not in the mechanics of what he does but in the mystery. It may be a generational thing. That evening I felt I liked—all right, loved—Ed as a particular human being.


The quiet hours of the night had begun to be interrupted by the early-morning activity of the hospital. Mr. Japhet had just been given permission to don a white coat and go into the intensive-care unit when Josephine arrived. Elsie hung in the background. The Japhets did not hug or kiss, because the corridor now had people passing. Elsie waved good-bye at them.

"She's just got a coat over her nightgown," said Josephine.

Mrs. Japhet was given a white smock to put on, and they both went in. Ed was in the second bed from the right.

They were told to be very quiet. The man in the next bed to their son was expected to die within the hour.

Ed's eyes were open. The orange tube taped to his upper lip went into his right nostril and then presumably down into his stomach. It was connected to a jar with a small amount of brackish liquid in the bottom.

Not only was his throat swollen, but the puffiness extended upward to his face.

Josephine remembered when she had been a religious woman, finding occasional peace in prayer.

Terence stole a look at the chart to see if it would tell him anything. He was about to touch it when he saw the nurse approaching, and his hand fell.

Ed moved his eyes as if to make up for his inability to speak. Then the nurse said to them both in a whisper, "The swelling hasn't increased. There's no sign of internal hemorrhage now."

Josephine started to take Ed's hand.

"No," said the nurse. "Sepsis. Wait till he's out of this room."

"Oh," said Terence, "when is that likely?" His heart bounded.

"If all goes well, maybe tonight."

Later that morning Lila came with both her parents, but

they were not allowed to see Ed. The Hursts, who did not really know the Japhets except by sight, chatted with them for a minute and then took Lila home.

Josephine persuaded Terence to go down with her to the hospital cafeteria for some food. The feeling had left that if he quit his vigil Ed would die. But when he returned from the cafeteria, the nurse had to reassure him that there had been no adverse change.

Frank Tennent came by in the afternoon. He thought Mr. Japhet looked like he was in a trance. He spoke to Mrs. Japhet, expressing his sympathy. When he left, she kind of waved stupidly to him. He hurried out to his car where his date was waiting.

It was late in the afternoon, when Mr. Japhet was trying to read the Sunday paper Josephine had brought, that he realized he was rereading the same paragraph over and over without catching its sense. He looked up at his wife and knew that unless he went to bed he might pass out. He had had no sleep since Friday night.

He didn't want to leave the car with the smashed windshield near the entrance to the emergency room; so Josephine drove it home. The snow had stopped, and with the heater going full blast, it was bearable despite the open windshield. Though he usually sat near the right window when she drove, this time he sat very close.

From the garage she took him to the kitchen, but he wanted no food. He undressed by himself, his limbs moving slowly. He slipped on a pair of flannel pajamas, crawled into bed, and was asleep almost instantly. Josephine watched him for a while, then went downstairs. Nothing on television held her attention. She called the hospital to check, distrusting the cheerful nurse, then went to bed, taking care to keep her distance from Terence so as not to disturb his sleep.

## COMMENT BY DR. GUNTHER KOCH, PSYCHIATRIST

On Saturdays there is much to do that cannot be taken care of in the week, some shopping for breakfast things and for the evenings when I do not want to go to a restaurant, picking up light bulbs and whatnot at the hardware store, then home, skimming through professional magazines I am too tired to read on a weekday evening, and finally, when I can no longer take all this nothing, a walk in Central Park if the weather permits, and perhaps a film.

I find myself going to older films at the Symphony or the Thalia, things I have seen with Marta, because when I see a new film that is really good, I find I want to nudge Marta in the ribs or talk to her about it, so I keep with things we saw together. The film world is for me finite, finished, no more that is new. Karl, whom I share an office with, teases me I should marry again and recounts always the possibilities among the widows we both know. But it would be a housekeeping thing, not a marriage full of the interchange of emotions I had with Marta for thirty-four years. It could not be fair to the woman I married, Marta's shadows everywhere, the constant mental comparisons. If I married a widow, she would have shadows, too. And who would want to marry a widow whose marriage had not been good?

Our big loss, of course, was grandchildren. Our one son, Kurt, married—was it in spite?—a young woman who had already had a needless hysterectomy. Was Kurt's childlessness a willful attack on us?

I am quite convinced, after all these years of tiring practice, that the societies which enabled generations to live together and the children to be tutored by their grandparents were the best of all systems, avoiding the oedipal clash. I was too young when Kurt was a boy to raise him with the understanding that came to me, as it does to all of us, too late in life really to be of use. And so the hope was for grandchildren, even for a solitary grandchild, with whom I would now have my principal relationship and for which I would reserve, at the very least, all of my Sundays.

For what is there to do on a Sunday except read the enormous paper, or nap, or ask at a restaurant for a table for one, which elicits always a look of pity. I cannot interfere in the Sundays of my friends who have families full of grandchildren. I remember when Kolvick was taking his training analysis with me, and against my better judgment I went to his house for Sunday dinner, how swept up I was with his little boy, becoming in one afternoon an artificial grandfather full of feeling. But this could only be a nuisance interference in Kolvick's analysis. I couldn't get involved with his son without unsettling something.

That Sunday evening, as usual, I went for a long walk, directing myself toward the newsstand on Broadway that gets the first edition of the Monday papers early. Over a cup of cocoa at home I flipped through its pages when my eye first caught the story about the Japhet boy. I read it six times. Was I making another mistake by becoming interested in something like this? Sixteen is not a child. And why do I find the fact that he is a magician so compelling? I really should do nothing until I understand this better myself, but my hand sweats to pick up the telephone.

At six A.M. on Monday Terence Japhet awoke with a start. He had slept a long time. When he came out of the shower, which he started warm and gradually turned cold, Josephine was sitting up in bed.

"What's the matter?" she said.

He didn't answer. The expression on his face terrified her.

While he dressed, she called the hospital.

"They say Ed had a good night. Why are you looking like that?"

"Can you fix some breakfast, any kind, anything, just quickly."

In five minutes he had finished only half his dish of cold cereal, coffee, and said, "I'm going to the police."

Driving to the station house on Croton Avenue, he kept his coat collar up. He worried for the first time about an object flying in through the open windshield and cursed himself for not taking his sunglasses from home.

"What's up?" said the policeman behind the desk.

"Is Urek locked up?"

The policeman didn't know what he was talking about. Mr. Japhet tried to explain calmly. The policeman dug around among his papers.

"Oh, we were waiting for you to sign the complaint."

"The what?"

The policeman showed him the form.

"But I gave the officer at the hospital all the information."

"His complaint isn't valid."

"What do you mean not valid?"

"He didn't see it happen. His complaint's got to have a deposition from a witness or the injured person."

"The injured person is a boy who can hardly breathe or talk, and you let all of Sunday go by. That maniac could run away. My son was nearly killed."

"Look, mister, calm down, we didn't let anything go by. If you were in such a hurry, why didn't you get yourself down here Sunday morning?"

"I didn't sleep all Saturday night. I didn't leave the hospital till late Sunday."

The policeman, used to half-hysterical parents, exaggerations by complainants, pointed to the form impatiently. "If you'll sign this one, we can tear the other one up. Yours doesn't need any depositions, you're an eyewitness, okay?"

Terence filled it out the best he could. While he was doing that, a sergeant came in. He was much more polite.

"I can okay this. We can get a judge to sign it at nine o'clock," he explained.

"That's a whole hour from now."

"We need a warrant to pick up the Urek kid at his home."

"But he'll be in school by then."

"Oh no!" said the sergeant. They hated to pick up kids at school. So many of them were hostile toward policemen. And they'd need the approval of the principal.

"We could wait till after school," said the policeman.

"Please," Mr. Japhet pleaded with the sergeant, "that boy is a maniac. You can't leave him on the loose another minute. He tried to kill my—"

"We'll handle it," the sergeant interrupted. "Why don't you go on home?"

Mr. Japhet's hands were still shaking when he turned the doorknob to leave. When he was out the door, the sergeant shook his head, and the other policeman shrugged his shoulders.

"We'd better fill the chief in," said the sergeant. "The school is his turf."

Mr. Japhet stopped at the glass place on North Highland Avenue. They said they couldn't get a windshield in till Friday. They'd have to order it. He drove to the hospital. They wouldn't let him see Ed just then, though when they saw how wrought up he was they did get the resident for him, and the doctor said the boy was not in danger any-more.

"Are you sure?"

"As sure as we can ever be."

The resident couldn't give him any more time because a carload of skiers returning to New York City in the early-morning darkness had skidded into a stone wall on Route 9, and all seven of the people jammed into the small car were on the critical list.

He phoned Josephine. He said he was going straight on to the school for his nine-o'clock class. Yes, he said, he could have called in to have a substitute take over for the day, but he wanted to be there when the cops got Urek.

All his rage was coming back.

# Chapter 9

THE THICK-PACKED AUDITORIUM bobbed with more than a thousand student heads, waves of chatter welling as Mr. Chadwick, the principal, tapped on the microphone for silence.

The entire faculty stood along the right and left walls under the high windows through which daylight streamed.

When Mr. Chadwick started his career nearly thirty years earlier, the appearance of the principal on the stage was enough to turn a room of youngsters into a catacomb. Now boys and girls raucoused freely, defying him. He had permitted the longer hair. He had allowed rock in the music curriculum. He kept his door open, always, to student complaints. They had wanted freedom, they said. He had harvested rebellion. Was it ever different?

"I do not like," he said into the uproar, "to allow the police into the school, but this morning we have no alternative."

As if on signal, Chief Rogers strode down the aisle, the rows growing silent from back to front as he came into view. Rogers looked now, as always, as if he had just shaved and bathed and pressed his suit, the appearance not of a cop but the uniformed administrator of the community's tensions. He spoke well, as if he had been to college, which in fact he had.

In five seconds he was onstage, facing the near-silent student body. Mr. Chadwick gladly relinquished the microphone.

"Boys and girls—a lot of you out there are my friends—I don't think the police belong in a school either to discipline students or to guard against trouble. If we have to do that here, as they do in New York City, which is only thirty miles away, then there will be little difference between schools and reformatories—except you get to sleep at home."

It got him a laugh, which was what he wanted. He thought of the thousand no longer chattering students as a mob, and the first thing to do with a mob is to relax it. Then he got down to business.

"Saturday night, after the midwinter prom, there was a serious occurrence just outside this building. It's all over the morning papers, which isn't good publicity for the community. Ed Japhet, an eleventh-grader, was beset and beaten by a gang of youths right outside these school doors. His father, who teaches here . . ."

All eyes turned toward Mr. Japhet, who was standing with his colleagues along the right wall.

". . . had his windshield smashed by the same boys. And Ed, who put on a magic show here that night, had his equipment smashed irreparably. I have always placed a much greater emphasis in this community on physical harm to human beings than to property damage. Ed Japhet is still in Phelps, though his condition is no longer critical."

Some students applauded the last statement, until the chief held up his hand.

"We believe that all four boys responsible for this attack are students of this school, and if so, are probably in this auditorium right now. I ask them to identify themselves."

## COMMENT BY GEORGE THOMASSY, UREK'S LAWYER

Now, I take very strong objection to this kind of thing. Under our laws a person is innocent until proven guilty. No one has been proven guilty of anything as of now. And a person cannot be made to incriminate himself. That's exactly what the chief did. He violated my client's constitutional rights.

"Mr. Japhet," said the chief, "has identified the alleged leader of the assailants as a student who was in his class last year, Stanislaus Urek."

Heads turned toward Urek, sitting in the fifth row. And Urek, with all the force his lungs could muster, stood and shouted, "Stanley!"

"Is this the boy?" the chief asked Mr. Japhet across the heads of the audience.

"Yes," said Mr. Japhet barely audibly.

Four uniformed policemen, who had been standing discreetly at the back of the auditorium, moved, three down the center aisle and one down the right-side aisle toward Urek. The students on both sides of Urek quickly spilled out in the aisles, leaving him alone in the row. The principal motioned them toward the empty seats on the other side.

"I didn't do nothin'," said Urek.

One of the three policemen in the center aisle started to sidle into the row toward Urek.

"I wanna talk to my father's lawyer," said Urek to the chief.

"As soon as we get to the station house."

"I ain't going to no station house!"

"Who were the other boys with you?" asked the chief.

"I ain't snitching on nobody," said Urek, suddenly darting

toward the side aisle, where the row was now blocked by a lone policeman. The faculty members standing nearby against the wall scattered. The policeman seized Urek's arm.

"Leggo my arm!" screamed Urek. Shaking free, he shoved the cop off balance, grabbed the high window ledge, and hoisted himself up.

The policeman tugged at Urek's leg. Urek kicked backward, his heel hitting the cop's face. A nostril gushed red blood as a moaning sound went through the student audience, suddenly all on its feet, with the chief yelling into the microphone, "Sit down! Sit down!"

Urek hoisted himself, first a knee, then altogether, up onto the windowsill, then turned, framed against the window light, shouting, "Let me alone!"

The hurt policeman wiped blood from his nose, cheek, and lip. The other three policemen were beneath the window ledge, looking up. One reached for his pistol.

"Put that away!" commanded the chief.

The policeman returned the weapon to the holster. Clearly, none of the three dared to try hoisting themselves onto the window ledge.

Mr. Chadwick whispered in the chief's ear. "Shall I clear the auditorium?"

"No," said the chief, "we'll lose the other three. This'll only take a minute." Then to the back of the room, "Somebody bring a ladder or a chair."

There was a bustling in back of the room as a chair from an adjoining classroom was brought down the side aisle by a faculty member.

"Now, you come down," the chief said to Urek.

"Fuck you!" screamed Urek. "Fuck all of you!"

The tallest policeman was on the chair, grabbing for Urek's leg. Urek stomped at the cop's hand, which was quickly withdrawn. Another chair was brought down the side aisle and placed on the other side of the window ledge, and mounted by another policeman. With a signaled nod, both policemen reached for Urek's legs at the same time, figuring he couldn't stomp at both at the same time.

Urek kicked out at one, then the other, hitting neither. Then he started losing his balance. One of the cops grabbed at his ankle, throwing him further off balance, and Urek went crashing against the window, his shoulders breaking the glass as girls screamed and a shout filled the auditorium. For a moment it seemed that Urek was falling backward out the window, but the quick policeman was up on the ledge, sitting, grabbing the flailing feet, holding on as the second policeman hoisted himself to the large sill, and together they pulled with all their strength, sending Urek pitching forward into the room. There was a rush of people toward where Urek fell, the chief abandoning the stage and the microphone, rushing up the aisle, yelling, "Give him room!" He thought Urek was unconscious, some bone broken, or his spinal cord snapped.

But in an instant he knew otherwise, because as the chief leaned over, Urek reached up and grabbed his collar. Before Urek could do any harm, a mass of hands had seized his arms and legs and held him pinioned beyond need, breathless, yelling, "Lemme go!" A minute later he was being led from the auditorium, his hands handcuffed behind his back, while the principal tried to restore order and get everybody to sit back down.

Monday in the early evening, Ed was moved out of the intensive-care unit because of hospital rules: as more-serious cases came in, less-serious cases were moved out.

The doctors thought Ed probably should be in a private room. Mr. Japhet's Blue Cross coverage provided for a semiprivate. Ed was put into a semiprivate room which was otherwise unoccupied.

Ed was glad to get away from the other people in the intensive-care unit whose grim state led some of them not to another room but to the morgue.

The overhead light hurt his eyes until it was turned out by the nurse. A floor lamp in the corner cast a yellowish glow. A television set was rigged five feet up on the far wall, its potential less interesting to Ed than the telephone at his bedside, which he could not yet use because of the orange tube in his nose that went down into his throat and stomach. But it was a connection with the outside world he welcomed.

Now that he was no longer doped up, he could feel the dull pain of his bruised throat. If he breathed deeply, his rib cage ached, but instead of a hurt bundle of pain sleeping fitfully, he now began to feel alive again.

Though it was past visiting hours, the nurse stood at the door of Ed's room with a very tall and seemingly shy young man in uniform. They were making an exception because the young man, who had seen the news about Ed in the *Times*, expected to be shifted out of Fort Dix by the end of the week. Ed was very glad to see Gil and motioned him to the bedside chair.

Gilbert Atkins, a stringbean six-foot-two, was three years older than Ed and had been inducted into the army some months previously. They had last seen each other at a meeting of the New York Chapter of the International Brotherhood of Magicians. The fact that they were the two "kids" in the organization had brought them closer than their three-year difference might otherwise have allowed. And they liked each other because they both did not merely buy or learn tricks to do, but experimented with inventing new ways of doing old tricks. Unlike some of the senior members of the brotherhood, they were both also intensely interested in the psychology of the audience, the willingness of most people under the right circumstances to suspend disbelief.

"Don't try to talk," said Gil. "They told me all about it. I brought you something."

Even before the young soldier had unwrapped the present, it was clear it was a book, small, without a dust wrapper, and obviously much used. Ed took it in his hand. The gold printing on the cover had flaked off long ago, but the embossing of the title and author could be read. It was a copy of Jean Hugard's little book of complex card tricks, the cornerstone of Gil's library of perhaps three dozen volumes of books on magic.

Ed, overwhelmed, tried to say, "But it's yours." The tube made his words unintelligible.

"I didn't have time to buy anything. Anyhow, I won't be back for two years."

Ed felt the cover of the book with the moist palm of his hand. "Thank you," he mumbled.

Gil sat for a bit in silence, uncomfortable with the obligation of having to do all the talking.

"The gang that got you, are they the ones you told me about?"

Ed nodded.

"You know," Gil said, "the army is full of guys like that. Rednecks, from every part of the country. Beer, bowling, hunting, car Simonizing. You should hear them talk about women, even their wives. Filling the old lady's hole, is the way they think of it. These guys don't even go to the movies, except drive-ins, and that's not for the movies. Biggest thing they miss in the army is TV. Booze and poker, that's it. I kind of keep to myself. If I weren't tall, I think I'd be in fights all the time."

The nurse came in to see if everything was all right and to tell Gil he'd have to leave soon.

"Before the army," said Gil, "I couldn't understand all the stuff you read about violence. I mean, I know about Hitler and all that, and assassinations and muggings, but after living with those guys for a couple of months, I wonder how come there isn't *more* violence, you know what I mean?" Gil studied the insignia on his cap. "Hearing what happened to

you makes me wish I'd had the nerve to head for Canada."
He laughed. "Wouldn't do any good. I'd wind up in jail
surrounded by the same types. Well, look, take care, will
you?"

He wrote on a piece of paper for Ed. "That's my address
for mail. I promise to write when your letters catch up with
me."

He stood up. "Maybe I can get transferred to some USO-
type outfit, doing magic. That'd be nice, wouldn't it?"

Ed held up the book, thanking him again for it.

"Take care," said Gil.

Going out the door, he looked very military, not just the
uniform, but the way he walked. Ed hoped the army
wouldn't kill him.

# Chapter 10

THE COURTROOM had fourteen rows of seats on both sides of a wide aisle for the townspeople to observe the administration of justice. The seats were usually empty. The walls, paneled with walnut veneer, gave the chamber a dark, brooding solidity. The one touch of color was the American flag, which drooped on its stand beside the black-robed judge. Some years earlier a village trustee had suggested that a quiet electric fan be hidden behind the bench, tilted upward at the flag so that it would seem to be waving, but the justices dismissed the notion as undignified.

Urek stood in front of the bench, no longer in handcuffs because his lawyer had assured the policemen that he wouldn't try anything funny. George Thomassy did not want to plead for low bail for a client under physical restraint.

Judge Clifford, a proud man, spent a good part of his time on the bench trying to control a human affliction: he had the habit of swallowing air and subsequently burping, which, though he had learned to burp quietly behind a hand held in front of his lips, disturbed him because it seemed inconsistent with the dignity of his office. Once, in the course of a prolonged and unruly trial, the affliction had distressed him so that he visited a doctor, who told him that air-swallowing was not an uncommon nervous habit among people; the less fortunate could expel their intake only through flatulence. The judge thought himself lucky because the indignity of passing wind in court would certainly exceed what he suffered as a burper.

The point at which the judge most tried to control his affliction was when a defendant first came before his view. The judge had developed a personal ritual of considering each defendant as if he were an employment applicant. During his initial study of a defendant's appearance, a moment that would last anywhere from five to thirty seconds, the judge's hands, pressed together before his lips, served not only the purpose of burp concealment but gave most defendants a sense that they were being studied by God in an attitude of prayer.

To Judge Clifford, Urek's face did not seem to be American, that is, clean-cut, short-haired, near handsome, with a look of innocent honesty. On the contrary, he looked markedly Slavic. The judge was also disturbed by the deep scar that ran vertically along Urek's right cheek and almost onto the ear. When he saw such scars on Negroes, he assumed them to be the result of knife fights, but in the case of this Slavic boy, perhaps it had been a spill from a bicycle. He wouldn't, of course, ask. The boy's hair had been plastered down in a way that betrayed uncustomary effort. Still, he was wearing a white shirt, with a striped blue tie, and his suit was pressed. The judge did not like to believe that he was influenced by dress, which could be contrived for occasions, as indeed Urek's had been by the lawyer who had brought the dress-up gear to the jail, but so many young people he saw these days just had no regard for their physical appearance.

Thomassy argued that his client was known to him for many years (true), that he lived at home with his mother and father (true), that he had not been in serious trouble before (false), and that bail should be nominal, considering all these points and the defendant's youth.

The police sergeant described the seriousness of the injury to Japhet, the smashed windshield, the fracas in the school auditorium, the difficulty in making the arrest, and the danger the police had been put in just in trying to get this young fellow to come along.

No mention was made of the fact that Urek's small, feared organization controlled the student body at the school more than the principal or the teachers could be said to do.

Judge Clifford decided that Thomassy was doing his duty in making Urek out to be a nice boy, and that the police sergeant was once again emphasizing the strain and danger of police work. As happens in smaller communities, the judge had Thomassy before him fairly frequently; in fact, at a mutual friend's party recently, Thomassy and the judge had gone off in a corner to discuss the recent Supreme Court obscenity decisions for a good part of the evening. Thomassy was probably the smartest trial lawyer in the community, articulate and charming in private, really knowledgeable about the law, and tough and earthy in front of a jury. The judge felt himself fortunate. Examinations of witnesses were never boring if Thomassy was defending somebody.

As for the police sergeant, the judge knew his opinion of adolescent kids. Their rock music late at night brought nuisance telephone calls to the police station. The kids broke street lights. They'd take the name shingle in front of a driveway and exchange it for another stolen somewhere. Always creating work for the department, then ending up with the parents coming down and saying, "Look, it's only kids having fun. It won't happen again." Of course, it always happened again; somebody's kids somewhere in town pranking, or smoking pot. The sergeant shouldn't feel that harassed. It was his job to deal with nuisances.

Taking his hands away from his face, Judge Clifford set the bail at five hundred dollars.

Thomassy felt relieved. Urek started to say something; Thomassy squeezed his arm hard to keep the boy silent.

The Yonkers bondsman Thomassy dealt with was very tough about going along with high bail for irresponsible kids. Five hundred dollars was okay. The kid lived at home, and he didn't seem to be the long-haired sort that might take off for Greenwich Village. The bond would cost Urek's father seventy-five dollars, and he'd probably have to sign the guaranty. The father wouldn't want to be stuck for five hundred. He probably didn't have five hundred. Paul Urek, Thomassy thought, would see to it that the kid didn't run off somewhere.

Almost as an afterthought, Judge Clifford said to Urek, "Remember, son, bail is a promise to return."

Back in his office, Thomassy sat Urek down on the leather couch. "You stay there," he said.

Thomassy hung his jacket on the back of his chair, revealing half-moons of sweat under each armpit.

"Be back in a minute," he said, heading for the men's room down the hall. This was his test. If Urek made a break for it, that was the end. He could break laws but not defy Thomassy. If Urek went for anything on the desk, or tried to relieve the jacket on the back of the chair of any of its contents, he was finished. A client had to realize that Thomassy was above all else immune from anything the client might do to the rest of the world.

Urek hadn't moved off the couch. Good sign.

Thomassy stretched his arms in front of him, fingers intertwined. Then he stretched his lanky frame, watching Urek all the time. This was Thomassy's silent treatment. Some clients filled the vacuum with talk. That kind was dangerous on the witness stand.

The boy was looking everywhere, except at Thomassy. Would he speak? Thomassy waited, thinking.

He had gone straight from the dean's list at NYU Law to Pritchard, Hutchinson, Batsford, & Morgan—but not before trying a little mischief: he had applied to Sullivan & Cromwell, been offered a job, then turned it down. He had been interviewed at Debevoise, Plimpton, & MacLean; they told him the salary they were considering starting him at, and he told the interviewer a day later it wasn't the salary, he didn't want the job. He did the same thing when he was offered an associate's position at Cravath, Swaine & Moore. Thomassy wanted Pritchard; they were the only firm of the bunch without a single non-Wasp name on its letterhead.

But he told Mr. Pritchard, who insisted on interviewing each successful applicant personally, of the offers from the other three firms. Pritchard liked the young man's nerve, raised the offer by a thousand dollars, and hired him as an associate. At the next partners' meeting, Pritchard made much about their having snagged that quick-witted Armenian who had turned down Sullivan & Cromwell, Debevoise, and Cravath. Within three years Thomassy had become the best tactician on the litigating side of the firm, when he was told by Pritchard personally that he'd have to resign.

"You might say," declared the seventy-year-old Mr. Pritchard, "that you are being fired for excessive competence. You're obviously the most valuable associate we've got. We can't promote any of the other associates into partnerships unless we promote you first, and we're not about to have a Boston Irishman, a Jew, or an Armenian in the senior ranks. They may be breaking ground in some of the other firms, but not here, not till I'm dead, anyway. Never mind, I'll give you a letter of recommendation that'll fix you up as house counsel at any American corporation you name at a higher salary. Good luck."

Thomassy didn't shake Pritchard's outstretched hand. He cleared his desk, said good-bye to no one, didn't wait for a letter of recommendation. In two weeks he was working a fanatical sixty-hour week at the American Civil Liberties Union, getting the guilty as well as the innocent off the hook. He started getting his name in the papers, became a master of press conferences as well as a crackerjack courtroom lawyer. Every year he sent old Mr. Pritchard a birthday card, his way of saying you're living too long, drop dead.

Finally, when civil-liberties cases became routine for him, Thomassy decided to devote himself to private criminal practice, with one intention: winning every time. He set himself up in the suburbs. Ossining had Italian lawyers for the Italians, Jewish lawyers for the Jews, Wasp lawyers for the majority, and so Thomassy concentrated his early practice on the miscellaneous ethnics who didn't have a lawyer in town.

Paul Urek was his first client. His television set had been repossessed by the finance company. Thomassy not only got him his TV back, he filed a claim against the finance company for removing the set in the full view of neighbors when the overdue check was already in the mail. They settled out of court for more than the television set had cost. Paul Urek spread the word: this new lawyer wasn't just good, he was great. Soon Thomassy was getting all the business he could handle, not only from the miscellaneous ethnics, but from Italians, Jews, and finally Wasps as well. The word was: if you want to win, get Thomassy. Defending Paul Urek's kid was something he had to do successfully.

During the silent treatment, Urek had kept quiet. Or was he about to talk now? Thomassy studied Urek's strange face. He saw the surface of animal agitation, an actual tic in one cheek, eyes that were never still, and behind them a feeling of lava. Urek, though still in his teens, reminded Thomassy most of a thirty-year-old anti-Semitic hooligan from Queens who had been accused of defacing the ark in a Queens synagogue. Somehow the case had gotten to the Civil Liberties Union instead of the Legal Aid Society. During his first interview with the man Thomassy had uncovered the fact that he was guilty not only of the charged offense but of several similar incidents in the past for which he had not been apprehended. Having defaced several synagogues without getting caught, he had gotten careless and taken too long on the inside, where he was seen through the window by three Jews, who waited for him to come out. They did not seize him but observed him carefully for identification purposes, followed him home, then reported the matter to the police.

At the trial, Thomassy showed that the black enamel used for the desecration could have been bought at any hardware store. The same for the brush. True, when the man was picked up by the cops, his hands, which had been thoroughly washed by then, still smelled of turpentine. But you couldn't convict a man on turpentine smells—not if Thomassy was defending him. When the three Jews testified, he tore their credibility to pieces by the use of easy law-school tactics. Everything was much too circumstantial for the judge, who let the man off with a warning to get rid of all the hate literature that had been found in his apartment. Thomassy had even objected to the warning, and the judge had withdrawn it.

Thomassy felt pretty good about that case. He surmised that the man had probably been guilty of a great deal throughout his disordered life. Something must have gone irretrievably wrong early, but you couldn't lock people up for life just to keep them in line. Society had to take its chances, and Thomassy was the instrument for protecting people like that from vengeance.

An expression of discomfort wrinkled Urek's features in what seemed to be the beginning of laughter.

"Listen, kid." Thomassy stabbed a finger at Urek. "You're in more trouble than you think. What's so funny?"

"Nothin'," said Urek.

"I don't want you discussing anything that happened with anyone from now on. That goes for your mother and father, too. Just shut up. You've said too much already. You got to get some facts straight. Japhet's father is a schoolteacher. That's in his favor. Your father is a millhand and a part-time gas-station attendant."

He wasn't getting through. Explaining such distinctions to Urek was pointless.

"They say you smashed the windshield of Japhet's car with a chain. If you did, that was stupid. That's property damage of an insured item. If the insurance company went after you, you'd be licked."

Thomassy rocked back on his heels. "Fortunately, there's a hundred-dollar deductible, and the amount that's over might not be enough for them to get excited about. How else did you damage the car?"

"Well," said Urek, uneasy.

"It's okay, you're telling me, not the judge."

"Well, I smashed one of the suitcases against the back fender. The other suitcase was done by one of the other guys."

"Did you dent the fender?"

Urek shrugged. He didn't know.

"Let's hope you didn't. We don't want the insurance company in this, right? Now, bodily injury. People damage. You jumped Japhet's kid and the girl friend."

"I didn't do nothing to the girl. I mean, I twisted her arm, but she didn't get hurt."

"That could be assault. In our society, we don't like women to get assaulted. Fortunately for you, the only witnesses on their side are the boyfriend and the boyfriend's father, and if she has no injuries that required medical attention ... Are you listening?"

"Sure," said Urek, twitching his nose. "What about the guy in the hospital?"

"He's going to be the chief witness against you. He's going to be asked to tell every detail of what he did and what you did, especially what you did to him. You damn nearly killed him."

Whatever Thomassy said from that point on washed over Urek, who was thinking he didn't like the idea of that Japhet superkid yakking about him on the witness stand. A few more seconds. If only he hadn't let go when the school janitor shone his flashlight, yelling. But there was Japhet's old man pounding his back, hurting.

"You're not listening," said Thomassy.

"You know somethin', that kid's father beat me."

"He what?" asked Thomassy.

"I didn't touch him. And he beat me."

"Very interesting," said Thomassy, making a note.

The woman at the hospital switchboard was very near retirement age. She had put in seven of her eight hours that Monday, and was looking forward to her relief. She mustered her strength for the last hour because she felt that in her job she could account for so many kindnesses if she handled each incoming call just right.

"Ed Japhet?" asked the caller.

"Would you spell the name, please," said the operator, immediately sorry she had given this stock response, because the caller seemed flustered. "Is it 'f-f' or 'p-p'?" She asked, then answered her own question, because she had just minutes before received the slip taking Japhet, Edward's name off the intensive list.

"Hold on, please. He's been assigned a room."

She always kept her Rollodex up to the minute, and there the card was, not keeping the caller waiting long at all.

"Room four-oh-two," said the switchboard operator proudly.

She was surprised that the caller did not ask to be connected. Urek, who had been released in the custody of his parents, did not even thank her before he hung up.

Dinner consisted of meatloaf and frozen corn on the cob. Urek watched his father put margarine on the corn. He could tell the old man was sore.

"What did ya get in a fight for?" he said at last.

Urek said nothing.

His father munched on the ear of corn, then wiped his mouth on a paper napkin. "Thomassy costs money. What'd ya get arrested for, are you gonna answer me?"

"Let him eat his supper," said Mrs. Urek.

"He can rot in jail, that's what I think."

Urek left his dinner on the plate. He went upstairs, saying he was going to listen to some records and then go to sleep. He put the record player on a long-play with the volume not too loud so that his father wouldn't come barging in, then fixed the record-player arm so that the record would be replayed again and again. Then he put on a sweater and went down the drainpipe as he had on many previous occasions.

It was a long walk, and Urek was out of breath by the time he got to the hospital and entered the side door marked "Physicians Only."

Once in the stairwell, he felt safe. He knew the room number from his phone call. Visiting hours were over, and with luck no duty nurse would see him going into the room.

Ed's eyes widened when he saw Urek enter the room. He wanted to yell, but the great sudden breath in his lungs, with the tube going down into his stomach, came out a useless gurgle. Ed reached for the nurse's call button, but Urek caught the wrist first in a fierce left-hand lock as his right hand fished for the knife in his pocket. He pulled the knife out, pressed the button that released the blade. Shit, thought Urek, he had to let go the wrist to grab the rubber tube so he could cut it.

The knife was just honed.

It cut through cleanly.

Urek dashed out of the room, thinking he had severed Ed Japhet's lifeline.

In the hallway just outside the room Urek ran into a nurse's aide carrying a tray of wrapped sterilized instruments which spilled, the clatter reverberating down the hall. Two or three other nurses on the floor turned in time to see Urek's figure dashing into the back stairway. Only the nurse's aide saw enough to be able to identify him later.

Ed pushed the nurse's call button. There was no need to. While the nurse's aide was picking up the instruments, two nurses rushed into his room. One saw what had happened and left to summon the duty doctor.

There was no urgent need to. The tube Urek had cut was there so the doctor could check for blood in the stomach that might have come from spleen damage or some other not easily detectable internal injury. It was a safety precaution, that was all.

But Ed knew that this time Urek had intended to murder him, and he couldn't for the life of him understand why.

# Chapter 11

THE NURSE AT THE DESK wished the telephone in her hands was the upright phone she remembered from her childhood, the kind whose cradle you tapped up and down to get the operator's attention. She had dialed 9 to get an outside line, and then O for Operator; it rang and rang and rang at the other end, ignoring her. Miss Murphy, as she was called by the younger nurses, saw the collapse of the modern world in such things as the increasing debility of the telephone service, as if it were an aged patient suffering from hardening of the arteries, loss of energy, the settling of cobwebs in the brain, the beginning of hopelessness.

Finally, an answer. The voice that said "Operator" was Spanish-sounding. Puerto Rican?

"Connect me with the police."

"May I have your number, please?"

"This is Phelps Memorial. Connect me with the goddamn police!"

"I have to have your number in case you hang up."

"ME-1-5100, hurry, it's an emergency."

For Miss Murphy, who was in her late fifties and nearing

retirement, the world had changed too much. Everyone—meaning the people she had come into contact with forty and thirty and twenty years earlier, other nurses, telephone operators—everyone had been of Scotch or Irish or English or German descent, could be relied on to be white, not slow. She spent so much of her life just listening to patients who wanted to talk, she thought of herself as being more understanding than most people. She knew that while Latin rhythms had a lot of bounce, the rhythm of Latin life did not, and that people coming up from Spanish America walked slowly, worked slowly, but did they also think slowly even in emergencies? They were quick-tempered, the adrenalin flowed, why couldn't they work efficiently, like the nurses she had gone to school with, the operators who used to work the telephones before the blacks and the Puerto Ricans took over in New York and its suburbs? All life was darker now, she thought, and somehow whiteness, the color of her uniform and stiff-starched cap, the normal color of things, was graying wearily.

"Tarrytown police, Sergeant Delaney speaking."

She tried to tell him quickly of the incident, the nose tube cut, the spilled tray of instruments, the short man rushing down the back stairs. Sergeant Delaney interrupted her, making her feel as if she were rambling. All she was giving him were the facts.

"Edward Japhet," she said quickly. "The patient's name is Edward Japhet."

"Christ!" said the sergeant. "I'll bet it's the Urek kid again."

She asked him what he meant by that, but the blasphemous sergeant wasn't even listening now. "My name is Murphy," she said.

"Got that," said the sergeant, as if it didn't matter, as if their common origin no longer counted.

He had hung up, leaving her holding the telephone receiver, with only her patients to attend to.

The police in Tarrytown and Ossining kept in close touch with their respective cases not only through the newspapers but through formal and informal procedures and friendships. The way that thermometer-shaker had gone on, Sergeant Delaney thought, the assailant would be too far from the hospital to be chased and caught.

When Delaney said it sounded like the Urek boy was on the loose again, the duty sergeant at Ossining called Chief Rogers at home. The chief ordered a squad car to the Urek house, then quietly thumbed through his telephone directory, found Thomassy *bus* and *res*, dialed the second number.

"This is a friendly call," said the chief.

"Not at this hour. What's up?"

The chief had a lot of respect for Thomassy. He would want him to defend his son if his son ever got into trouble. He told the lawyer what had happened at the hospital.

"Couldn't have been Urek," said Thomassy. "I left him at home with instructions not to leave."

"Listen," said the chief, "I've got a car on the way down there now. For your sake, I hope that kid hasn't fucked up again. If he's not there, I hope you find him before we do."

"I appreciate the call," said Thomassy.

"Clifford'll double the bail if it turns out—"

"I'll handle Clifford. I appreciate the call," he repeated, and hung up.

Thomassy dialed the Urek house and glanced over at the bed, where Jane Purdy had the sheet pulled up to her chin. Jane and her husband, who was a long-distance truck driver, had both been caught with pot, and Thomassy had gotten them off with a warning. Since then, Jane had regularly showed up on Tuesday evenings because her husband called home collect on Mondays and Wednesdays. The end of the week could be dangerous, and more particularly because

Thomassy had another girl he saw on Fridays, he tried to get it off twice on Tuesdays, once right after she'd whip up a dinner at his place and then again after a short nap. He was just stirring a second time when the chief called.

Sex for Thomassy was the perfect form of exercise. Perhaps swimming limbered up more of the muscles, but you couldn't swim during eight months of the year except at the crowded Y. Besides, it was the fantastic mind-releasing exercise that made sex work. You *felt* better afterward. All you had to do was organize it right. Use steadies to minimize the courtship crap. Alternate partners to prevent boredom. Do what she likes so she'll do what you like—and remember, every woman likes something different better. Minimize the risks. Do it in safe places. Leave no grounds for revenge. Leave no evidence for revenge, in case it breaks up.

Paul Urek answered the phone. He immediately went up to check the boy's room.

He came back to the telephone breathless.

"He's gone."

"I'll be right there," said Thomassy.

Jane looked petulant. Thomassy shrugged. Even a quick one wouldn't work now. His mind was racing in other directions.

"Make up for it next Tuesday," he said, buttoning his shirt.

He pulled down the sheet and gave her a darting kiss on her belly. He didn't know why she liked that, but she did.

"Please get dressed fast, honey," he said. "I've got to make time." He *never* left a woman alone in the apartment.

He watched her drive off and waved before he got into his own car and headed for Urek's.

Urek, on his way home, stopped off in the kraut girl's place. She was surprised to see him.

"What do you want?"

He couldn't tell her what had just happened. Or how excited he was.

"Well?"

He tried to make his shoulder shrug casual.

"You look all . . . something. Where you been?"

He was thinking of what he might say.

"Never mind," she said.

"Look," Urek said, "I gotta talk."

"What about?" she said, not really curious.

"I just did somethin'."

"You rob someone?"

"No."

"What are you so worked up about?"

"Jesus, I gotta talk to somebody."

"How about your mother?" she said, a skin of derision over her voice.

"Yeah," he said, "sure."

"Well, okay, talk to me." She locked the door of her room, then sat down in front of the vanity mirror. He watched her run a comb slowly through her blonde hair. He liked it when they were alone. When the gang took her on, Urek usually went first, so he didn't get the kick they did before they took her on.

"I really gotta talk to somebody," he said.

"It's your dime."

"Cantcha even turn around?"

"How can I comb my hair if I turn around? I can hear you."

He touched her hair.

"Well, you're getting real romantic," she said.

"I just thought your hair looked, you know, nice."

She turned to face him. "You ever talk to a priest?"

"You mean in the box. Sure. It's no good. Whatever I tell him, he always makes me say the same fucking thing. I could tell him I killed my mother and father and half the

town and he'd say, say ten Hail Marys. I can talk to myself
for all the good it does."

"Come here."

Urek took one step toward her. Sitting, she was able to
put her hands around his waist, then laid her cheek against
him. She could hear his heart, the rhythmic thump-thump,
thump-thump.

"Hey, you're alive," she said, letting her hand drop and
just brush the front of his pants.

"Whadya do that for?"

She laughed.

"Say," he said, "are you really a nympho? Some of the
guys say . . ."

He thought she was going to make him get out. Instead
she said, "Your mother and father, they don't like it when
they do it, do they?"

"I never thought about it."

"You had to. Everybody does. You think any of the old
people *like* to do it?"

"How would I know?"

"You ever watch them?"

"What do you think I am?"

"I do. I got a way. It's what gave me the idea before."

"Before what?"

"Before I ever did anything with anybody. Everybody's
mother and father does it. *I* enjoy it, I like it, don't you like
it?"

He wished she would stop talking now.

"You and your guys think you know something when you
know that I do it. That's like thinking the President doesn't
do it. It's stupid."

He was so touchy. She hadn't meant to get him angry. She
unbuttoned her blouse. He watched her.

"You know something?" she said, as she unhooked her
bra. "You never once kissed me."

"You mean on them?"

"On the mouth, stupid."

He had never kissed any girl on the mouth.

When he didn't move, she moved to him, and put her arms around his neck and brought his face down to her and held her lips against his tightly closed lips.

"Do that again," she said, "only relax."

His head was in a roar. He could feel the needling in his groin, the signal, but couldn't connect the idea of kissing lips and a feeling half his body away.

"Do it to me," she said.

He looked blank.

"What I'm doing to you."

Their mouths met, and despite the slaver and terrified thoughts in his head, he felt himself stiffening with an urgency, the need to rush.

She slipped off her shoes, unwrapped her skirt, let it drop, and stepped out of it. She took her half-slip off.

"You don't have to take everything off," said Urek.

She took her socks off, and then stepped out of her white panties; the hair where her legs met was dark, not blonde like her long hair.

"Arencha going to turn the light off?" he said.

She shrugged her shoulders and turned the switch. It merely dimmed the light, one of those three-way bulbs now at its lowest setting. Then, completely naked, she sat down in front of her dressing table again, and again combed her hair. He could have killed her.

"You afraid of catching cold?" she said, turning. "Take your clothes off."

He got down to his shorts and socks, then stood adamant.

"Take your socks off."

He took off first one, then the other.

"The rest, too," she said. "Want some help?"

He wasn't going to have any girl undressing him. He let his shorts drop to the floor, the hairiness of his body now wholly exposed to her view.

"Well," she said at his preparedness.

He gestured toward the bed.

"What's your hurry?"

She came closer to him, and he gestured toward the bed again.

Her hands were on him, stroking, and he tried now with force at her shoulders, to push her to the bed, but it was suddenly too late, and like an idiot he stood there, coming in spasms.

The kraut was frightened at his anger. He didn't say anything. She put her arms around him, it seemed to him tenderly, and sat him down on the edge of the bed. She kissed the side of his neck, then his cheek, and then his closed mouth.

He motioned for her to turn the light completely off, which she did, so that she would not see him, but when he lay down, his face in the pillow, she could hear him smothering the shame of his sobs.

# Chapter 12

ON THE OPEN ROAD in daylight, when Thomassy was relaxed, he drove with his left elbow on the window or on the armrest, his right hand lightly on the wheel, feeling the responsiveness of the car as he had once the controls of a light plane when he took a few flying lessons. But when tense, he clutched the wheel with both hands, apprehensive about oncoming traffic, each car a new threat, worrying about the brakes' sudden failure or a tie rod going, the auto out of control and veering him, trapped in his seat belt, toward a yard-wide tree. Tonight Thomassy drove through the night with both perspiring palms on the wheel, all the way to the Urek house.

His most frequent fantasy while driving was of himself cross-examining a witness. Other lawyers he knew dreamed of being admitted to practice before the Supreme Court— perhaps just once. That was not Thomassy's aim, though he didn't doubt for a moment that he could get there if he wanted to. In front of the high court he couldn't cross-examine in the way that intoxicated him, setting up the witness for a laugh from the jury and spectators, even at his own expense, so that the momentarily relaxed witness, enjoying the sudden release of tension, perhaps even joining in the laughter, would be suddenly faced by the most crucial question Thomassy had to ask of him. The witness, chilled in mid-laugh, would have to compose himself, *think* to answer the shocker, and it was the pause that Thomassy went for most. Because when a man took too much time in framing an answer, the jury thought he was lying. Or making it up. Or partly. And Thomassy would turn from the hesitation, and stroll to the jury and say, "Please take all the time you need to think of your answer," which the jury always understood to mean *Take all the time you need to make up your lie.* How Thomassy loved that, the director of a play played just once, the other lawyer rehearsing the actor only to have Thomassy produce a stage wait, a silence that damned.

Sometimes Thomassy would find himself imagining a crime not yet committed, the criminal being chased and caught and brought to trial, to be defended by him, as if *that* were the purpose of the crime in the first place. If, he was thinking, a sudden hazard caused him to carom into a yard-wide tree, would anyone be guilty or innocent of his death, which would seem so pointless otherwise? He laughed at—and relished—the absurdity of his fantasies.

He saw the police car in front of the Urek house. Paul Urek was in front of the doorway arguing with the two cops.

"The boy isn't home," he was saying. "There's Mr. Thomassy."

Both cops turned.

"What's up?" Thomassy asked them.

"Just want to see for ourselves. He won't let us in the door."

"You got a warrant?"

The cop squirmed. "It'll take an hour to get one this time of night."

"Get one," said Thomassy.

"We'll have to wake the judge up."

"Wake him up."

"All we want to know is if the kid's in there."

"Mr. Urek told you he wasn't."

"Well, that proves he was over at the hospital. . . ."

"Proves nothing. If you want to play lawyer, go to law school. Meanwhile, go get a warrant. *That's* the law."

Thomassy knew he had gotten the cop sore, but he liked getting people with authority sore. The cop went off to get the warrant, leaving the other one in front of the house.

"I see you have a doorman now," said Thomassy to Paul Urek as they closed the door behind them.

Urek walked home not on sidewalks but down the middle of each successive street, too late for traffic now, but hoping a car would swing around a corner suddenly, giving him a chance to sidestep out of death's way like a bullfighter, then laugh at the frightened driver.

No car came.

From a block away he could see his own house ablaze with light on the darkened street. He began to trot, hoping that his absence hadn't been discovered, that he could get up the drainpipe as he had so many times in the past. He saw the cop in front of the house just in time.

He stopped, caught his breath.

The cop in front of the door, a car—Thomassy's car—in front of the house.

Run? Where to?

Into the bushes, over a hedge, quietly, then close to the house he could hear his father's voice and Thomassy's voice, arguing. Up the drainpipe? They wouldn't hear him because of the noise they were making. But the cop would hear him.

Around the back, he lifted the metal cellar door, glad it wasn't kept locked. He slipped down the stairs to the cellar, carefully lowering the metal door so it wouldn't bang shut. He came up through the kitchen and into the living room. His father, his mother, and Thomassy all stopped talking.

He followed his father's right hand as it reared back and came around in a half-circle, the palm open, smashing into the side of his face. He felt the pain jab up into the top of his head, and the thought flashed through his mind that he should pack a case and go off with the kraut somewhere.

"You're a shit," his father said.

Urek looked to his mother, hoping for something.

"I'm dropping the case," said Thomassy.

Urek felt a family alarm, his, his father's, his mother's. Without Thomassy they were unprotected.

"Please, Mr. Thomassy." His mother was finally speaking.

"Be a sport," the father fumbled. "I'll see the kid behaves."

"Yeah," said Urek.

"You shut up," said his father.

"You know what he's done now?" said Thomassy quietly.

Clearly they didn't.

"He tried to kill the other kid in the hospital."

"He what?"

"He cut the tube going down the boy's throat."

Thomassy took the father's arm before he could strike again. "Hold it!"

The father subsided, a gray bag collapsed of wind. Thomassy let his arm go and turned to Urek.

"You were in enough trouble already. What the hell did you do it for?"

All three waited for an answer.

He had no answer he could articulate.

Paul Urek, feeling no strength in his arms, slipped his belt from his pants, folded it in two, and then swung the folded strap against the boy's upraised arm again and again and

again, Urek yelling, "Cut it out!" but defending himself only
with his arms, the mother crying out, and finally Thomassy
shouting, "For Christ's sake, stop!" The puffing man no
longer swung his rage against his son. He turned to Thomassy, saying, "Please, please, you got to handle this case,
maybe he should get out of school and get a job, or enlist, or
go to a nut house, maybe that's where," and then at the very
top of his strident voice, "*I don't know what to do!*"

Thomassy took the strap out of the father's hands and put
it down on a table.

"Looks to me like he's in a nut house already."

Urek's mother spoke seldom. Now she said, "I beg you,
Mr. Thomassy, help Stanley."

"I'll pay you anything," said the father, a comment
Thomassy ignored.

"I beg you," Mrs. Urek repeated, holding her hands out
like a frightened peasant woman entreating aid. "He's my
only boy."

"You have all of you got to do everything I say," Thomassy said.

Mr. and Mrs. Urek nodded, then looked at their son. He
nodded too.

"Okay," said Thomassy, just as they all heard the sound of
a car drawing up.

Paul Urek opened the door, a belittled man. The policeman who had gone for the warrant was striding toward the
house, followed by Chief Rogers.

The cop who had guarded the door shouted toward them,
"The kid's in there, I could hear his voice!"

Thomassy stepped forward with assurance. "Everything's
under control," he said.

# Chapter 13

ED SAT BACK against two propped pillows. The bed rose under his knees, then sloped to the foot, where his chart hung for the inspection of the white-coated men and women who came by in shifts, flicking a glance toward him (to see if the bed was occupied? to see if he was alive?). Ed thought it would make you feel better about what these people were doing to you (pills, tubes, temperature, pulse, needles) if they'd pretend you were really there.

The new waitress in Walker's Diner was like that. She took your order, brought your food, wouldn't notice if you had two heads. He'd had breakfast there with Lila—it was a great illicit feeling to have breakfast in a diner instead of at home—and Lila, when she'd seen the glazed look of the blonde waitress, said, "Meat," and the waitress answered, "What kind, honey?" and Lila said, "Human," and the waitress said with her pencil, "Just point to it on the menu, honey."

"If I'd made enough trouble," said Lila, "she would have looked at me."

School was the same. When a new term started, thirty

kids would be looking at the teacher to see who he was, was he worth learning from, did he seem smart or interesting or just a time-server. Did the teacher look at his new students, wondering which of these teen-age nobodies was a potentially interesting person, maybe even now? If someday Japhet, Edward made a breakthrough in the teacher's own field, would the teacher then say that kid was in my class, I taught him, I got him interested in this subject? They won't remember what I look like even, they'll make it up, invent what I was like. Or had the magic show and the newspaper story changed that? Was he now the kid magician who got beat up, rescued from anonymity by what? Alcoholics Anonymous get driven there by drink after being driven to drink by anonymity: Look at him, he's a drunk, look at him, he's an alcoholic, see how he avoids *touching* booze. Maybe Urek's not so bad, he's picking on *me*. Only see, I end up in the great hospital specialty. Patients Anonymous.

His father said hospitals *had* to be impersonal, so much death and misery passed through them they couldn't be efficient if they thought of patients as people. Could generals be efficient if they thought of the troops they were sending into the bush or out on patrol as real people? Hospitals aren't any more efficient than armies, are they?

His father said hospitals charged too much because they were inefficient. But were they any more inefficient than the phone company, or the railroads, or the other institutions that had you by the short hairs because you needed them and you had no alternative? Freedom, his father had said, was the availability of alternatives. Hospitals were not free institutions.

"Hi," said the head looking at him over the top of his chart.

White jacket, white pants, bushy hair, full sideburns, stethoscope, big peace ring on finger, name tag "Karp."

"Hi," said Karp again. "How do you feel?"

"About what?" said Ed.

The doctor looked up over his stethoscope. "About your health."

"How do you feel about your health, doctor?"

"Look," said the doctor, "you're in the hospital, I'm not in the hospital."

"If you think you're not in the hospital, doc, you're in trouble."

The doctor laughed. "I asked how you feel."

"Oh," said Ed. "I thought you were just discussing how I felt about health, and I wanted to know how you felt about health, to see if we had a philosophical basis for a discussion."

The doctor laughed again. "Hey, who are you?"

"It says on the chart."

"You got a pretty good sense of humor for a kid, Japhet."

"It's nice to be appreciated by an adult."

"How come you're putting me on?"

"Well, I need to get some information. How come you look like Woodstock instead of medical school?"

"I wasn't born looking like either. I went one place and my father sent me to the other."

This time Ed laughed. "I thought all you medical-school types were members of the crew-cut generation."

"Thanks. What do you want to know?"

"Well, my own doctor won't tell me."

"Tell you what?"

"Like, am I going to die?"

Young Dr. Karp paused for just a split second. "Eventually."

"Well," said Ed, "that doesn't make me especially different, so why am I still in bed, I mean, can you tell me something about why I'm still here?"

"They haven't told you?"

"Who's they?"

Dr. Karp's eyes passed over the chart again, reverse chronological order. He looked up, glanced at his watch to make sure he had time, then sat down on the edge of the bed.

"You don't look like a kid that picks a fight."

"I got picked."

This doctor enjoyed laughing.

"Okay," said Karp. "You seem to have some trauma, damage, on your neck. That's no problem. And in your throat, that was a problem because of the swelling, possible broken blood vessels, difficult to see in there."

"A real pain in the ass."

"Wrong," said Karp. "Actually, it's much easier to see inside the other end of the alimentary canal. We have something called a proctoscope."

"Sounds great."

"You get used to it."

"You've just talked me out of a medical career."

"Do you or don't you want to know—"

"I do."

"In throat trauma there's an actual danger that the tissues swell up so much you choke to death, maybe while trying to eat. The X-rays show no permanent damage to the trachea, which is lucky. You ought to be out of here in a couple of days more." He got up to go.

"I appreciate the information." Ed paused. "Doctor?"

"I'm listening."

"How did you feel when you cut up cadavers in medical school?"

Karp sat down again. Then, thoughtfully, "I hated dissections. At first."

"But you got used to it."

"Listen," said Karp, "I'm going to come back and see you again when I'm not making rounds."

He smiled and shook Ed's hand. "Just don't get into any fights."

"Does that include self-defense?"

"Nobody wins," said Karp. "Not even in self-defense." He held a thumb up as he went out the door.

After a while, two nurses came in to shift Ed to a rolling bed as they had two days ago.

Ed said, "I can get over onto it myself."

"You're not allowed to," said the older nurse.

"It's got something to do with the hospital's insurance policy?" said Ed.

They were unlaughable. Not everyone was like Karp.

They shifted him to the rolling bed clumsily, then wheeled him up to X-ray, where he went through the same uncomfortable procedures; then they wheeled him back down and transferred him to his own bed again.

"Can I turn on the television for you?" asked the younger nurse.

"No, thanks."

Was the nurse offended by his refusal? He tried to make amends by asking her for a deck of cards.

"Oh, solitaire," she said.

He didn't contradict her. A few minutes later a nurse's aide brought a deck of cards. He slipped them out of the case gingerly, getting the heft and feel of the particular deck the way a gambler might. He held the pack high in his right hand to see how steady he was.

Holding the pack between thumb and forefinger, he cut the cards with one hand by letting the bottom half drop, and then, in a maneuver that had once cost him many hours of practice, lifted one side of the bottom half up until it passed the side of the top half and landed neatly on top.

Ed then passed half the pack over to his left hand, which he thought of as his second-hand hand, the hand that would never measure up to the right. As he had developed his sleight-of-hand, he had been able to teach the clumsy left hand to cooperate, but always the right hand, not to be outdone, was a step ahead in agility.

Now with half the pack in one hand, his eyes shifting from one to the other, Ed slowly cut both half-packs with each hand at the same time.

For a second he thought the cards might spill. They didn't.

He hadn't lost his touch.

Now, more quickly, he repeated the maneuver, gaining certainty as well as speed. When he looked up, a stranger was watching him from the door.

"Could you please do that once more?" asked the man.

Ed felt sheepish, wondering who the grandfather was. What kind of accent was that?

"Please?"

Being watched while performing was expected. Being watched while practicing made him feel queasy.

"Just once?" asked the man.

"Oh, sure," said Ed.

First he cut the pack single-handedly with his right hand. Then with his left. Then simultaneously with both hands.

The old man seemed genuinely enchanted. "Very good," he said, pulling up a chair by the side of the bed, sitting closer than a stranger usually would. Why was he looking without saying anything more? Ed felt that he was supposed to talk, but didn't know what to say.

"Your parents said I could visit with you. I'm from New York. My name is Koch, with a 'ch,' Gunther Koch. I came up on the train this morning. I really don't trust myself to drive any more long distances. Around the city is all right, not thirty miles straight. My reflexes are not what they used to be."

What did this guy want?

"I have been doing a study," Koch continued. "I am interested in your case." He saw Ed's puzzled look and continued, "Never mind, it's not important for now. This cutting the cards, that is all skill? I mean, there's no trickery?"

"No," said Ed.

"Why do you think people like to watch magic?"

Every once in a while someone asked Ed how he did a particular trick. The code was strict: tell no one anything. But a few times the code had seemed unimportant, as when his father had asked him about the rope trick. When he had explained the mechanics, the expression on his father's face was one of disappointment. How a trick was done always brought less pleasure than seeing it done and being mystified. Knowing how made the spectator seem foolish for not having guessed. The explanation always seemed obvious, simple. And explaining a trick made Ed feel uncomfortable because it took not just the puzzlement but the magic away, made it all seem so ordinary.

His mind had been drifting. "Excuse me," he said.

He found himself explaining what he had just been thinking about to Koch, but it came out simpleminded, not precise as it had seemed to him when he was thinking through the answer.

"Perhaps I can help," said Dr. Koch. "In psychiatry . . ."

So that was his bag.

"When we analysts talk to each other about cases, it seems routine because the problems people have seem unique to them, great personal pain, and we see the explanation often so much alike for people who think that they are alone in the world with their differentness. The explanation of therapy is boring, not only for us but the patient too, especially the patient. Perhaps magic is the same?"

Maybe this Dr. Koch was all right.

"When I was young," the doctor went on, "Houdini was a big name. I mean, even his name was important. I hated to hear that his name was Ehrich Weiss. Anybody could have such a name. But Houdini, that is almost extraterrestrial, perhaps satanic, godlike, out of the ordinary. Such a man would be tied up in chains, put in a box, the box lowered into water, and we hoped he would not die, perhaps we hoped he *would* die but fought against our hope, and he never disappointed us. He always escaped. My wife Marta used to love it, I used to love it. We'd talk about it afterward, theories, the chains were specially made, there was an air tube, no, an air tube wasn't possible, but I believe we really didn't want to know. The real explanation had to be disappointing, don't you agree?"

"Oh yes," Ed said. He had never discussed magic this way before, with anyone.

"According to the paper," said Dr. Koch, "the last trick you performed—you don't like me to call it a trick?—the last thing you did in your show at the school was with a guillotine, yes? Is it supposed to have a second blade?"

"If I tell you, it will disappoint you."

A smile flecked the corners of the doctor's mouth. "Right, do not tell me." The doctor held two fingers against his lips, reflecting. "Why do you think the Urek boy tried to kill you?"

The nurse who interrupted them asked Dr. Koch to leave the room for a minute. She took Ed's temperature, felt his pulse, had him urinate in a bottle, marked the chart.

When Dr. Koch came back in, he was at once apologetic. "I did not mean to bring up an unpleasant matter so abruptly."

"That's all right," said Ed. Then, after a moment, "Is it important—I mean, for whatever you are studying?"

"I cannot tell yet. It may be."

Ed liked the doctor's uncertainty. Or was it honesty?

"You are thinking," said Dr. Koch.

"I try never to do that in school," Ed said.

"Oh?"

"If they catch you thinking, they say your mind is wandering."

"What were you thinking?"

"About you."

"Good or bad."

"I guess good."

"You were going to tell me why the Urek boy . . ."

Ed explained to the doctor how Urek's gang ruled the locker rooms at school and how Ed had defied them by buying a lock they couldn't hacksaw through.

"Well," said Dr. Koch, "that certainly gives Urek an economic grievance against you!" Dr. Koch reflected a moment. "That doesn't, however, account for the fact that you were attacked the night of the magic show."

"No."

"Something triggered that boy's response."

Lila was standing at the door, a yellow embroidered headband on her hair, a yellow blouse, and jeans.

"Hello," she said.

Ed thought she looked beautiful.

"Hi. This is Dr. Koch. Dr. Koch, this is my friend Lila."

Dr. Koch disengaged his heavy body from the chair and struggled up to shake Lila's hand elaborately. He seemed embarrassed.

"We were just talking," said Dr. Koch.

"Don't let me stop you," said Lila. She curled herself up on the foot of Ed's bed.

"I was saying," said Dr. Koch, "that something triggered his action. Most actions are in some ways a reaction to something. His was to your performance, would you say?" He looked at the girl. "We are talking about the Urek boy."

"I'd have guessed," she said.

Ed suddenly thought that Dr. Koch might leave before he could ask one question.

"Dr. Koch?"

"Yes?"

"From what you know, can you tell *why* Urek did it?"

"Ahh," said Koch, "I know at this point little, but I can speculate."

"I didn't mean to put you to any trouble."

"No, no, it is the *business* of human beings to speculate."
He folded his hands in front of his face, wondering how
much he might say. Then he looked up. "There are," he
began, "three kinds of people. What I call category-one
people go through life like solo athletes, at their own fast
pace, toward their own goals, setting up their own obstacles
to conquer. Independent people who are not in competition
with others but their own capacities." Dr. Koch took a deep
breath. "Does this make sense?"

Ed said nothing.

"Category-two people are followers. They are content to
obey instructions, are very good assistants to those with real
leadership qualities. Category-two people are potentially
dangerous because they are entirely dependent on others for
their instructions."

"I don't like putting people into categories," said Ed.

"Yes, yes, I agree," said Dr. Koch. "I don't even like
putting *things* into categories. There are so many surprises.
But ..."

"Aha," said Lila, "here come the categories."

Dr. Koch laughed. "You see, a woman's intuition. Yet, if
we say women have superior intuition, we are categorizing.
If we say men have better musculature, we are categorizing.
Thinking would be an unstructured mess if we did not poke
around in this anarchy and find some guides, even if in time
we adjust and change them."

"My mother's family came from Germany," said Lila.

"I've heard her on that subject," said Ed.

"Well," said Lila, "people always say the Germans are like
your category twos, dangerous because they follow instructions."

"*Most* people are category two," said Dr. Koch. "You have
them here in America, Russia, all over. Every business has
them. The Germans make a specialty of it."

Lila started to protest just as the nurse came in. "I have to
interrupt," she said.

"Please interrupt later," said Ed.

The nurse seemed startled.

"This is Dr. Koch," said Ed. "He's here for special consultations."

"Oh, I'm sorry, doctor," said the nurse, "I thought you were a visitor. I'll come back later."

The moment the door closed behind her, all three of them laughed.

"You," said Dr. Koch, "are definitely not category two."

"What category is Oswald?" asked Ed.

"The Kennedy man?"

"Yes."

"Three."

"You haven't told us about category three," said Lila.

"The man who shot Martin Luther King," said Ed.

"James Earl Ray," supplied Lila.

"Is he category three?"

"I think so. I think the boy who attacked you . . ."

"Yes?"

"He is category three. That is what I am studying. That is why I am here."

Dr. Koch saw how Ed and Lila, quite unconsciously, moved closer together.

"I will tell you," he said, struggling out of his jacket and hanging it on the back of his chair. "My hope is that if you understand you will not object if I study this case further. The public cases, assassins and so on—there is too much one cannot know. It is possible here I can develop something."

"Who are the category threes?"

"Very restless people."

"I'm restless," said Ed.

"No. I mean, yes, but in a different way. You are restless to do, to stop being sick perhaps, to get on with your life. Category threes do not set their own goals, like category ones. Their achievements are not in response to some inner drive or talent. They burn with frustration at not being category-one people because they don't know what they want."

"Well," said Ed, "I'm not sure I know what I want. Most of the kids I know don't know what they want."

"Yes, yes," said Dr. Koch, impatient now, "I was not clear. You want something that you will do, that you will make, that you will be, yes? Threes cannot tolerate category ones because ones make them feel shame about their lack of purpose. They are not content to follow, like category twos. They have no inner drive toward something—achievement, study, success, whatever. Because category ones have this drive, threes hate, I mean really hate, category ones. They are angry. They want to govern the followers, but to no end, you understand, no constructive purpose. And so they feel they must destroy the category ones in order to have power over category twos."

"What's this got to do with Urek?"

The doctor's excitement was visible. "Everything. Somewhere inside him he knows—perhaps without thinking it—that his gang, his followers, will one day very soon leave him to take a job or go into the army and become good category twos like the majority of humanity. And that majority is led by category ones. Look, let me explain. Category ones do not, as a rule, commit crimes because they are too busy, right? Category twos are, well, policemen are category twos, they can obey the chief or the mayor or whoever, or the law, following instructions. The category threes is where the real criminals come from. Their lust is to destroy."

Koch stood up. "They cannot tolerate a society which allows category ones to humiliate them simply by existing. You are the enemy!"

"I think I see," said Ed. "If it's true."

"You were defying this Urek by your unbreakable lock—but on top of that, by your magic show, you were doing something which requires a facility—which he sees as a power he cannot understand. You threaten him. That is why he must get rid of you."

"That's a horrible way of looking at humanity," said Lila, dropping Ed's hand and uncurling from the bed.

"Perhaps horrible. Perhaps also useful. It is easy to take in the beauty of life. It is difficult to understand its viciousness. I must go now."

Dr. Koch put his jacket back on, Lila helping him with it. "This," he said, "is one of the clearest instances I have come across. When something like this happens with adults, it is complicated because they are in business together, or rivals over a woman, or political adversaries, but this is such a clear case, so simple. What do you think will happen to Urek now?"

Ed thought a moment. "I guess it's up to the judge."

Dr. Koch let a deep sigh escape him. "Alas, not. The law is powerless over category threes. It cannot punish them. It cannot deter them. Even in jail they will find number ones to attack. Society has not yet learned how to live with them."

For a moment Dr. Koch seemed lost in thought.

Ed wanted to whisper something to Lila, but she raised a finger to her lips. Koch was coming out of his reverie.

"It is possible I will be allowed to talk to Urek, perhaps before the trial—if not, after. Would you mind, can I then come to see you again, perhaps at home when you are better?"

Ed wasn't sure.

"I can see you hesitate. I know it is an imposition."

"I wouldn't like to become a case history in some book."

"If I write this up, it will be for a medical journal only, and if I do, I promise no real names."

"People can guess."

"Yes, I suppose that is always a risk."

"Is it important?"

"Yes."

"Very?"

"Yes, very." Dr. Koch got up to go.

"Sure," said Ed. "Come back anytime."

Koch seemed pleased. "A thought has just occurred to me which I do not like to have thought of," he said with a slight smile. "Your lady friend . . ."

"Lila," said Lila.

"Looks, from the side, a little like my Marta did—when she was young, of course. My wife, Marta, was a category one, and that is a very difficult thing for a woman. When she has no profession, I mean. And when she is married to a category two like me. A plodder with theories who follows the steps of Freud."

"Frankly," said Lila, "I wish my teachers in school were like you."

"You are very kind. Almost like a European woman."

"You see, you're categorizing again."

"Enough," said Dr. Koch. "Here I am a *tertium quid*, a third party you two do not need." He waved with open palm, first at Ed and then at Lila, in whose direction he also bowed.

# Chapter 14

THE CAGE in the village lockup, empty except for Urek, seemed huge for the short boy, who didn't fall asleep till morning, and then slept fitfully because of the barracks chatter in the police squadroom next door.

Through the bars, on the wall opposite, he could see the large clock with the slow-moving hands. It annoyed him because it was the only thing to look at besides the plaster walls and the humiliating bars of the cell he was in. He'd open his eyes, his back aching from the hard bench, and the clock would tell him it was only fifteen or twenty minutes later, that he had dozed, not slept. He had refused breakfast at six A.M. Now it was nearly ten, and he was hungry. Where was Thomassy, who his father said was a wheel in this goddamn town?

He banged on the bars with his shoe, producing a dull sound that attracted no one's attention till one of the cops walked through headed elsewhere.

"Put your shoe back on," the cop said.

Urek looked at him. He stooped to put his foot into the shoe.

"That's a good boy," said the cop.

"I didn't get breakfast."

"Wait a minute."

The cop returned. "You turned down breakfast."

"I was trying to sleep."

"This isn't a hotel. You eat when we bring it."

"Could I get some coffee? Please, huh?" He hated saying please.

"How old are you?"

"Sixteen."

The cop came back with coffee a few minutes later.

"What about cream and sugar?"

"Drink it the way it is."

Urek sat on the bench, hunched over the black coffee, which he had always diluted before with milk and three spoons of sugar. He realized for the first time that jail meant restriction.

In another hour he was ready to crawl the walls with boredom, hating Thomassy. He called many times before someone came.

"What are you yelling about?" said the sergeant.

"Do I get to exercise in the yard?"

The sergeant said. "Look, kid, this isn't a jail, it's a lockup."

"You got a yard."

"Do push-ups if you need exercise. Beat your meat." The sergeant laughed and left.

You have to be crazy to beat your meat with all those open bars in front of you. Anybody could come by. What do you do in jail? He had to beat this rap. Why didn't his father or mother come to visit him? What was he supposed to do all day? He looked at the walls, the bars, the locked door, the high barred window. You couldn't even escape if you wanted to, he thought, his rage rising.

Then voices and footsteps promised a distraction. The

policeman let Thomassy into the cell, locking it behind him. "Take as long as you like," said the cop respectfully.

Thomassy motioned Urek to sit down on the hard bench. The lawyer remained standing.

"You look like you're glad to see me," said Thomassy.

"Where you been?"

"I brought you a couple of magazines." Thomassy put down mint copies of *True* and *Popular Science*, which he had recorded on the expense page of his pocket appointment book.

"Do you need your glasses for reading?"

"Who told you that?"

"Your father gave me these." He put the eyeglass case down on the bench next to Urek. "I want you to listen carefully now."

"When do I get out of here?"

"Your arraignment is tomorrow morning."

"What about the bail?"

"Well, we could go before the magistrate. He'd probably raise the bail to two thousand dollars to let you out. I don't want you out."

Urek tried to keep his anger down. Cool, cool, he thought.

Thomassy tried to explain. "Cutting the kid's tube in the hospital would not be considered an aggravation of the first assault, it's a new crime, and with two assaults, the judge would set a higher bail. It's normal."

"My old man would sign for it."

"His signature wouldn't be good for two thousand."

"He's got the house, there's a lot paid on the mortgage. He told me he'd get me bailed."

Thomassy let his breath out slowly. "I want you in here for another reason."

"I promise I won't try anything."

"You promised the last time."

"This time I swear."

"It doesn't matter."

"What the fuckin' hell do you mean?" Urek regretted the words the moment they spilled out.

Thomassy came over, put one foot up on the bench Urek was sitting on, and leaned down close. "You listen."

"I'm listening!"

"Try to get this into your head. When you're arraigned tomorrow, I'm going to insist on a preliminary hearing. I want to find out what the village prosecutor has in the way of witnesses. It'll be useful to us. I want that before we go to White Plains."

"What's in White Plains?"

"County Court. If you're charged with a misdemeanor, the trial would be here in town. If it's a felony, it'll have to be in White Plains. Maybe we can keep it here."

Urek wasn't understanding.

"A misdemeanor means you're charged with something that's good for no more than a year in jail. A felony is first-degree assault. I'll try to get you third degree. In fact"—he looked at Urek's uncomprehending face—"maybe I can get this whole thing quashed. Dismissed."

"Yeah?" Urek was interested.

"You've got to cooperate."

"Sure."

"You've got to stay put. Here. I'm going to make a thing at the arraignment about a sixteen-year-old kid having had to spend two nights in the lockup. It might help. It'll give me a chance to do a little digging, too."

"Like what?"

"The nurse's aide can identify you."

"I don't get it."

"You don't have to get it. You don't have to learn anything or say anything. If you want to get off, you're just going to leave it to me."

"You really can get me off?"

"Your father wants me to try."

"*I* want you to try."

"You're not paying my fee."

"Look, Mr. Thomassy, you get me off, and I'll turn all I earn over to you—for the whole year."

Thomassy laughed. "The quarters?"

"What quarters?"

"The dough you get from the kids? For their lockers?"

"No, I'll get a real job and . . ."

"You're going to finish high school."

Urek sat back down.

Thomassy thought for a moment. "I don't want you giving anything—I mean anything—away in court. When the arraignment's on . . ."

"Yeah?"

"You look down at your hands. Try it. Okay, that's good."

"How long?"

"When you get tired of looking down at your hands, look at a spot on the table. When you get tired of that, go back to staring at your hands. I don't want the judge to see your face. I'm going to try something, and I don't want him to see your reactions to it."

"What would I do?"

"I'm taking no chances. You look down at your hands, understand?"

"Yeah."

"Even if you're bored, keep looking down at them, don't look up, don't look at the judge, don't look at any of the people who are talking, don't even look at me, understand?"

Urek thought about how long he could avoid looking at anyone. It was crazy.

"Answer me!"

"Okay, okay!"

"Now, cheer up. I'm doing all I can for you."

Urek looked up at Thomassy's thin face with the high cheekbones.

"Mr. Thomassy?"

"Yes?"

"Thanks for everything. I mean it."

Thomassy called to be let out of the cell, patted Urek on the shoulder, a conscious gesture intended to relax him for tomorrow. He looked to see if anything could be improved in the boy's physical appearance. "I'll have your mother send some fresh clothes in the morning."

"I could use some underwear."

"The judge can't see your underwear."

Thomassy saw the pulse leap in the side of Urek's forehead.

"Okay, son"—he hated to use that word—"You'll get your underwear."

Urek, suddenly young, said, "Mr. Thomassy, can they come today, my mom and dad?"

"I told them to stay home. It's better for your case." When the parents saw him in court tomorrow, he wanted them to come rushing up spontaneously.

Urek didn't understand.

"Well," said Thomassy, "just leave it to me."

# Chapter 15

IN MID-AFTERNOON Urek was awakened from a deep sleep by someone shaking his shoulder. He sat bolt upright, the copy of *True* dropping to the floor from where it had rested when he read himself to sleep. The two men looming over him came into focus. He recognized the sergeant. The man with the sergeant picked up the magazine and handed it to Urek.

"This is Mr. Metcalf, the village Prosecutor," said the sergeant.

Mr. Metcalf, sixty, short, gray-suited, had a red-orange-yellow gash of tie-color down his front. His wire-framed bifocals looked to Urek like the kind of glasses you could smash with one stomp of your foot.

"Young man, I'm here to try to be of some help. Are you fully awake?"

Urek nodded slowly. The sergeant poised his pad and pen.

"You were taken into custody by the Police Department pursuant to a warrant issued by Judge Clifford at one A.M. this date alleging that you committed the crime of first-degree assault on the persons of Edward Japhet, his father, Terence Japhet, and Lila Hurst on or about eleven P.M., January 21, and upon the person of Edward Japhet in Phelps Memorial Hospital on or about nine P.M., January 24."

Mr. Metcalf looked away from his notes. "Now, young man, it is quite possible that a plea of guilty to a lesser offense would enable you to be tried in the local court—your counsel can waive the jury if he likes—which might effectively reduce your chances of drawing a long sentence in the Elmira Reception Center. One of the three boys allegedly with you on the night of the original assault has a past conviction and may want to turn state's evidence and be a witness against you. Before discussing the matter more fully with you, I must advise you that you have a right to remain silent and refuse to answer questions."

Urek stared at him as if he were crazy.

"Anything you say," continued Mr. Metcalf, "may be used against you in a court of law. As we discuss this matter, you have a right to stop answering my questions at any time that you desire. You have a right to talk to a lawyer before speaking to me, to remain silent until you can talk to him, and to have him present during the time you are being questioned. If you desire a lawyer but you cannot afford one, the Legal Aid Society . . ."

"Mr. Metcalf," said the sergeant, "he's represented by Thomassy."

"I see. Do you understand each of these rights which I have explained to you?"

Urek looked blank.

"Answer yes or no."

"Well, I—"

"Now that I have advised you of your rights, are you willing to answer my questions without having an attorney present?"

"I want Mr. Thomassy."

The sergeant glanced at the wall clock. "He's probably in his office."

"Do you want to talk to Mr. Thomassy on the telephone?"

Urek nodded.

The sergeant unlocked the cell and, holding Urek by the arm, led them into the squadroom next door and to a phone. The sergeant looked up the number and dialed. When the phone started ringing, he handed the instrument to Urek.

"Mr. Thomassy, this Mr. Metcalf is asking me questions. He says one of my friends is going to rat on me." Urek, his heart drumming, listened, then handed the phone to Mr. Metcalf.

"Metcalf here."

Metcalf's face slowly turned pink.

"Yes," he said.

"All right," he said.

"Yes, certainly I understand, Mr. Thomassy," he said and hung up, pointing to Urek and motioning to the sergeant to take him back to his cell.

Thomassy put the phone down on the cradle and thought, that son of a bitch Metcalf, trying that Junior League ploy on a sixteen-year-old kid, he ought to be disbarred. If he'd gotten anything resembling a confession, I would have got the whole case thrown out faster than a finger-snap. I should have let him try. So he's going to charge the other kids and get one of them to cop a plea. That warning is very much appreciated, Mr. Metcalf, thank you.

As Judge Clifford looked about the courtroom, he thought that some of these people were going to be disappointed by not being called, especially those who had brought lawyers with them. He probably could dispose of the trivial cases quickly, but it was difficult to predict when some minor offense would draw a contest. In any event, habit directed him to deal with serious matters first. Maybe he could get this Urek case out of the way. He asked Mr. Metcalf and Mr. Thomassy to come up to the bench.

"Gentlemen, I'd like to send this matter on to County Court. George, have you considered waiving a preliminary hearing?"

Metcalf prudently stood silent. He turned to get Thomassy's reaction.

"Well, your Honor," said Thomassy, "if you were to suggest that, I don't think I could accept your Honor's recommendation."

"Because?"

"Naturally, my client would insist on a preliminary hearing."

Judge Clifford sighed. This wasn't going to be a one-two-three. "Have you seen the information and the depositions?"

"Yes," said Thomassy, "but I think we have a dearth of objective witnesses to the alleged offense."

"Oh, come on now," Metcalf broke in.

Thomassy raised his voice just enough to override. "We don't have to trouble the County Court—"

"It's not a question—"

"I think the whole matter should be dismissed right here," said Thomassy.

Judge Clifford leaned forward on his elbows.

"As far as I can see," Thomassy said, "no crime has been committed."

Mr. and Mrs. Japhet, in the second row, strained to hear.

"If we start sending fist fights between school kids to the grand jury—"

"I object!" said Mr. Metcalf.

"Well, we're trying to keep this informal," said the judge. "But state your objection."

"The assailant—"

Thomassy cut in, "The defendant!"

"The defendant," continued Metcalf, "is sixteen years old. Under the law, he's an adult, not a 'kid.' "

"Your Honor," said Thomassy, his voice suddenly quiet, "this defendant is less than sixteen and two months old. If this alleged offense had happened sixty days ago, it'd all be a juvenile matter for quick disposition in the Family Court."

"There has to be a demarcation line somewhere," snapped Metcalf, "and the law says—"

"I know what the law says, Mr. Metcalf," said the judge. "The bench would like to send this on, to see if the grand jury in White Plains would find a true bill because frankly I see the possibilities of a borderline here."

"Oh, your Honor!" said Thomassy.

"What is it, Mr. Thomassy?"

"I'm sorry, your Honor. It's just that I hate to see things blown up. Assault third is a misdemeanor which can be disposed of right here. It seems to me that a schoolyard fist fight—"

"Your Honor, Mr. Thomassy is forgetting the second assault in the hospital, with a deadly weapon—"

"Now, hold it, Metcalf, the hospital is in a different jurisdiction and—"

"Gentlemen, we are jumping way ahead," said the judge.

"That's exactly my point," said Thomassy. "I think this ought to be heard in an orderly fashion, here in this court."

"Assault first and second are felonies and would have to be heard in White Plains anyway," said Metcalf.

Thomassy figured the case must have some extra significance for Metcalf. He was an amateur, who let his real feelings show instead of limiting his expressions to those that might prove useful.

"I was trying to point out that Phelps Memorial is in the village of North Tarrytown, and whatever allegedly happened there is not in this jurisdiction."

"Well," said the judge, "I'd have to consider other offenses by the same defendant in setting bail."

"I don't want to prejudice my client's position with regard to bail, your Honor," said Thomassy. "Cutting a tube, as it is alleged happened in the hospital, is not physical injury to a person. We're prepared to show that no physical injury did or could come about through the cutting of the tube."

"Your Honor," said Metcalf, "the victim was severely injured, confined to the intensive-care unit of the hospital for days, and—"

"Hold everything," said Thomassy. He had the eye of everyone in the courtroom. "Mr. Metcalf knows, I am sure, that we're dealing with two separate allegations. There was allegedly a fist fight which ended with one of the combatants in the hospital. A fist fight will usually be third degree, in the absence of intent to cause serious physical injury by means of a deadly weapon or dangerous instrument."

"But the knife!" said Metcalf.

"The knife," said Thomassy, "has only to do with the second allegation, in another jurisdiction, and no one, I repeat, no one was hurt, much less hurt seriously, by the incident in the hospital."

"Your Honor, the defendant went into that hospital with intent to kill—"

"We are not dealing with intentions right now, Mr. Metcalf, we're trying to get at the facts."

"The fact is—"

"The fact," said Thomassy, "is that we haven't even established *who* was in the hospital."

"Your Honor, the nurse's aide can identify the defendant."

"Who did you say?"

"The nurse's aide, Alice Ginsler."

Thomassy repeated the name to himself twice. Then he spoke, even more quietly than before. "Your Honor, Mr. Metcalf can call whoever he wishes to testify in due course, but before we get lost in the fantasies of what might or might not have gone on in the head of someone in the hospital that night, shouldn't we be clarifying the incident at the school?"

Judge Clifford said, "Mr. Metcalf, I think the defense has a point. We have to keep the two incidents separate."

"But, your Honor, the same people were involved in both incidents."

"The fact that one assault allegedly followed another assault upon the same person is a matter for separate consideration." In mid-sentence the Judge noticed a man in the second row whispering agitatedly to the woman next to him.

"*This is insane,*" said Terence Japhet to his wife. "It's so clear what happened."

Mrs. Japhet tugged at his sleeve. The judge was staring at him.

"I had hoped," said Judge Clifford, "to save the people and the defendant time, but it looks now as if we can't shortcut the procedures." He looked at the people who had hoped to have their cases tried that day. "You'd better reschedule all these other people for Thursday," he said to the police officers.

There was a low moan in some parts of the room.

The judge tapped his gavel once, lightly. Four or five people left the room. Several others consulted in whispers with their lawyers, and the policeman ushered them out as well so that they could talk beyond the doors and not disturb the court.

"Well, then," said Judge Clifford. "We're not trying the case now, we're trying to determine whether he should be bound over. If by any chance the results of the preliminary hearing show the possibility of first- or second-degree—"

"I believe we can," said Mr. Metcalf.

"Now, let's wait," Thomassy thundered. Even the policeman at the door turned to look.

"I'm sure Mr. Metcalf didn't mean to interrupt."

"I thought your Honor had finished."

"All right," said the judge. "Now, I don't want to make things complicated. There was allegedly a fight. Mr. Metcalf, you've got to satisfy me by evidence that this is a case of first- or second-degree assault, and that there is reasonable cause that the defendant named in your complaint is guilty. If what you produce convinces me that the grand jury might indict, I'll pass it on. If not, I'll hold him here for trial on assault third. I'll have to determine where the case will be tried, and then—"

"I'm sure your Honor means," said Thomassy, "that he'll first determine whether there is anything to try."

"Yes, of course, Mr. Thomassy. If there seems to be a case, and we determine the degree of assault involved, I'll decide whether we'll hear it or whether it goes to the grand jury in White Plains. What is your pleasure?"

"I hope we won't have to go all the way for a grand-jury indictment to be dismissed for lack of evidence. I believe," said Thomassy, "that it can be done right here."

"You are going to argue . . ."

"I am asserting that no crime has been committed and the distinguished attorney for the people cannot so prove."

"Mr. Metcalf, how many witnesses do you intend to call?"

"Five."

Thomassy quickly ticked them off in his head: Ed Japhet, the father, the girl friend, the nurse's aide, and—it had to be one of Urek's gang, offered a deal and squealing. Something will have to be done about that.

"Can you have your witnesses here at two o'clock?"

"It'd be easier tomorrow morning," Mr. Metcalf said.

"Are they all local people?"

"Yes, your Honor."

"Are any of them employed?"

"Two, your Honor."

"By?"

"The high school and the hospital."

"I'm sure their employers will sympathize with the calendar problems of the court. Let's have your witnesses here at two."

Judge Clifford felt satisfied. It was easier to find out what went on if the witnesses couldn't be rehearsed at length.

"Mr. Thomassy," said the judge, "I notice the defendant has been staring down throughout this hearing. Is he ill?"

"I don't believe he's ill, your Honor."

Urek glanced at Thomassy from under his hands. Thomassy nodded. Urek let his hands fall and looked around for the first time.

"I hope the judge hasn't inconvenienced your afternoon," Thomassy said to Metcalf.

"Not at all, Mr. Thomassy," said Metcalf, feeling desperate about collecting his people by telephone on such short notice with no chance to brief them properly.

Everyone stood so that the judge could leave the courtroom. The last to stand was Mr. Japhet, whose head clanged with the words, "No crime has been committed." Nothing mattered now, he thought, but that justice be done. Or was it vengeance he wanted?

# Chapter 16

"Do you promise to tell the truth, the whole truth, and nothing but the truth, so help you God?"

"I do."

Mr. Metcalf laid the Bible aside carefully, as if it were a living thing. "Name and occupation," he asked.

"I'm sorry, I didn't hear you."

"Please state your name and occupation."

"Terence Japhet. I'm a teacher at the high school."

"What do you teach?"

"Biology."

"You are the complainant in this case?"

"Yes, I signed the complaint."

"How long have you been at the high school?"

"Fourteen years."

"Do you know the school well?"

Thomassy was on his feet.

"Now, gentlemen," said Judge Clifford, anticipating Thomassy's objection, "this is not a trial. It'll take forever if you constantly object to each other's questions. We're only trying to hear from the witnesses themselves, in order to find out whether we've got a felony that needs moving to County Court or a misdemeanor that can be handled right here."

"Or nothing," said Thomassy.

"Or whether the case is dropped, correct. Mr. Metcalf, let's find out what happened at the school and in the hospital. If you want to make a record, make it at the trial."

"If there is to be a trial," said Thomassy.

"Mr. Thomassy, I have very much in mind your feeling that there may be no case at all. Any further reminders will constitute an annoyance."

"I'm sorry, your Honor."

"Let's just find out as quickly as we can what the witness saw and heard. Mr. Japhet, can you describe in your own words what happened on the night of January twenty-first?"

"My son was to do a—"

"Your son is Edward Japhet, the person who was injured in these incidents?"

"Well, he was the principal victim."

Judge Clifford could see Thomassy bristling. "Mr. Japhet, we're trying to narrow things down."

"I understand, your Honor, but while my son's injuries are the primary concern, his friend, the girl he took to the dance, was molested, and my automobile was damaged."

"Well, let's go on."

Thomassy relaxed in his chair, his feet stretching to their full length under the table. If opposing counsel had to tread warily in order to avoid constant objections, the man would have to concentrate on the formulation of his questions rather than their effect, which was what counted. Metcalf could be kept in line. But the judge could get annoyed. There was a fine line between keeping the pressure up and antagonizing the judge.

Metcalf resumed. "You were telling us that your son was going to do something on the particular evening in question."

*Jesus,* thought Thomassy, *kids in law school can pose questions better than Metcalf.* He liked a tough opponent. Metcalf was sponge cake.

Japhet was talking. "My son, Ed, that is, was going to do a magic show for the school dance. I've seen his magic tricks, and I wasn't one of the faculty people assigned to chaperon that evening. So I was going to drive Ed and his girl, Lila, to the dance and pick them up afterward."

"Did you do so?" asked Mr. Metcalf.

"Yes. He had two suitcases full of equipment, and I helped get those to the school, too. We picked up Lila— Miss Hurst—on the way. It was snowing."

"Go on."

"Well, nothing untoward happened on the drive to school. I dropped the kids off. Ed was to call me to pick him up."

"Did he in fact call you?"

"Yes."

"What time was that?"

"I'm not sure. I'm afraid I had dozed off in front of the television."

"We can establish the time in other ways. What happened when you arrived at the school?"

"To pick them up?"

"Yes."

"I didn't see them at the front. I assumed they'd be inside because the snow was still coming down."

"Did you see anyone else when you drove up to the school entrance?"

"No, no one. I parked just past the school-bus zone, I'd say fifty feet past the entrance, where the driveway starts to go down."

"And then?"

"I went inside the school building and saw my son and his girl down the hall. Ed had the bags. I took one, and Lila followed us."

"How long would you say you were inside the school building?"

"Three or four minutes, no more."

"And then what happened?" asked Mr. Metcalf.

"We came out of the building. The drifts were knee-deep, and the bags were heavy. We were nearly to the car when I saw that it was occupied."

"Your car?"

"Yes."

"By whom?"

"By that Urek boy and three of his friends."

The sound of Thomassy letting his pencil fall to the table top was enough to attract the judge's attention.

Judge Clifford said, "May I, Mr. Metcalf?" He turned to Mr. Japhet. "We are trying to establish facts, informally it is true, but it is important that you try to discipline yourself to stick to what you actually saw. Did you know that it was the Urek boy at the moment that you saw your car was occupied, or a moment later, or when?"

"Later, I think."

"I see," said the judge. "Then how did you know the other three were his friends?"

"Well, they're all part of a gang at the school which—"

"Your Honor," said Thomassy, approaching the bench. "I can't in good conscience let this pass. Whatever Mr. Japhet knows about any gang goings-on at the school is probably hearsay and shouldn't be developed here, any more than it should be allowed at a trial."

"I respect your view, Mr. Thomassy," said the judge. "Any evidence concerning a gang at the school must be developed by questioning of a police officer or school officials and connected to this assault, unless Mr. Japhet knows about this gang firsthand."

"I know about it from my son and from other students and from faculty members, we've talked about it, and the principal has talked to all of us about it."

"I'm afraid," said the judge, "that's what we call hearsay. Could you go on with what you yourself saw that evening."

"Urek smashed the suitcase, one of the suitcases, with the magic equipment up against the fender, the rear fender of the car, and then he attacked Ed and Lila—"

"He or one of the others?" asked Metcalf.

"No, I'm quite sure it was him. When he was on top of Ed choking him, I remember beating on his back or doing something to make him stop."

"Did you stop him?"

"Yes, but not before Ed was pretty badly hurt. It was a brutal beating. That boy has caused more trouble at the school. . . ."

Mr. Japhet stopped himself. He looked at the judge, Metcalf, and Thomassy. "I'm sorry."

"It's perfectly understandable," said the judge.

"What happened when Urek let go of your son?" asked Metcalf.

"He smashed the windshield of my car."

"How?"

"With a chain."

"What kind of a chain?"

"Well, I'm not sure. It must have been a strong chain because I believe the windshield smashed with the first blow."

"And then?"

"The janitor appeared in the doorway of the school building with his flashlight, yelling."

"What did he yell?"

Mr. Japhet thought for a while. "I honestly don't remember."

Mr. Japhet saw Thomassy grin and despised him for it.

"Then what happened?"

"The four boys ran off. Lila and I got Ed into the back seat of the car—he insisted on taking the suitcases with us though I was anxious to get him to the hospital."

"Did you go to the hospital?"

"It was a terrible drive, the windshield was open, there were glass shards all over the front of the car, the snow was coming in."

"Did you drop the girl off on the way?"

"No, no, my son was badly hurt, and we had to get to the hospital right away."

Metcalf knew enough to quit when he was ahead.

"Your Honor," he said, "I have finished my examination of this witness. I'd like to call the girl."

"Do you have any questions you'd like to ask the witness, Mr. Thomassy?"

Thomassy put his hand on Urek's shoulder. It looked like a consoling gesture, but in fact it hurt a bit, and was intended to keep Urek looking down. Then Thomassy stood and very slowly approached the witness chair.

"Mr. Japhet, did your son at any time hit the defendant?"

"Well, yes, I suppose so, they were fighting—"

"I see. Do you know why the defendant and your son were fighting?"

"He was attacked!"

"Mr. Japhet, please try to understand that we are not interested in your characterization of what you saw. Just tell us what you saw. My question was, do you know why the defendant and your son were fighting?"

"My son was defending himself."

"Against all four boys?"

"Against Urek."

"Did Urek fight with you and with the girl, or only with your son?"

"He went after the girl and then my son."

"Not you?"

"No."

"But you attacked him?"

"I was trying to defend my son, to get that boy off—"

"Urek didn't hit you, you say, but you beat your fists on

his back, that's clear. Now, for the third time, will you answer—if you know—why did your son and Urek fight?"

Mr. Japhet felt he was being a terrible witness. If only he remembered what Ed had told him Dr. Koch had said in detail. But he couldn't speak that, could he, that would be hearsay.

"The question is, why did your son and Urek fight?"

Mr. Japhet hated saying it, but what else could he say? "I don't know."

"Your Honor," said Thomassy, "I think Mr. Metcalf had better call the girl."

# Chapter 17

LILA WAS CALLED from the adjoining room. She entered, nodded in the direction of her mother and father, saw that everyone else was watching her as the policeman led the way to the stand. She did not like being conspicuous.

The judge thought she was a very pretty girl, not one of those that ironed her hair straight and affected jeans and beads. She looked like what he still thought of as a nice girl, and he hoped that she would testify straightforwardly.

The judge told Lila to put her left hand on the Bible and asked her to raise her right. "Do you promise to tell the truth, the whole truth, and nothing but the truth?"

"Yes."

Mr. Metcalf began his examination.

"Please tell the court your name and occupation."

"Lila Hurst. I'm a student at the high school."

"You've undoubtedly heard others discuss the events of January twenty-first. May I caution you that you are not to use anyone else's recollections as your own, but to say independently what you saw and heard."

"Okay."

Mr. Metcalf covered the ground between the time Mr. Japhet picked her up and dropped her and Ed at the school. Then quickly he asked, "After the dance, what happened?"

"We were going toward Mr. Japhet's car—"

"Who's we?"

"Mr. Japhet, Ed, and me."

"All right, continue."

"The snow was kind of deep, and I had this long dress on so I wasn't looking up. I was watching where I was going, and I didn't see the boys in the car until Mr. Japhet saw them."

"Did you recognize any of the boys?"

"Not right away."

"When?"

"Well, Urek just before he grabbed me."

"Tell us what happened."

"He was being smart aleck with Mr. Japhet and Ed, and then he rushed at me and twisted my arm behind my back and pulled my hair until Ed made him stop, and that's when he whipped the chain against Ed's face."

"Chain?" asked the judge.

Mr. Metcalf spoke to the girl in quiet tones. "The court is interested in what you said because, under the law, fighting with hands or fists is very different from using a deadly weapon."

"Your Honor!" said Thomassy, on his feet.

"Yes, I know, Mr. Thomassy, but this is an important piece of evidence. I don't remember a chain being mentioned in the police depositions attached to the information. Mr. Japhet merely testified that one was used to smash the windshield, not against a person. You can develop whatever you like after Mr. Metcalf is finished with the witness."

Thomassy, pricked, sat down.

"Miss Hurst, what happened when Urek produced the chain?"

"Well, he didn't produce it, I mean, he had it wrapped around his fist from the beginning."

"I'm not sure I understand. Could you explain?"

"Like this." She made as if she were wrapping something around her fist.

"Exactly what was Urek doing?"

"He was pulling my hair with his left hand. The chain was on the other hand."

"Were you hurt?"

"It hurt when he pulled my hair."

"And when he twisted your arm?"

Thomassy scraped his chair back as if he was about to stand.

"Mr. Metcalf," Judge Clifford said, "I think you're leading the witness. Would you let her tell it her own way, please?"

"I'm sorry, your Honor."

"Just go on."

"I was glad he had let me go, but then I saw the terrible blood on Ed's face. He knocked Ed over and was choking him."

"With his hands?" Metcalf corrected himself. "I mean, how did he choke him?"

"With his hands. He still had the chain in one hand, but both hands were around Ed's throat, and he was beating Ed's head against the ground and choking sort of in spurts, like this." She demonstrated with a squeezing motion of her hands.

"What did you do?"

"I screamed. I guess the janitor heard me."

"Let's not jump ahead. When did the Urek boy stop choking Ed?"

"Well, Mr. Japhet was trying to get Urek off, but it wasn't till the janitor appeared in the school door that Urek let go of Ed. You see . . ."

"Yes?"

"The janitor said he was going to call the police. I think that did it."

"Think a moment. Have you left anything important out?"

"Not that I remember."

"Your Honor, I have no more questions of this witness."

"I have one," said the judge. "Young lady, what you saw—would you describe it as a fight?"

"Well, they were fighting." She looked at the judge and felt she wasn't being helpful. "Ed was defending me, I suppose. That's why he punched his arm."

"Punched whose arm?" asked the judge.

"Ed punched Urek's arm, to get him to let go."

"Was that the first blow between Urek and Japhet?"

Lila felt very uncomfortable. "Well, my back was sort of to them, but Ed was trying to get Urek to let go of me."

"By punching?"

"I think so."

"What do you mean, 'I think so'?"

"I didn't see the punch or anything. I think that's what happened."

"All right," said the judge. "Are you ready for cross, Mr. Thomassy?"

"Your Honor," said Thomassy, "some of the answers given by this witness require me to bring some physical objects to the court. I wonder if I might have fifteen minutes? I need to shoot down to Main Street and pick up a few things."

"Which are necessary?"

"Yes, sir."

"All right, court is recessed for half an hour. I don't want you to get a speeding ticket, Mr. Thomassy."

Lila's parents came over to her when the recess began, but she wanted to be alone. She put on her coat and went for a walk, her hands stuffed deeply into her pockets. It was cold. She heard the footsteps in the snow behind her.

"You have to be back in the courtroom when the recess is over," said Mr. Hurst.

Lila looked at her father, his face red from catching up to her, his breath visible in the cold. Mr. Hurst, who had wanted to be a doctor or a dentist, had been beaten down by the depression, and had settled for becoming a dental technician, a craft that had plagued Lila all through school because kids sometimes wanted to know what your father did, and if she could have said "dentist," that would have been that, but "dental technician" sometimes made them laugh, and so Lila anticipated their laughter by saying, "He makes teeth," but she never got used to it. In fact, Mr. Hurst had built up quite a business and now had ten or twelve dental technicians working for him in three locations, but to Lila he was a boring man. He bored her mother and her with small, technical talk about improvements in his trade, new ways of making bridges and things. He never seemed to talk about anything that mattered. Nevertheless, she loved this large, red, puffing man in front of her, anxious to help.

"Want to walk with me, Dad?"

"Not too far."

"Just around the block."

They walked side by side.

"It's crazy," said Lila after a while. "I mean, it all seemed so simple what happened, but their way of looking at it in court is so different. They made me feel as if anything I say might be a lie, and I'm not lying, Dad."

"I know you're not, Lila."

They went on in silence for a while and then he said, "I think we'd better turn back."

Thomassy arrived at the front doors of the courthouse just as they did, carrying two loaded paper bags. He stepped aside to let Mr. Hurst and Lila enter first.

In a few minutes the hearing was reconvened, and Lila

resumed her place up front facing the spectators, still shivering from the cold outside.

"Proceed with the cross," said Judge Clifford.

"With your Honor's permission," said Thomassy, "I would like to develop a point that involves some characterization by this witness. I think it essential to understanding her testimony, but more important, I think it speaks directly to the purpose of this hearing."

"Well," said Judge Clifford, "we'll make allowances. Either Mr. Metcalf or I will stop you if it's nonproductive or prejudicial. Please go on."

Thomassy walked away from the witness stand so that he'd have to speak his questions louder. He doubted the girl would project the same way, which fitted his intentions perfectly.

Thomassy turned to face her. "Would you say that a gun was a dangerous weapon?"

"Oh, yes," she said quietly, uncomfortable at the distance between herself and her questioner.

"Would you say that a knife was a dangerous weapon?"

"What kind of a knife?"

"Any knife."

"Yes, I guess so."

Thomassy went to the table and took an object out of the paper bag. It was a rolling pin.

"Would you call this a dangerous weapon?"

It seemed as if everyone in the courtroom laughed, including the judge.

"No," she said. "Well, I guess you could get hurt if someone bashed you with it."

"But if you saw this, would you think of it as a dangerous weapon?"

"Would you call this"—he reached into the bag again—"a dangerous weapon?"

"No."

It was a screwdriver.

"No."

Judge Clifford ahemmed. "I'm not sure I'm following what you're trying to develop, Mr. Thomassy."

"One moment more, please, your Honor." Once again he took an object from the bag, a garden trowel made of green metal with a wood handle.

"Would you call this a dangerous weapon?"

"No."

Quickly Thomassy reached in for the last object in the bag and showed Lila a bicycle chain.

"Would you say this was a dangerous weapon."

She said "No" almost as a reflex, then quickly said, "Yes."

"Well, which do you mean, yes or no?"

Lila was silent, hoping the judge or Mr. Metcalf would say something.

"I'll rephrase that. What makes a chain any more a dangerous weapon than a garden trowel or a screwdriver or a rolling pin?" He didn't wait for an answer to his rhetorical question, but asked the judge, "Your Honor, in your determination as to whether the charges against the defendant should be quashed or tried as first or second or third, the question of whether a dangerous weapon was involved is important."

"I agree," said the judge.

"Well, your Honor, this witness thinks correctly that a gun or a knife is a dangerous weapon but says that household or garden articles in common use are not dangerous weapons. . . ."

Mr. Metcalf interrupted at last. "Your Honor, we are supposed to be gathering firsthand facts from the witnesses, which the attorney for the people has tried to do. The attorney for the defendant has a right to question the witness about anything I questioned her about—"

"Well," said the judge, "in this hearing, he really has a broader latitude—"

"Not to bring a hardware store in here and—"

It was the judge who noticed that the witness was in tears. "Gentlemen," he said, "please let us remember that the witness is a young girl—how old are you, Miss Hurst?"

"Sixteen."

Thomassy was excited to the bursting point. "Your Honor, the defendant is sixteen years old. The Japhet boy is sixteen, too. Sixteen-year-olds, whatever their responsibility under the law, are adolescent children who laugh and cry and fight, yes fight, with each other, and these things cannot be seen in an adult context. May I ask the witness a few questions?"

Metcalf was flabbergasted. He didn't know how to stop Thomassy.

"Are you and Ed Japhet good friends?" Thomassy asked.

"Now, wait a minute!" Metcalf was losing his temper.

"I'll wait as long as Mr. Metcalf likes, but the line of questioning I'm developing now is extremely pertinent." To the girl, "Are you and Ed Japhet good friends."

Lila nodded.

"Please speak up."

"Yes," she said, the word filling her throat.

"How good?"

"I don't know what you mean?" She was on the verge of tears again.

"Why didn't you go directly home after the dance?"

"Mr. Japhet was giving me a lift."

"And while you were waiting for Mr. Japhet to come, were you being good friends?"

"We are good friends, that's all!"

"Would you lie for his sake?"

"I'm not lying."

"You said the defendant pulled your hair. Did anyone else ever pull your hair?"

"Well, in school—"

"In school what?"

"The boys used to pull your hair."

"So hair-pulling is not so unusual among kids in school. Yet Ed Japhet attacked young Urek when he was pulling your hair, according to your testimony?"

"I don't understand."

"Did you and Mr. Terence Japhet ever discuss the events of that evening, the evening of the fight?"

"Yes, in the hospital."

"You heard his version of the story, and you told him your version?"

"It wasn't a version. We talked about what happened."

"Did you talk about what happened between you and Ed before Mr. Japhet arrived to pick you up?"

"Of course not."

"Why not?"

"It's none of his business. It's none of your business." Tears flooded her eyes now, and she could barely see the moving, pointing, stalking figure in front of her.

"Your Honor," said Thomassy, "I think there's a real question here about the charge, about whether in fact the alleged victim struck the first blow. There is also a real question as to whether this girl, in her close relationship with the boy that struck the first blow, should really be considered an objective witness. I have no further questions."

# Chapter 18

JUDGE CLIFFORD had asked to see counsel in chambers. The small conference room also served as the law library, three of its walls lined with tomes. On the fourth wall, next to the entrance door, hung portraits of Clifford's predecessors, painted in oil by a local artist.

When Metcalf and Thomassy came in, Clifford had already removed his robe and lit up a cigar.

"Thomassy," he said, "what the hell's gotten into you?"

The lawyer chose to be silent.

"You got a rod up your ass? You were very rough on that girl. What were you trying to do out there?" In the face of Thomassy's silence, he went on. "I'll tell you what I think. You were trying to scare the hell out of her and her mother and father so that the next time she's on the stand, in front of a jury, you'd have a frightened, thoroughly intimidated witness." He turned to Metcalf. "You've got nothing to grin about. Your performance out there's been C-minus."

Thomassy stretched his legs under the table. He intertwined his fingers, thrust the palms of his hands toward Metcalf, and stretched his arms. "I was just feeling my way," Thomassy said. "I'm sorry if I stepped over the line. Metcalf's got a nice boy victim, nice girl friend, nice school-teacher-father, and I've got an inarticulate, hostile kid with a scar on his face. If nature stacks the deck, I've just got to work a bit harder."

Judge Clifford couldn't help chuckling. Thomassy was really something.

"I guess you know where we're at," he said.

"I guess," said Thomassy.

From Metcalf's expression, it was clear he didn't.

"The nitty-gritty," said the judge, "is the tire chain. I appreciate your floor show from the hardware store, but I think we're into a potentially deadly weapon."

"And a knife," said Metcalf.

"Yes, how're you going to handle that, Metcalf?"

"The nurse's aide, Alice Ginsler. The one Urek bumped into. She can identify."

"Tell you what," said the judge. "You fellows are keeping me awake, for which I'm always grateful. But I see a grand jury finding enough to indict for first-degree assault. I'm passing you on to White Plains."

"I see," said Thomassy, wondering how he might keep Urek from making an outburst in the courtroom when he heard the news.

"No hard feelings, I hope," said the judge, stubbing his cigar out carefully so he could relight it later. "It must have been obvious to you, George, that I would have to hold him." He slipped his arms into the robe, which Metcalf held out for him.

"No hard feelings," said Thomassy. He looked at Metcalf, who was now well out of it. All he'd have to do was to pass on his notes to the D.A.'s office. This case was over his head, anyway.

The judge went out into the courtroom first, the hubbub instantly hushing.

"After you," said Thomassy, letting Metcalf precede him through the door.

Thomassy went directly over to the defense table, where Urek, like everyone else in the courtroom, was standing. The judge sat. They all sat.

Thomassy whispered to Urek. "Take that pad. Write down the names and addresses of the three kids who were with you at the high school that night. If you remember any of the phone numbers, write them down too. Write down a description of each kid, as best you can." That would keep him busy.

"I have advised counsel," said Judge Clifford, "that from the information produced thus far, it seems to me necessary to pass the case on to the grand jury. The defendant is continued in bail." He tapped his gavel once, a note of solemn finality rendered out of habit.

The spectators jabbered. Thomassy constructed the local newspaper headlines in his head. Urek, busy writing on the pad, hadn't even heard. But his parents got the message, and they were heading toward the defense table. Thomassy rose to meet them.

"Let's discuss this in your home, not here," he said to Mr. Urek.

Inside the Urek house, Thomassy said, "No coffee," before it was offered. "Let's all talk."

"Is this very bad?" asked Paul Urek.

"There are two ways of looking at it," said Thomassy. "I could see early on that the judge wasn't going to dismiss the case as a schoolyard fight. Clifford's not stupid. He sees the possibility of first-degree assault with a dangerous instrument, which is a felony and might mean a year in jail or more if we lose. But . . ."

He could feel them hanging on to his words.

"I think I can handle both Japhets and the girl on the stand, no problem. That nurse's aide worries me some. The big question mark is one we haven't faced yet. Metcalf was going to get one of the other kids, one of your friends, to cop a plea. That means plead guilty to a minor offense in exchange for testifying against you."

"They wouldn't dare," said Urek.

"We've got to be realistic. Someone always dares. The negative thing now is that in White Plains the prosecution's case isn't going to be handled by a bumbler like Metcalf. It'll be one of the young assistant D.A.s for the county. They're smart and ambitious, but don't worry. We've got a big plus on our side from now on."

Urek's father couldn't see what was hopeful.

"I think our case rests on the issue of reasonable doubt. If we stayed in this court, I'd have to convince the judge. Tough to do. If he decided on third degree, which is a misdemeanor, we'd have a six-man jury. All I'd have to do is convince one of them that there was a reasonable doubt as to your son's guilt to get him off. That's a six-to-one chance in our favor. But if the grand jury in White Plains finds a true bill, then we get a twelve-man jury. And all I have to do is convince *one* of them that there's a reasonable doubt. That doubles the odds in our favor. It's much easier, believe me, to hang up one juror out of twelve than one judge."

Urek had a nervous smile on his face. His father said, "This is going to cost a lot more, isn't it?"

"Don't worry about that," said Thomassy. "When I enjoy something, I charge less. We can always stretch out the payments."

"Thank you," said the father.

"One more thing. This is a long shot. I've had a call from a New York psychiatrist who's been studying this case for reasons of his own. I'd like him to have a chat with your son. Depending on what he comes up with, we might call him as a defense witness. The prosecution wouldn't be allowed to call him, so there's no risk. Okay?"

All three Ureks nodded, though Thomassy wasn't certain

they had understood. He thought it best to avoid the word "insanity," especially since he'd only plead it if the Japhet kid died.

"The doctor's name is Koch. I'll give you a ring and let you know when he can come." He went over to the boy. "Remember one thing. The odds are more in our favor in White Plains. Don't screw up. Don't run away. Don't get into any kind of new trouble."

When he left, Thomassy felt good. He wished it was Tuesday.

Dr. Koch took a taxi to the Urek home. The driver asked for seventy-five cents. Koch gave him a dollar bill and hoped it would be enough. As the taxi pulled away, the driver waved, which was most unusual and friendly compared to New York.

The white frame house appeared whiter on the left side than on the right, and as Koch walked up the flagstone path he surmised that the house was in the slow process of being repainted a part at a time. The empty flowerpots on the two windows on either side of the entrance would, when spring came, contain geraniums. This so-called classless society in America had class distinctions even in the choice of flowers. Ah, well. He pushed the doorbell.

It was awkward at first, as he expected it would be, shaking hands with the father and the mother (when would he remember that in America one doesn't shake hands with the women!) and then being introduced to the boy, who kept perhaps ten feet away as he nodded in response to Dr. Koch's hello. The doctor thanked them for suggesting coffee, but said he didn't really want any, nor anything else, and after a bit of shuffling they excused themselves, leaving the uncomfortable boy and the equally uncomfortable interviewer face to face.

"Mr. Thomassy said I have to talk to you," said Urek.

"Only if you wish." Then, after a moment, "How would it be if we took a walk?"

"Where?"

"Oh, no place in particular, just some air and exercise."

"They think I'd run if I got out of the house."

"If you ran away, where would you go?"

"I'm not running away."

"I believe you."

"Yeah."

"Why should I not trust you?"

The boy didn't move.

"Would you *like* a walk? It's not greatly cold, just brisk, quite nice."

"I'll get my coat."

What if the boy did run? Thomassy had made a big point of that. The father appeared just before they left the house.

"It's all right," said Koch. "We'll walk awhile and then come back here."

Outside they both walked with their hands rooted in their pockets, the leftover snow crunching under their feet.

Urek didn't know what to say, certain only that Koch's silence was an invitation for him to speak.

They turned the corner. The sidewalk was less wide, and they were forced to walk closer together.

"How is it for you in school? Do you like it?"

Urek hated questions like that.

"What kind of answer do you want?"

"The truth."

"Well . . ."

"Yes."

"School's a bore."

"All the time?"

"Most."

"Whose fault do you think that is?"

Urek thought. "The teachers'."

"Are they all boring?"

"Some of the things are okay, but they do it in such a boring way, it's hard to stay awake."

"Do you sleep enough at night?"

Urek laughed. "Sure."

"Boredom is man's worst enemy."

The boy looked blank.

"Is there any teacher who isn't boring?"

"Look, I don't want to get in trouble."

"No one is going to repeat what you and I say together."

"Sure, sure."

"Can you tell me your first name?"

"Stanley. Everybody calls me Urek."

"Stanley, do you know what a psychiatrist is?"

"Are you a shrink?"

Koch laughed. "Yes, sometimes."

"You listen to people?"

"Yes."

"Why do you want to talk to me?"

*Be patient,* Koch told himself. *He is frightened.*

"Have you ever gone fishing?"

"Sure, what's that got—"

"You fish, hoping the fish—"

"I ain't a fish."

"No, no, Mr. Thomassy would call this a fishing expedition for ideas, hoping to find some that might be of help to him in defending you." A moment's silence as they slowed their walk. "We were talking about school."

"Okay."

"Which was boring to you because of the teachers. All of them?"

"Not all the time. Gym's okay, but the teacher doesn't talk much. There was one teacher who got sort of interesting."

"A gym teacher?"

"No."

"What subject was that?"

"Science."

"Oh, are you interested in science?"

"What I mean is, the teacher made it sound like it was exciting, you know what I mean?"

"I think I do. Who was it?"

"Mr. Japhet."

Dr. Koch didn't want his surprise to show.

"You're not going to tell anyone, are you?" asked Urek.

"No, no. How did you do in Mr. Japhet's course?"

"He didn't like me."

"Why would he not like you?"

"Look, I could tell from the first day. Some of the kids he was chatty with, you know, the ass-kissers, the kids who get dressed up for school like it was church, when he came around the room looking into their notebooks he'd say, 'Good, good,' and crap like that."

"Did he say, 'Good, good,' to you?"

"He said, how come you don't use the English language right. I said what the hell did he think I was talking. He said I didn't have a single sentence right. I said I had studied the lesson, I dared him to show me where I was wrong, and he said it was wrong because it wasn't literate, some shit like that."

Koch stared at the boy.

"I didn't mean to say 'shit.' "

"That's all right. You mean you had the content right?"

"Every fact was right out of the book he assigned. I had nothing wrong—"

"Except the words you put it in."

"What difference does that make?"

"Did he tell you to take remedial English?"

"He gave me a flunk on the paper. So I cut his class."

"Yes?"

"I mean, he asked me why I was absent when he saw me in the hall. I couldn't say I was sick or anything. So I said the truth."

"You said what?"

"I said he put me down. He acted surprised. Surprised! He said he wanted to see my mother or father. I told him my father worked and I didn't want my mother to come to yessir him. He said I was insolent, I'll never forget that word he used. I told him *he* was insolent. I didn't even know for sure what it meant. I cut his class the rest of the week. That finished it. He sent the principal some kind of note that I wasn't prepared to take a science course. Shit!"

Dr. Koch walked along with the boy in silence; then he said, "I would like to ask you about something difficult."

"Like what?"

"Do you think you can talk to me about that locker-room business?"

Urek said nothing.

"Why don't we turn around and walk back to the house."

They walked uphill now, in silence. After a while Urek said, "The boys paid me a quarter a month. Everybody knows it."

"How many boys did you collect from regularly?"

"Well, Mr. Chadwick, the principal, he exaggerated like hell. It was only sixty-one."

Dr. Koch did the figures in his head. "That's fifteen dollars a month."

"Not even, because some of the kids owed it to me when they didn't have it. It's hard to collect from some of them, even though they promised to pay. I never beat a kid up for not paying."

"Do you think you could have earned fifteen dollars a month by working?"

"That *was* work, doc. I had to patrol. I had to keep my guys in line. And did you ever use a hacksaw—it's a lot of work."

"Hacksaw?"

"To cut open a lock if they didn't pay."

"Did you have to do that often?"

"Till they caught on it's cheaper to pay than to buy a new lock. That Japhet kid, he paid five dollars and seventy-five cents for that tempered lock I couldn't get through, isn't that crazy? I figured out he could have bought twenty-eight months of protection for that money. Nine months to the school year, he'd of graduated and be ahead of the game if he wasn't so stubborn."

"I see. If you got a job in a grocery on Saturdays, or mowed lawns in spring and summer, or did something regular after school for a storekeeper, swept up, anything, deliveries, couldn't you have earned a lot more per month?"

"Yeah."

"What does that mean?"

"I *tried* it."

"Well?"

"You know how lousy people are when you work for them, do this, do that, never say nothing when you do something right, they don't tell you how they want something done, then criticize you if you do it wrong. I worked for Pete's Hardware, and they accused me of stealing parts!"

"You didn't, did you?"

"I was going to pay for them out of my pay. I was just putting them aside because my father was fixing up the downstairs bathroom, and he told me the parts he needed. My father would have paid me back. They had no business accusing me of cheating. You know, Pete told the employment office at the school on me so it'd be impossible to get another job? What was I supposed to do, go on relief, they wouldn't give me relief. I'm sixteen! They give niggers relief, and I wanted to work!"

"I understand what you are saying."

"You don't think I did something wrong?"

"That is not for me to say."

"I'll tell you something. It wasn't the fifteen bucks, it was being my own boss. But every time I passed Japhet's locker with that tempered lock on it, I would get so mad I could have— I'm saying too much."

"It's all right."

They were in front of the house, about to go in. He'd better finish before they got back inside.

"How would it seem, how would you feel, to have had Mr. Japhet as a father?"

"I got a father."

"Yes, but just suppose circumstances were different."

"I don't get it. I like my old man."

"Of course."

"Mr. Japhet hated me."

"I'm sure he didn't hate you."

"How would you know?"

"He doesn't seem like a hateful man."

"He didn't give me a chance."

"Why did you resent Ed Japhet's magic show so much?"

"What do you mean, 'resent'?"

"You had your fight with him right after the show."

"Listen, that kid is worse than his father. He thinks he's king or something just because he knows some tricks. There's a lot of things I know he don't. He never had a piece in his life. He can't weight-lift. I seen him try in the gym, what a laugh!"

"If he was inadequate in some ways, didn't that make you feel good?"

"He—"

"Yes?"

"He—the—son of a bitch!"

"We have to go inside now. I think your mother and father would be upset if they thought I had upset you."

"You don't upset me, I just can't stand thinking of that kid."

Dr. Koch wanted to put his hands on the boy's shoulders. "Even if Japhet is completely wrong, your feeling toward him has hurt you more than it has hurt him. Yes, you had a bad fight, and he was in the hospital. I have talked to him, too. He may not be as bad as you think. I don't want to change your mind about him, just to ask you, would *you* not be better off if you put him out of your mind?"

Dr. Koch realized that he was asking the impossible.

Inside the house, he accepted Mrs. Urek's repeated offer of coffee, and the four of them sat in the living room. Finally Mr. Urek suggested that his son go upstairs, and then he said, "Mr. Thomassy said you might be able to help get the boy off."

"Yes. I'm afraid I don't think I have heard anything today that could be very helpful."

Mr. Urek rose. "If that kid was smart-alecky to you—"

"No, no, Mr. Urek, he said nothing wrong. It's just that the only way the testimony of a psychiatrist can sometimes be helpful is if there is a question as to the sanity of a defendant. Your boy is not insane, I assure you."

"You're damn right he's not! If I knew that was what Thomassy was up to—"

"Please be calm. Mr. Thomassy is trying to help you."

Mrs. Urek came over to stand behind her husband's chair. Dr. Koch felt he should go. He asked them could they please telephone for a taxi. It took exactly seven minutes to arrive, and in that time not a single word passed among them.

# Chapter 19

THOMASSY PARKED HIS CAR a block away from the small, sad-looking house he thought was Alice Ginsler's. The gray-green paint reminded him of the colors one saw in the stairwells of institutions. The outside of the house must have seemed dreary even before it had weathered and flaked. He checked the number on the front against the one he had found in the phone book. It was the right house. There were lights on wherever there was a window. Was she alone, or were there others inside? He looked in vain for figures in the windows.

Thomassy walked up the path to the front door. The nameplate under the bell was empty.

The door was answered by a man of about thirty or so, in his undershirt, not bad-looking. His long hair was a bit wiry and his lips thick. Some black blood somewhere along the line, thought Thomassy.

"Mr. Ginsler?" he asked.

"We're not buying anything."

"I'm not selling anything, Mr. Ginsler. My name's Thomassy." He handed the young man one of his "B" calling cards, which gave only his name and the business address.

"What do you want?"

"I've been asked to investigate the incident at the hospital the other night, Mr. Ginsler. May I come in? I tried to phone first—"

"It's disconnected. We don't like being bothered."

Thomassy wondered if the faint smell coming through the open doorway was pot.

"It's okay," said Thomassy, smiling, "I'm not a cop."

"You don't look like a cop."

*You don't look like a white man,* Thomassy thought.

"Bill, please let him in." The voice turned out to be that of a pleasant-looking but not terribly attractive girl in her late twenties in the process of removing her apron as she joined the young man at the door.

*If she was washing dishes, she wasn't smoking pot,* thought Thomassy. *But it's her house, and she's responsible.*

"Bill, please," said the girl.

The young man reluctantly stepped aside to let Thomassy in. Thomassy put his hand out to shake. "Name's Thomassy."

"I read the card. I'm Bill Carey."

"I'm Alice Ginsler," said the girl. "I don't remember seeing you at the hospital."

"I'm not on the hospital *staff,*" said Thomassy, hoping the stress would suggest that perhaps the hospital had employed him. "I'm an investigator. That's my office in town." He pointed to the card.

If she testifies, thought Thomassy, she'll say that I visited her and posed as an investigator. The prosecutor might develop it on direct or re-cross.

He was shown past the dining table on which six plates with leftover food were still sitting, into the L of the living-dining room, and to an overstuffed sofa.

The girl and Carey each pulled a chair away from the dining table, to sit directly opposite Thomassy on the sofa.

"I apologize for taking your time this evening," said Thomassy, "but I think you know it's important."

"It's about that boy who cut the tube, isn't it?" said Alice Ginsler.

"Yes."

"Am I going to have to be questioned by the police again?"

"Perhaps not."

"I don't see what they want from Alice," said Bill Carey.

"Shhh," said Alice.

"Did you actually see the tube cut?" asked Thomassy.

"No, I told the police all I saw was this young fellow bursting out of the room. He knocked over a tray of hypodermics I was carrying, and he just went right on down the back stairs."

"Could you identify him?"

"He was shortish and had a scar on his face, I saw that. There wasn't all that much light in the hallway. It happened quickly, you see, but I think that if I were to see him again, I could—"

A three-year-old dark-haired girl came around the corner of the room and stood staring at Thomassy.

"Hello," said Thomassy.

The child looked away shyly.

"Yours?" asked Thomassy.

Miss Ginsler smiled pleasantly. "No, that's Harriet. She belongs to Milton and Barbara. They share the house with us."

"I see," said Thomassy, who was getting more than he bargained for. "That's not your daughter, it's Milton and Barbara's daughter."

Bill Carey laughed out loud. "Actually," he said, "that's Barbara's before she met Milton."

"Well, never mind," said Thomassy. "I take it," he said, addressing Alice, "that Mr. Carey is your common-law husband?"

Carey laughed out loud again.

Miss Ginsler explained. "We don't call it that anymore."

"If the D.A. calls you to testify, which may not be necessary because there's so little that you actually saw, he would have to establish your credibility as a witness, or it might be dealt with on cross-examination, do you follow me?"

Miss Ginsler nodded, but she looked unsure. Bill Carey had moved forward in his seat. He seemed much less naïve than Miss Ginsler. Thomassy would have to be careful.

"The fact that you're a nurse's aide in the hospital is a big plus in your favor because nurses and their assistants are held in high repute in the community."

"Yeah," said Carey.

"But," continued Thomassy, "it would develop that you were illegally . . ."

Carey was standing. "Say that again."

"I meant no offense. I'm trying to be helpful. On the witness stand Miss Ginsler would have to tell the truth, that's all, about living here out of wedlock—of course there's nothing wrong about it, but you know how backward many people in this town are about that, and also with another couple in the house with a child that is not issue of a marriage between that couple, I think you begin to see the complications. The newspaper people are always looking around for juicy tidbits for their readers. My main concern, actually, is that the hospital staff—"

"I try to keep my private life to myself," said Miss Ginsler.

"Exactly. That's why I'm trying to prepare you for what happens in a courtroom."

"Suppose she doesn't want to testify?" said Bill Carey, sitting down again.

"Well, the district attorney could always subpoena her, but I think he might not want to do so because it would come out in the cross-examination that the witness did not come voluntarily, and—look, I want to give you my assurances. I don't want to see your private life aired any more than you do."

"What you're saying," said Bill Carey, "is—"

"I think we all know what's being said," said Miss Ginsler. Maybe she wasn't as naïve as she looked.

Thomassy stood. For a second he wondered if Carey was going to hit him. But he had misinterpreted a tic that creased the skin near Carey's eye. Carey had a good thing going here. He didn't want to leave. He didn't want anything in the newspapers.

"I won't take your time anymore," Thomassy said. "I'm sorry if I interrupted your evening." They caught him staring at the six dinner plates on the table. Milton and Barbara make four, the child five, who's the sixth, another child? Maybe a baby would cry. That would tell him nothing. A baby didn't sit at the dinner table.

"I guess you're going," said Bill Carey.

"What I've said can only be of benefit."

Carey's laugh was very nervous. Thomassy wondered if Alice Ginsler had access to other drugs at the hospital. Never mind, he'd probably found out all he needed to.

"I don't have anything against you. Believe me, I'm trying to be helpful."

"Sure," said Carey, moving toward the door.

Thomassy stopped. "By the way," he said, "I wouldn't leave things like that lying about."

Alice Ginsler's face flushed. Bill quickly took the roach holder off the sideboard and out of the room as Miss Ginsler let Thomassy out the front door.

# Chapter 20

THE TALK ONE HEARD about the case depended on which of two shopping areas one frequented. The Warmark Shopping Center was patronized principally by middle-class and upper-middle-class wives, well-groomed ladies who would never wear hair curlers to the marketplace or bring young children in their sleepclothes. These women did not stop to gossip on their rounds, but saved their conversation for the Saturday or Sunday cocktail hours, when they could talk about controversial matters in an atmosphere of discretion.

In the bustle of shops near Fulton and Plane streets, hair curlers, half-camouflaged in bandanas, were much in evidence on a Saturday morning, as were occasional unkempt children in nightclothes plunked onto their mothers' shopping carts. These women would frequently stop to chatter with a familiar face, and it was here that one heard the names of Japhet and Urek and Thomassy as well, with gossip asserted as fact. Elaborate stories developed nuances enriched with detail on each retelling. A half-accurate sentence in Friday evening's newspaper would seed several hundred words passed from shopper to shopper. Thus were the apocrypha of the Japhet-Urek case made.

Several newspapers from towns in the surrounding area had sent young reporters to the courtroom, and their copy, edited by older but not necessarily wiser men, was, as usual, a pastiche of fact and fiction. Had anyone checked the direct quotes against the stenographic transcript, he would have been hard-pressed to find two successive sentences on which the papers and the transcript agreed. Though the fuel of conversation was fed also by observations of those who had attended the preliminary hearing, each person had remembered what he wanted to remember.

Judge Clifford had guessed that papers in Mount Kisco and Pleasantville and Tarrytown would play up the after-dance attack and its consequences as a local affair, and he was surprised to be told by his wife, whose fellow club-women came from all over the county, that Larchmont, Mamaroneck, Yonkers, and Peekskill had covered the story on the front page. The references to his studied conduct of the difficult proceedings would surely enable him to think of countywide office more optimistically in the future.

In the school itself, talk outside the classroom was of nothing but the case. The teachers, even in civics and social studies, tried to steer clear of such discussions because they sensed, accurately, as it turned out, that the student body had polarized on the issue, the majority of course siding with the Japhets but a fair minority of the boys, not girls, sympathizing with Urek: Japhet was a teacher, and therefore the enemy, and Ed was a teacher's son, and therefore a candidate for a good college, and what would happen if tiffs and fights and pranks and occasional window-breaking mischief became a matter for the courts? The school was a repressive body against which all adolescence had to try its horns, and how could one do this in the shadow of the law? It was like having invisible policemen on the premises. Even some of the boys who had been forced to pay locker-room

tariffs to Urek and his friends held this view and were beginning to think of the Japhets as cop-loving finks.

## COMMENT BY LILA

I just can't take it in this school anymore, or even after
school, the girls are impossible, and when Ed and I are
together, if anybody sees us it's as if we were freaks. Even
when we're in his house or my house, it's like having cam-
eras watching you like a shoplifter in a store. We haven't
even kissed since the court thing. It isn't the same anymore.
It can only get worse when the trial is on. I don't want to
tell that story again. I don't want to testify. *I don't care,* I
just want to be left alone, please God, starting right now,
even if it means Ed and I have to break up. I never thought
I'd think that, but I think like that all the time now.

## COMMENT BY MR. JAPHET

At first it was only the fact that I couldn't keep the experience from coming to mind in the middle of lectures or
class discussions, my mind would wander, I didn't feel the
beautiful tension of an attentive class anymore. I've tried to
put this all out of my head with thoughts that it could have
turned out so much worse, Ed could have been perma-
nently injured, I might have hurt the Urek boy in my rage. I
have always said to the kids, at least to the ones I felt I was
leading along, I always said it wasn't their answers that
counted as much as the questions they asked me, it was
asking the right questions that would lead them beyond the
subject matter of biology or any other, to what? The begin-
nings of wisdom? Now I find myself nagged by impossible
questions! How could I have prevented this from happening? What is the use of teaching, or parenthood for that

matter, if you can't anticipate trouble and avoid it? I try to tell myself it's like sickness or injury, you try to be careful, and if it happens, you try to correct, to fix, to heal, to adjust, to make a comeback to normalcy, but is that now possible? If Urek had stayed in my class last year, could I have gotten a grip on his attention? Would this have happened? Why did Ed develop an insane interest in a hobby that bothers people?

"Dad, did you talk to the insurance man about replacing the tricks? The guillotine is thirty-seven fifty."

"I told him you didn't save the receipts."

"And?"

"He said he'd allow the replacement cost less forty percent depreciation."

"Depreciation? On magic tricks?"

"On everything. Ed, you really want to replace all those . . . I guess you do. All right, I'll make good the difference."

"Can I go to Tannen's Saturday?"

"I'll give you a check."

"Lila digs Tannen's, remember she went with us when—"

"I can't drive to New York Saturday."

"I was going to take the train. I thought I'd ask Lila and we could go to a movie afterward."

A cheerful Ed dashed to the kitchen phone to invite Lila.

"I'd just as soon stay home," Lila said.

"But you loved wandering around Tannen's. We could go to a movie after."

"No, really."

"Well," he said, "Saturday's out."

"Yes."

"What about a movie tonight?"

"With school tomorrow?"

"That never bothered you before."

"I'd really rather not."

"You sure?" he said, his voice gravelly and indistinct.

"What'd you say?"

"Never mind."

"I didn't hear you."

"It's okay."

He went upstairs to his room because he couldn't stand being near people, especially his own parents.

The letter appeared in the local newspaper on Monday.

To the Editor:

We appreciate the opportunity provided by your pages to reach the citizens of our community.

We, the undersigned, are all students at the high school. We are law-abiding, and none of us has ever been in serious trouble. All of us are having lots of trouble at the school we didn't ask for.

For a long time the school has been divided into two groups. Those of us who think of the school as a place to get an education have been disturbed in and out of the classroom by the greasers.

"Greasers" is a term that is misunderstood by many adults. It doesn't mean Spanish-Americans or Mexicans (to the best of our knowledge, there are none in the school). Nor does it mean members of any minority group or ethnic group because there are blacks who are on our side as well as in the greaser group, and students of Italian extraction who are with us and others who are greasers. A greaser is someone who does not care about school, who feels it's just a place you have to go to for so many years. A greaser lives by the opposite of the golden rule. He tries to do unto others whatever he can get away with. According to the greasers, doing something bad or illegal is wrong only if you get caught and punished for it.

We think it is unfortunate that the law requires everyone to attend school up to age seventeen. It means that those of us who are trying to learn something are interfered with all the time by greasers and their like, who are just passing time.

We are addressing this appeal to the parents of this community to help us, because the teachers can't. It is a fact of life in many communities throughout the country that the teachers have no control over the divided situation. The few really good ones give up and go elsewhere. The majority of teachers are afraid and do nothing.

We are afraid also, but we want to do something about the situation before we become adults. The reason is that adults are afraid or don't care. Adults are hypocrites. If any student who wants to find a pusher can find one, why can't the teachers or the police or the adults find them? The answer must be that they don't want to. If students have to pay protection money to greasers in school, let us remember that they see adults doing the same thing because it is easier to pay protection than to risk anything.

We know we are taking a risk by signing this letter. Actually, we were turned down by nearly seventy students who approve of what we're doing but who didn't want to sign this letter. If we are taking a risk by signing, who can say it isn't a risk worth taking?

| | |
|---|---|
| Leon Abels | Inge Jansen |
| George Crockett | Edward Japhet |
| Elizabeth Crowell | Abraham Lefkowitz |
| Dominick Deluria | Bertram Lilo |
| Fred Frankel | Kevin Mooney |
| Lila Hurst | Chisholm Motherwell |

Edgar Motherwell          Sheldon Summerville
Thomas Olafsen            Patricia Toombs
Morey Ruff                Richard Tubbs

That evening, Paul Urek sat in his living room after dinner, skimming the evening paper. He checked the front
page, sports, what was playing at the local movie houses,
and then his eye lit on the letter, which was on the page
facing the editorial page. Normally he would not have read
a letter in a newspaper, but the long list of names caught his
eye, and when he saw Ed Japhet's among them, he read the
letter, quickly the first time, then more slowly. He got up
and put the paper down in front of his wife and son, pointing.

"Son of a bitch," he said, "they're talking about us."

# Chapter 21

PAUL UREK climbed into his blue Chevy coupé, glancing as always at the odometer, the numbers now at 82,991, deriving the familiar good sensation from the knowledge that he had disassembled and reassembled practically every part of that car, that he had personally replaced, as they wore out, muffler, tailpipe (twice), rings, carburetor (rebuilt by himself), starter, shocks (all four), radiator belts, brake linings, everything but the transmission, which, thank God, hadn't needed major work, that on his wheeled creeper he had checked, lubed, rechecked, drained, then, standing up, refilled the oil, pampered, anticipated, refined, sandpapering body spots, applying filler, sandpapering again, spot painting, then Simonizing all over with paste, not liquid wax. He'd dare his friends to find the nicks.

Sixteen years ago the car and his son were both brand new. He had watched his wife change the diapers and had tried it in front of her, laughing at his clumsiness, but after that first time he didn't like the mess of it when, instead of pee it turned out to be a near-loose yellow crap he had to get unloaded into the john without spilling, and hoping the kid wouldn't fall off the bassinet in the meantime. When the baby was to be fed, he tried several times to take a turn at it, but the little bastard kept letting the stuff dribble out of the mouth at about the same rate that he was shoveling it in. Finally, after junior had sideswiped a nearly full jar of strained carrots onto his father's suit pants as well as the chair, he decided it was time to make a clear division, and he told his wife, "You feed and change the kid, I'll take care of the car," and since he didn't take any back-talk from her, that was that.

He had asked for and gotten each empty Gerber's jar for cotter pins, tacks, nails, wood screws, machine screws, brass screws, lock washers, and other small whatevers so they'd be neat and handy to the grasp whenever something needed fixing. He'd bought the Chevy when his wife had announced she was pregnant, and for nearly seventeen years now he had nursed and tended it, brought it to its present proud state as the cleanest, smoothest-running, most trouble-free automobile owned by any of his friends, including, he laughed to himself, Scarlatti's year-old Mercury lemon that still wasn't working right.

Paul Urek's touch was gentle as he lifted the gear lever into neutral, turned the key while his toe applied minimal pressure to the pedal, and listened for the instant hum of the smooth start he expected and got almost all of the time. He put the car into reverse, backed out of the driveway, checking oncoming traffic both ways, then slipped the gear lever into drive. With the comforting, automatic shift into second, he picked up speed on Route 9, satisfied at the shift into high, no jolt, smooth, from a car with—he glanced at the odometer again—82,992 beautiful miles on it, a delight.

Paul Urek saw the light turn yellow, glanced quickly in his rear-view mirror to make sure he didn't have a tailgater ready to go up his ass, and braked just as the light turned red. He'd nearly lost his license for three infractions during one eighteen-month period long ago, and his desperation at the time that *he wouldn't be able to drive* nearly drove him insane. Luckily, the judge gave him one more chance, and since then he hadn't had a ticket.

It was a long light. When he had briefly had a job at the wire works and joined the union, he had gotten the booklet which described the grievance procedure. That night, thinking about the booklet as he dozed off to sleep, he had dreamed about every goddamn grievance he had against the world, until he woke at two A.M. and couldn't really get back to sleep before dawn. He hated the roustabout nature of his work, not knowing what to do when a good job was heard of and then lost to someone else, hated the penny-counting, no-chance-to-save round of buying the first and second television set on time, converting the boiler to oil because coal was hard to come by and his wife kept pushing, then the clothes washer and dryer combination, which was just no damn good, and he finally gave up on getting less than a third of what he had paid for it and putting that down on a separate washer and dryer from Sears, who had gotten very tough about delays on the monthly payments. He was furious every time he saw the hole in the new counter for a dishwasher. He had wanted to buy it for cash to avoid the chance of his credit application being turned down and ended up not buying because he couldn't get his hands on that much cash and, furthermore, he'd be damned if he'd be beholden to the dishwasher-repair service coming in every few months, as he'd heard, for this and that costing twelve or fifteen dollars, lifelong servitude he didn't need and want, and wondered now, as many times before, if Japhet worried about these things. It wasn't fair that Japhet, whose schoolteacher income couldn't be all that great, *looked* as if he never had to worry about bills, wore dress shirts that needed laundering every day, shoes that must have cost twice what his work shoes cost and lasted half as long. People like that either had the money or knew something he didn't know, and he didn't see himself or his son ever getting out of that bind.

Cars honked behind him. The light had changed. He took off with a roar.

He parked in the bowling area parking lot carefully, not too close to any other car whose opening door could mar the finish on his while he was inside.

At the desk Al waved hello and reached for size tens, but Paul brushed away the offer of shoes even though, as a mark of long patronage and respect, the proprietor no longer charged him the twenty-five-cent rental fee. He wasn't bowling tonight.

He used to come regularly on Friday nights like this, bowling with the same group, beering, living off a high he had reached some years back when he had for the first time in his life struck oil, a 299, luckily with the whole mob watching, stamping, and applauding. His name had gone up on the board of perfect scores since Al always made the one-point allowance, on the assumption that anyone with his name on that board would never play at a competitive alley if he could help it. Then Urek had cut down and almost cut out his Friday-night appearances for a reason he would not admit: shortness of cash. His share of the game never came to more than a couple or three dollars, but the beer would go fast and could come to five or six, especially when a good mood or a series of strikes made him overdo the buying of rounds for others. He hated coming home high and going through the money routine with the old lady, who'd talk about how she had saved six cents here and seven cents there by careful shopping, and then he'd blow ten dollars on what? A night at the bowling alley?

Urek slapped a back and palmed a greeting all around. Scarlatti offered him one of the uncapped, still-chilled bottles of beer, which he accepted because he hoped he wouldn't be around long enough to have to buy an exchange. He watched along with the others, kidding, laughing out loud when he was supposed to, wondering how many of them he could count on. Eldon's kid was a friend of his son, and the father was okay, a riveter who worked the I-beams on office buildings in New York, fearless about walking on steel thousands of feet in the air without support, a regular Indian, which he might have been with those high cheekbones, and they kidded him about it. Feeney's kid was also one of the gang, a coward according to his son, but the old man was all right, a twenty-year teamster who could handle big ones, including a two-trailer rig. Corrigan would do anything the rest of them did.

So when they were taking a breather, Urek asked if they had seen the letter in the newspaper. Scarlatti was the only one who had. Urek brought out the neatly folded clipping and opened it up on the table in back of their alley so that the others could read while he and Scarlatti fed the fire by pointing at the names on the bottom.

"Five of 'em are Briarcliff Jews."

"None of our kids would sign a thing like that."

"I make three Jews."

"They change their names."

"Crockett's a nigger."

"You sure?"

"Sure I'm sure."

"There's the Mooney kid."

Mooney's father, though R.C., was a traitor. He had worked a pump at the Sunoco station, then somehow got financed to a half-ownership position, no one knew how, and now talked about sending his kid, who got straight A's and hung out with the Protestants, to Yale or Amherst! What shit! Mooney had had the nerve to keep coming to the alley —they all knew why, he had never learned to play golf— and one day they had paid their respects to his snobbery. Mooney had gone to the crapper, and four or five of them had waited until he got behind the booth door. Then they took turns pissing on the tile floor which slanted slightly so

that the river of piss ran right into Mooney's booth. They
had waited and waited for Mooney to come out, but he had
outwaited them, and they had gone back to the game, and
after a while Mooney came out, avoiding their alley, finished his game with his stuck-up son, paid off, and left without a glance in their direction. Later that week, Eldon,
goaded by the rest, had driven into the Sunoco station when
Mooney was on, Eldon's car stayed parked at the pumps for
fifteen minutes while Mooney ignored it, taking cars that
came after, till another customer, seeing what was going on,
had laughed, and Eldon had gone caroming out of the station yelling he was going to report the station to Sunoco.

"Japhet put his name on it," said Urek.

"Yeah."

"I got an idea," said Scarlatti.

"I bet I know," said Feeney.

"Do Japhet's garage."

A garage hadn't been done in town for nearly a year. The
last time, none of the five had gotten to participate though
some of their friends had. Somebody had crossed somebody
else, and one morning had arisen to find that his weed-killer
bags had been slashed and some dumped into other bags so
you couldn't tell how much of what was in what, and all of
it useless unless you wanted to risk your grass—and the
rotary nut had been loosened, which would have sent the
blade spinning off when the machine was started up, though
on that occasion the victim had checked everything carefully out of caution and had tightened the mower nut so
that no one was hurt. The police, of course, said it must
have been vandals, meaning teen-agers.

"Doing a garage doesn't reach the kids," said Feeney. "I
was thinking of the new rec hall."

Urek was quick to agree. He'd had the rec hall in the back
of his mind all along.

"My kid was in there once," said Scarlatti. "They got
peace posters and all that Communist shit on the wall."

They talked some more, had some more beer, let the plan build, went back to the game, which seemed less interesting now, decided finally to give up their lane, talked some more at the bar between beers, hashing out what they'd need to do the job properly.

When Corrigan said, "Well, we're not going to write a letter to the paper, right?" they all laughed.

"What are we waiting for?" asked Urek.

The five took off in three cars, headlights on, tailgating each other like a short funeral procession.

The bartender at the alley was on the phone to Thomassy the minute they left. Mike was Thomassy's favorite stool pigeon. Most people in town who got into trouble were bowlers, not golfers, and if Thomassy had had his tipoff man at the Sleepy Hollow Country Club bar, he wouldn't have seen any clients out of it. Those people, on the rare occasions when they got into trouble and couldn't sweep it under the carpet, used multiple-named New York City law firms to stand up for them. On the other hand, the people who bowled produced almost all of the first-, second-, and third-degree assault, manslaughter, and wife-beating cases, their offspring the car thefts and late-night break-ins that brought them to court in handcuffs, Thomassy at their side.

Thomassy tipped Mike the bartender enough to make Mike think of himself as a moonlighting staff member instead of a squealer. Mike had gotten so proficient he no longer reported bar talk that would lead nowhere. He knew the difference between mischief and trouble better than most cops. Thomassy was a good teacher.

"Scarlatti, Eldon, Corrigan, Urek, and Feeney, destination the new rec hall for a paint job," he reported.

"You sure it was Urek?"

"These fellows is all regulars around here for years."

"Was the kid with him?"

"No kids."

"Why the rec hall?"

"A clip from the paper, something about a letter signed by a bunch of kids, make sense?"

"How much they have to drink?"

"They were pretty beery."

Thomassy glanced at his watch. The kids would still be there. Did the rec hall have a phone? Would the kids believe him? If Urek's old man got in trouble with the cops, it'd kill his chances with a jury for the kid. If Ed Japhet got hurt again, it'd tear the case to pieces.

"You still there?" asked Mike.

"They know you know?"

"You know me, I serve drinks and I'm deaf."

"Okay."

"Yeah, well, maybe you'll get a homicide out of it."

Thomassy hung up on Mike's chuckle. Within minutes he was speeding toward the rec hall.

The five men had to stop at two of their homes before they had enough supplies, a four-inch paintbrush for each of them, two half-full gallon cans of black paint, a steel rake for ripping, a hammer, a crowbar.

Corrigan wanted to add an ax.

"No axes," said Paul Urek, clearly the leader.

"I got something better than that in back of the car," said Corrigan, pointing to the five-gallon can of gasoline. It's full."

"You leave that in the car," said Urek. "The rec hall's got houses on both sides. A fire would sweep the block. Besides, half the volunteer firemen are still at the alley, and you don't want them to lose all their business tonight."

The men laughed. Urek said, "Let's get moving. They close the place at eleven."

Thomassy was racing up South Highland, anxious to get

to the rec hall as far ahead of the men as he could, when suddenly a yapping brown mongrel darted off the sidewalk. Thomassy couldn't swerve either left or right because of the oncoming traffic and the parked cars, so he jammed the brake to the floor, glad his seat belt was buckled because his body rose toward the windshield as the car screeched to a stop, rocking forward, and from the clunk and the hideous dog-cry he knew he had hit. No car was behind him. He looked left and right. Was it possible no one had seen?

He reversed the car ten feet till he could see the thrashing animal, which needed a bullet through its brain but Thomassy had no gun and didn't dare phone the police. He shifted the gear lever and, with tires squealing, drove around the helpless dog and away from his first hit-and-run accident.

Outside the rec hall Thomassy mopped his dripping face with his handkerchief, feeling the sweat all over his back and chest and even inside his pants legs. But maybe he could make up for the hit-run with what he was about to do if God gave him the time.

The kids were startled to see Thomassy come in the front door. Adults rarely visited the place.

Thomassy peered into the throbbing noise of the large room. It was hard to see. The colored lights had some kind of device in front of them to make the colors seem to whirl and blob in random shapes on the kids dancing and on the postered walls. Thomassy scanned the dancers for a familiar face.

Ed and Lila both recognized him immediately. He saw them about the same time. Since he didn't know who among the kids was in charge, he threaded through the dancers toward Ed. The rock blast from the corner stereo was deafening. Thomassy said practically into Japhet's ear, "You've got to clear the place out fast."

"Why?"

"Where's the phonograph?"

Ed pointed. Thomassy strode over to it, avoiding the dancers. Gently he picked the arm off the record. The dancers gradually stopped, though the colored lights continued to swirl.

"What's the matter?" said Ed.

"Can I have your attention," said Thomassy into the leftover babble. "There's very little time. A group of men who are high on beer are overreacting to the letter in the paper today. They're on the way over here right now, looking for trouble."

A red-headed boy clenched his fists.

"Now, we don't want any trouble," said Thomassy.

"We can take care of ourselves," said the red-headed boy.

"I know some of these men," said Thomassy. "You can call the police if you want, or you can clear out of here."

He noticed that some of the girls were heading for the door. "That's good," he said. "There's been enough trouble in this town."

Thomassy took the red-headed kid by the arm, figuring that if he could get him moving, the rest would go too. He whispered something in the kid's ear.

"Gasoline?"

"Maybe."

One girl said, "It's crazy. Why would they do anything?"

"Shut up," said her frightened escort. There was a general move toward the back door.

Thomassy didn't like the way the Japhet kid was looking at him. He could get into real trouble if Urek and his friends found out who warned the kids.

"Please," said Thomassy, "trust me," not knowing why they should trust him.

But they did.

He made sure they locked the front door before they left through the back. He turned the lights off himself, after someone had pointed to the switch box, which was around the corner near the small kitchen. He had to hurry one boy along who was slow about putting his records back into their jackets. When he was sure they were all out, he closed the back door.

His heart still pounding, Thomassy found his way in the darkness around the side of the rec hall toward the front where he had left his car. He was about to cross the sidewalk to it when the three-car procession came around the corner almost directly at him. He stepped back into the shadows, hoping the men had not seen him.

# Chapter 22

Behind the bushes, uncomfortable on his haunches, Thomassy watched the cortege of cars stop, five doors swing open to let five men out, the distinctive, different slams of the car doors, the momentary huddle at the lead car as they looked at the darkened building, and then Paul Urek motioning them along.

"What do they do in the dark?" said Scarlatti.

"It's usually lit up," said Eldon.

Paul Urek knocked on the door.

It was Feeney, brave in company, who kicked in the small window. The sound of glass was music. The other four laughed, and it took only a second before they were battering the door, and the hinge gave.

Urek lifted the bolt on the second hinge, and they were in.

He flipped the light switch, expecting to see a mob of scared kids backing against the walls.

The fucking place was empty.

Thomassy, unused to squatting, was glad to stand. He edged around the bush. Something caught his left shoe, and he went forward, breaking his fall on both hands. He brushed away the dirt he could not see and careful not to trip again, found his way to the side window.

The five faces, frozen in anger, at that moment broke their surprise. The men went into action, ripping down posters, spinning records like thin discuses across the room to split and shatter when the edges hit the far wall. Paint cans opened, they dripped and smeared LOVE AMERICA across the wall. Each streaked obscenities of his own devising, except Paul Urek, who waited till they had exhausted themselves, and wrote, neater than the others, across the wall facing the window through which Thomassy peered: KIDS ARE SHIT.

As they closed their paint cans and assembled their things near the front door, Thomassy saw Eldon wipe his brush on the floor in the unmistakable shape of a swastika. Scarlatti and Eldon laughed. Then they were gone through the rectangle from which the front door swung.

Three sets of sealed beams went on, the third car lighting the second, the second the first, and the first the road, as they drove off.

Inside the building, Thomassy stepped over the torn posters on the floor to study the mess on the walls. He took the white, neatly folded handkerchief from his breast pocket and, knowing it would never be usable again, smeared the still-wet drawing on the floor in the hope of making it indecipherable.

# Chapter 23

LILA ANSWERED THE DOOR, a finger to her lips, and motioned Ed toward the living room where the meeting was already under way. He sat down on the floor next to some of the other kids.

The Motherwells had a hopeless proposition. They wanted to hit every door in town for a donation for redoing the new rec hall. It was dismissed on the grounds that it would take too long and that most people wouldn't give anyway.

Morey Ruff, who turned up a minute after Ed, jumped in with an offer of five bucks if ten of the other kids would match it. "We could buy the paint and do it ourselves in a weekend."

Frankel protested. Why should some pay and others not, when they all used the rec hall. He suggested a dollar each, but compulsory.

Liz Crowell asked what about the kids who couldn't afford it.

"Everybody can afford a dollar," said Frankel.

"It'll take too long," said Morey Ruff.

Ed didn't know where the idea came from, but it came into his head while the others were talking, and his first instinct was to leave, to just excuse himself, say he wasn't feeling well or something, and go. He listened some more. He hated committees. Nobody was taking the lead. There were now more proposals than people. The conversation was getting heated, and then Liz said, "Ed, you're the only one who hasn't spoken up. Do you have any ideas?"

He wished Lila wasn't in the room. "Well, I don't know if you'll like my idea."

"Can't tell until you say it," said Fred Frankel.

Ed got up. You couldn't speak sitting on the floor. He had an impulse to pace. He felt nervous, which was ridiculous. He put his hands on the back of Pat Toombs's chair. "I think we ought to leave the rec hall as it is," he said.

There were half a dozen questions all at once, like how do you dance in a wreck like that, rain would come in the broken window, and so on.

Pat Toombs turned around in her chair and said, "Why?"

"Look," said Ed, "I haven't worked out all the details, but I think we ought to keep it as a museum."

They were all looking at him.

"It'll help us remember. Listen, they kept some of the Nazi camps as museums, but they cleaned them up first, which was a mistake. Don't you think they ought to have roped off the grass at Kent State and put four dummies on the grass where the students fell? How else do people remember, unless you leave reminders."

He looked at their faces as his idea sank in.

"I mean," he said, "you can put a plastic sheet outside where the window's broken to keep the rain out, but keep the broken glass as it is inside. Leave the torn posters hanging. Keep 'Kids are shit.' "

"Where'll we dance?" asked Pat Toombs, looking up at him from the chair.

"I don't know. We'll have to fix up another place, I guess."

There was another silence in which people avoided each other's eyes, and then Kevin Mooney, who hadn't spoken before, said, "Wow, a museum."

"My father won't like the idea," said Ed, "but I'll bet anything it'll have an effect on him."

Perhaps that was the conclusive argument because in their entire lexicon of teen-age strategies, the most difficult was to come up with something their parents couldn't argue down.

"I think it's looking for trouble," Lila said.

"We've had the trouble," said Ed. "This may be a way of avoiding trouble like that in the future."

There wasn't much discussion. Lila voted against the proposal. Everyone else voted in favor.

# Chapter 24

ED JAPHET KNEW he could not make the withdrawal without his father, and his father refused to accompany him to the bank. "It's my money," said Ed. "All you do is sign the slip."

Mr. Japhet couldn't disagree about that. All the money Ed had saved from his allowance and later, sums he had made from delivering newspapers, mowing lawns, raking grass, and finally from giving magic performances for children's birthday parties, had gone into the savings account. But the account had prudently been set up as a trust account so that Mr. Japhet would not be taxed on the interest that accrued.

"A hundred and eighty dollars," said Mr. Japhet, "is more than half of what you've saved in four years."

"It's my money."

"You've got to learn to be cautious about money."

"I'm taking it out for a useful purpose."

"I consider karate lessons a dangerous purpose. I'd just as soon let you buy a gun with it."

"You can't go to that school without knowing how to fight back."

"Take boxing lessons, then."

"Oh, Dad, you can't box with kids that carry knives. You're living in a dream world."

"You think everything was invented yesterday. We had hoodlums in school when I was a boy."

"And what did you do?"

"I stayed clear of trouble."

"I mean, when they came after you."

"I stayed out of confrontations."

"You mean you ran away."

Terence Japhet watched Ed leave the first unpleasant conversation they'd had in a long time and go up the stairs to his room. Was his son accusing him of having been a coward? Had he been? Never mind, he was convinced that the karate lessons were not a solution to anything. It was to him like the escalation of an arms race.

At moments like this he wished that they had had a second child, because when one was being impossible, it was probably nice to be able to turn to another, to have an alternative. He had never been able to bear a quarrel that lasted beyond the speaking point.

Mr. Japhet was conscious of each step as he drift-walked up to Ed's room and patted the door with his fingertips. It took Ed a long time to answer. Then he said merely, "Yes?"

"It's me. Please open up."

Terence Japhet would never have opened the door of his son's room unasked, any more than he would have walked into a friend's house if the door were open.

"Come on in," said Ed, sighing.

The walls were covered with a collection of bright posters, some in luminous oranges, yellows, and reds, a few garish and ugly to Mr. Japhet's eye, and some certainly obscene by the standards of an earlier time. Mr. Japhet did not understand the attraction of posters to almost all of the young. Once a middle-class boy's room might have had a triangular banner of the college the boy hoped most to go to, a framed photo of a girl, and that was all. Here it seemed that all visible space had been allotted to—what? Hendrix, dead. Joplin, dead. Zappa sitting on a toilet. The idiot boy from *Mad* magazine, wearing an Uncle Sam uniform and saying, "Who Needs YOU?" And on the facing wall, Dennis Hopper and Peter Fonda on their strangely shaped cycles, smiling easily as they ride toward a gratuitous death. And on the door itself, an election poster which had once said under the candidate's picture, "Make America Great," and now, with the last word obliterated, said "Make America."

The posters had offended at first as they had been intended to. But Mr. Japhet had gotten used to them. Some he had actually liked from the beginning: the one in Miró-like colors that said "To Love Is Enough" and another one, "War is unhealthy for children and other living things." It would be an idea, thought Mr. Japhet, if the delegates at the United Nations made posters instead of speeches.

He was staring at the last one when Ed said, "You like that one, don't you, Dad?"

"Yes," he said.

They sat at opposite ends of the bed, facing the same poster-filled wall and not each other.

"I don't want to be unreasonable," said Mr. Japhet. "I was trying to make my point of view clear."

Ed wondered when his father would capitulate. He usually did.

"Dad, I didn't mean to imply that you were a sissy or anything. I'd just as soon duck trouble as face it myself." He closed his eyes. "The trouble is, you just can't anymore. It's not just our school, it's all over."

"Couldn't you just try a lesson or two and see if you really do find it useful? Maybe a couple of lessons'll give you more physical self-confidence, keep people from picking on you. I mean, why commit a hundred and eighty dollars at once?"

"If you pay in advance, they give you your karate suit, a white gym suit, free. You need the suit anyway, and if you pay piecemeal, it costs you an additional twenty dollars."

"It sounds a little like a racket to use your money before they've provided the services. How long is the course?"

"Four months."

"You see!" Terence leaped at the point. "It's like a bank deducting interest in advance. It actually means you're paying more than a hundred eighty for the course. And suppose you decide to quit—will they refund?"

"I suppose they'd have to give you some back pro rata, I didn't ask. But they'd make you pay for the suit you got free."

"It's not just the money. I don't like the psychology of prepayment."

"It's an advantage to me, Dad. It'll make me go."

"Why should you take on something that requires forcing?"

"Because I know it's something I have to do."

The cash withdrawn from the savings account was deposited by Mr. Japhet, who gave Ed a check for a hundred and eighty dollars so they would have a record of the payment. "I don't trust people who run a school like that," Mr. Japhet said.

The owner, Mr. Fumoko, was also the instructor. The ad for the school had billed him as a black-belt holder and a third-generation instructor in the Japanese arts of self-defense. Mr. Fumoko, a fortyish, soft-spoken nisei, was a very short man with a broad flat face and shiny black hair. He registered Ed in the cramped cubicle that passed as a front office, told him he could pick up his suit after three days, when the check had cleared. A new course started each Monday. In the meantime, would the young man mind filling out this questionnaire?

Ed glanced at the questions. Gently Mr. Fumoko said, "Insurance company wants no trouble. This is educational institution." He smiled, and Ed filled out the form, which included such questions as, "Have you ever been arrested? If yes, please explain." And he had to give three adult references, who, Ed soon learned, actually were called by Mr. Fumoko.

Mr. Fumoko introduced the other new students elaborately, each to the group and then each to each. The Baxe boys were brothers, one Ed's age, one two years younger. One tall, skinny boy of nineteen had kept himself apart. He had a pronounced Adam's apple that went up and down when he mumbled a "how-do-you-do" in response to the other people's "hi" or "hello." One of the boys Ed's own age was Japanese, like Mr. Fumoko. And there was an older man, past forty, with a very white face and white legs. Ed hoped he wouldn't have to pair off with him.

Perhaps because the nineteen-year-old was shy, Mr. Fumoko picked him as the model to point out the vulnerable parts of the body. In a dispassionate voice, Mr. Fumoko explained how a blow to the bridge of the nose would drive the bone back into the brain, stunning, or paralyzing, or killing the victim, depending on the strength of the blow. He showed how to strike the windpipe and explained the consequences. He dealt with the temple, the ear, under the jaw, the side of the neck, the Adam's apple, the hollow of the throat, how to grasp the shoulder muscle to cause great pain, the solar-plexus strike, the vulnerability of the side just below the last rib, how to cause pain in the back of the hand, the wrist, the forearm, how to crack fingers that came within one's grasp, how to kick the upper and lower thigh, the shin, ankle, and instep, and then, turning the nineteen-year-old around, Mr. Fumoko indicated the vulnerable base of the skull, the center of the neck, the seventh vertebra, the back between the shoulderblades, the back of the arm and the back of the elbow, the kidney, the back of the upper leg, the back of the knee, the calf, and the vulnerable tendon called the Achilles' heel.

Mr. Fumoko had them pair off, then point to the vulnerable parts of the partner's body as he called off the places, murmuring, "Very good, very good." Finally, as the hour drew to an end, he warned them of the dangers inherent in the sport of self-defense and devoted himself to the description of five degrees of force. A moderate blow would cause moderate pain. A sharp blow would cause sharp pain. A hard blow would stun or numb in the head or neck area and would interfere with an opponent's ability to strike back for anywhere from several seconds to several hours. A really hard blow in several spots would probably cause a temporary paralysis—very useful in self-defense—and he was quick to point out that temporary meant not a few hours always but perhaps only a few minutes, time to get away, or call the police. Then, watching the faces of his pupils with greater attention than some of them were paying to him, using his hand against himself with pretended ferocity, Mr. Fumoko showed how hard and where a blow would cause a severe and possibly permanent injury, or kill. In a whisper he said, "You think of this only if life is in danger."

Ed was glad the lesson was over. Perhaps his father's advice had been right: he would not want to force himself through the entire course; maybe just a few lessons would suffice. As he changed in the back room with the others, a room that had the pungency of a locker room, though there were no lockers and all their clothes were hung on hooks along the wall, he was aware of all of the parts of his body that might be struck, and also of his hands, which might strike, and a memory crossed his mind of seeing a nuclear physicist on television, a famous one—he couldn't remember who at the moment—explaining the sense of guilt that the developers of the atomic bomb felt, of having tasted the apple in Eden. During the disruptions in school that followed the assassination of Martin Luther King, Ed had taken the position that owning a gun meant having the means to kill. Now, Ed thought, he was developing those means in his own hands, which Mr. Fumoko had urged them all to harden by hitting against hard objects.

Dressed in his street clothes, his gym suit rolled in a bundle, Ed was walking past the door of the cubicle that was the front office when out of it came Urek, angry, carrying the questionnaire. Ed hurried to get out the front door before Urek could see him, but there was a hand on the door as he reached it, and then Urek slid in front of it, his face in front of Ed's face.

"Hello, Japhet," he said.

"What are you doing here?"

"I heard you were taking the course, Japhet."

"So?"

"I thought I'd take it, too."

Urek opened the door to let Ed through. Ed went out, frozen, saw his mother in the car at the curb, tried not to walk too fast to its door, got in beside her.

"Isn't that—?" said his mother, looking over her right shoulder.

"Yes, it is."

"What's he doing here?"

"Don't start the car." Ed turned the rear-view mirror so he could watch Urek go down the street toward the bus stop. Luckily, there was a bus just pulling into the corner, and Urek got on.

"Please wait here for me," said Ed, and he ran from the car back to the judo school and found Mr. Fumoko in the office. "That boy who was just here," he blurted out, then realized he had better calm down, "is he enrolled?"

"He take questionnaire home."

"He can't answer some of those questions truthfully."

"Please sit down."

Ed sat on the edge of the chair, his hands folded in his lap to keep them from trembling.

"The question about whether you've been arrested, et cetera. He's been arrested. He's up for trial."

"For?"

"Assault."

"That boy?"

"Yes."

"Who he assault."

"My father. And me. If he gives Mr. Thomassy as a reference, ask Mr. Thomassy. He's his lawyer. He wouldn't lie to you."

Ed thought Mr. Fumoko was about to touch his hand. "Please, judo-karate is sport, build self-confidence, not for trouble. Only for emergency. Insurance company say no troublemakers. Bad for other students. Bad for school. I wait till questionnaire returned."

Mr. Fumoko seemed satisfied that he had stated his case perfectly. "Okay?" he asked.

"If he gets in," said Ed, "I quit."

When Urek returned his questionnaire by mail, he lied about being arrested, but Thomassy, whose number he listed, confirmed to Mr. Fumoko that the boy was in trouble. Moreover, Mr. Thomassy made it quite clear that enrolling Urek could mean problems for the school. Mr. Fumoko didn't want any trouble. He sent a polite, oriental turn-down letter, so discreet that Urek couldn't figure out that he was being refused until he read it the third time. He took his mother's paring knife and jabbed the letter to the cork bulletin board so hard that the knife went through the cork and embedded its point in the wall behind.

# Chapter · 25

DESPITE THE COLD WIND, the sun shone. Out in the open, one could feel the chill, and then suddenly, in the lee of a building, surprising warmth. Thomassy, his raincoat collar up, hunched down into the coat when a street crossing brought him into the path of the wind, which he knew from the morning news was sweeping in from the northern Middle West, across New York, and out to sea, carrying London-bound planes to Heathrow in less than six hours.

He had been thinking of a quick trip to Europe all morning, no special purpose—why? To drop out for a fortnight?

He opened the door to his office and stooped to pick up the mail that had been put through the slot. The envelope he was waiting for was there, and he slit it open with a quick forefinger. The grand jury had indicted Urek for first-degree assault.

He picked up the phone to let the family know. It rang once, when he decided to hang up. He'd better do this piece of newscasting in person. On went the belted raincoat he had just hung up.

Marvin Cantor, the assistant district attorney assigned to prosecute The People *vs.* Urek, was disappointed in the assignment. Cantor, a gangling six-feet-four, looked a young version of Kenneth Galbraith, not handsome, but certainly not Jewish—a factor Cantor had always thought a big plus for his prospective political career. A lot of Jews would vote for him because of his name, and Gentiles would feel comfortable about him. As they had often let slip at cocktail parties, he looked, well, neutral.

People in groups liked Cantor; at a party, when he talked, it was not only his looming size that gave him a built-in podium, but his gentle voice had a way of carrying its richness to the far corners of a room without amplification. People listened, and paid him the compliment of seeing unintended depths in his comments on public affairs. But Cantor's size, an advantage in crowds, made men avoid him in private. At twenty-nine, he did not have a single close friend. Once, just out of Harvard Law, he and a journalist named Henry Siller had seen a lot of each other, but Siller, then working as a desk man at *The New York Times*, had stopped his vertical ascent into manhood at five-foot-seven, and the two of them together looked ridiculous. It was not only the occasional cliché remarks of rude people; even when they talked alone, Cantor was conscious of looking down at Siller, just as he was certain that Siller was aware of looking up. Despite an easy rapport, the silly difference in height ultimately proved an insuperable obstacle, and they drifted apart.

Having passed his bar exams at twenty-five, Cantor had assiduously pursued his well-placed relatives and managed to become the youngest candidate ever to run for trustee in the Westchester village he'd grown up in. Running as a Republican in a Republican community, he thought, would make his first small step into the political arena a shoo-in, but his opponent kept referring to him as "the tall kid who's running for my seat," which made people chuckle. In a Sunday-night bandstand speech, Cantor had pointed out, he thought cleverly, that another Republican lawyer, Abe Lincoln, had been on the tall side. At the first opportunity, his Democratic opponent had labeled Cantor as "the tall kid who thinks he's Abe Lincoln," and that did it. Cantor went into a week-long depression when he lost.

Cantor gave himself three years to build his political connections, learn how to campaign, and develop a program that would mark him as an up-and-coming liberal Republican. In school he had suspected that he had the gift of wit, but was leary of using it often; being a head taller than your classmates was rough enough, he didn't need the reputation of being a smart aleck. His fiancée, however, laughed at his verbal play, which encouraged him to take her seriously, and now that she was his wife, she encouraged him to develop his verbal agility as a public speaker. She even teased him with the possibility that he might become the kind of senator who didn't need a speech writer. As for Cantor, he found himself thinking that if he ever got elected to Congress and then to the Senate, he might realize his most private goal: to become the first Jewish President of the United States.

During what Cantor thought of as his monkish period, he studied the early law careers of recent lawyer-Presidents and came to the conclusion that what he needed was a famous—or infamous—case to make his name known to the public beyond the courtroom. People *liked* to vote for someone famous. The D.A.'s office was a natural stepping-stone, but so far, the right case hadn't come his way. The publicizable plums were taken by older men. Now, having reached twenty-nine, Cantor felt he was at the great divide. He had to make his second bid for office within a year.

He didn't see the potential in the Urek case, but you never could tell how a trial like that might develop on the witness stand. He spent a weekend digesting the material in the large manila folder, taking notes, jotting down points to follow up, plotting tactics, checking out the judge with his colleagues, and, with a few discreet phone calls, getting a line on Thomassy. Sunday night he joined his wife on the love seat in front of the television set, and during the first commercial break told her he'd get a conviction.

Cantor started to build his case in the process of selecting the jury. He asked each prospective juror in turn, "If justified by the evidence, would you be unwilling to bring in a verdict of guilty just because the man on trial is sixteen years of age?" Only two or three hesitated. In the end they all agreed they would not take the defendant's age into consideration. Cantor knew some of them were lying. They were bored hanging around the jury room and just wanted to get on a case and get it over with.

In Thomassy's questions to potential jurors he got in quite a few references to "this boy on trial" and once, even, "this schoolboy."

The jury was picked in much less time than usual. Thomassy and Cantor went by the same unspoken rules: no professional men, no intellectuals, no one with a graduate degree except in acounting or engineering, no one accustomed to abstract thought or moral subtleties. They each wanted the same thing, a human orchestra to play.

Thomassy tried for a black with an Afro haircut, assuming him to be militant and hopefully someone who might hang the jury, but Cantor allowed color on the jury only in one sixtyish, retired Uncle Tom and one black woman who smiled her agreement even before questions were put. In addition they got a Finast manager, an unemployed steel worker, a building janitor, an insurance salesman, a childless housewife, a cemetery groundskeeper, the owner of a fruit and vegetable store, an oldish man who had been a bank teller and cashier in his working days, a crane operator, and a Sears, Roebuck stock clerk.

Thomassy took a liking to Cantor, even during the boring

process of picking a jury. He enjoyed the young man's style, and thought his height useful: in confrontations, though Thomassy was tall, the other man was so much taller, that the jury might like to see them toe to toe. He would cream Cantor when the time came. In the meantime, it might be a good idea to put him on edge a bit.

"You're doing fine," he told Cantor in a break.

"Thanks," said Cantor. "They tell me you've got a lot of experience."

"Just in winning," said Thomassy, ready to move off.

"Winning what?" said Cantor.

Thomassy was going to answer him, then thought the better of it. He winked at Cantor.

Cantor knew the wink was meant to be condescending. And so, in return, he winked both eyes together.

*Son of a bitch*, thought Thomassy, *this is going to be fun.*

As a young lawyer Judge Brumbacher had quickly learned to have all of the boring research done by a subordinate, concentrating his own efforts on preparation, the strategy of a trial and the tactics of each day. He liked the actual courtroom work and was constantly surprised at how quickly a recess or adjournment came, and getting back to the courtroom was for him a welcome anticipation. He liked his work, and thought that only the justice on the bench, the referee and judge of all that went on before him, had a richer experience of the law at work. And so when he got his deserved judgeship, he was stunned to find at the end of the first week that he had committed himself for many long years to the most boring job of all.

Much that he did in the courtroom, his "style," as lawyers would refer to it, grew out of his own desperate need to make the day pass with as much liveliness as he could summon. He kept adversaries on their toes by taking over the questioning from time to time. He made the sheriff's deputies sit or stand at the back of the court, out of sight, so that spectators would feel that the defendant was not yet a prisoner.

Mainly Judge Brumbacher tried to enliven his life by being very tough and very fair, which helped to shape his calendar. Neither Thomassy nor Cantor had tried to get before another judge. They obviously had guts. *This might be an interesting case*, he thought hopefully, knowing that if it didn't turn out that way, he'd wind up the trial fast, and as he sometimes said to his colleagues, go to review another play.

He struck his gavel to command attention and instructed Assistant District Attorney Marvin Cantor to begin his opening statement.

"Your Honor, members of the jury, I've been assigned to this prosecution by the Honorable Charles C. Lane, district attorney of Westchester County, to represent the People of the State of New York."

Now that he had their attention, Cantor took advantage of his six-foot-four frame to tower over the seated jurors from as close to the box as he could get. "I have sworn," he said, "to do my duty to society, as you have."

That, thought Cantor, puts me and them on the same side.

"My first duty," he continued, moving along the jury box, "is to tell you that the indictment charges Stanislaus Urek with four separate and distinct counts of assault in the first degree. That's a felony. A felony means a major crime."

Cantor paused just long enough to see if the judge would stop him.

"The people propose to show by clear-cut evidence that on January twenty-first of this year, at Ossining High School, the defendant Stanislaus Urek, without any justification or provocation whatsoever, did assault Edward Japhet, a high-school student, with intent to cause serious physical injury with depraved indifference to human life. He committed the assault with his fists and with a chain, a dangerous instrument, striking Edward Japhet about the head and body and choking him, injuring Edward Japhet so seriously that he required confinement in the intensive-care unit of Phelps Memorial Hospital, with a severely injured throat."

He let that sink in. "Moreover, the People will show by evidence that at the same time and place, the defendant, Stanislaus Urek, did willfully and intentionally without provocation assault Lila Hurst, also a high-school student, and at the same time and place, the defendant, Stanislaus Urek, did commit assault against Mr. Terence Japhet, a schoolteacher.

"And that is not all. We will show you, as the fourth count of assault, that when this grievously injured boy, Edward Japhet, was a patient in Phelps Memorial Hospital in North Tarrytown in this county, he was once again willfully assaulted by Stanislaus Urek, with intent to cause serious physical injury with a dangerous weapon, a knife, with depraved indifference to human life.

"Perhaps you will be able to determine a motive for these criminal assaults. I have been unable to.

"I expect to call as witnesses the injured boy and his father and Miss Hurst, all of them eyewitnesses. Also, as an eyewitness, the school custodian, Felix Gómez. Dr. Morton Karp of the staff of the hospital will testify as to the injuries inflicted. As to the fourth count in the indictment, the People will call nurses Murphy and Ginsler of the Phelps staff, eyewitnesses to the assault inside the hospital itself.

"The People seek justice. If, after listening to the evidence, you do not find that we have proved the defendant's guilt beyond a reasonable doubt, I ask you to acquit him, but if we do so prove"—he took in every juror's face, one at a time—"the People ask for a verdict of guilty."

Cantor took a deep breath. "We live in a period not only

of mounting crime rates and escalating violence, but one in which the laws that protect us from each other are derided and vilified and held in contempt. There are some who would say that the whole country is sinking into anarchy. This may be your concern as citizens, but, ladies and gentlemen, it is not your concern as jurors. You must keep from your mind everything but the facts relating to *this* defendant and the crimes of which he is guilty."

Cantor sat down, pleased with his delivery and how he had managed to end with the word "guilty." The jury seemed excited by the prospect of the trial, and that was what he wanted.

Thomassy got to his feet slowly. "Your Honor," he said, "I would normally waive my opening statement in a case as ordinary as this, but in view of Mr. Cantor's remarks, I have no alternative but to address the jury."

"Please proceed," said the judge.

"Ladies and gentlemen," said Thomassy as he walked toward them, stopped in front of the jury box, and leaned both of his hands on the railing. His voice, in contrast to the assistant district attorney's, was relaxed and casual.

"Please understand that Mr. Cantor is one of thirty-five assistants we've got in the district attorney's office assigned to try to get convictions, and he's just trying to do his job.

"You know," he said with a light shrug, "they sometimes accuse the defense attorney of trying to win sympathy for the accused. Well, that's wrong, of course. You're here to find out if the facts stack up, to decide whether the accused is guilty or innocent. But I wonder if it isn't also wrong to try to win sympathy for these young fellows in the district attorney's office. Here's this nice young lawyer attempting to make a track record, to please his boss, to work his way up. He talks fine, he tells you the country is falling into anarchy or whatever, and these fine fellows in the district attorney's office are trying to keep that from happening by filling up the jails."

Thomassy scratched his ear. "I've been around the people of this county long enough to know that all of us are guilty of one thing or another, and if all nine hundred thousand of us got put away in jail, the district attorney's office would have a perfect record"—one of the jurors had trouble stifling his laugh, and Thomassy winked at him to tell him it was okay—"but we'd have to get our jailers from outside the county, and if any of the jailers did something wrong, like all of us do from time to time, why, we couldn't get up twelve innocent people in this county to try him.

"We're not here to fill the jails—I read in the papers that they're pretty full up anyway—nor to give these nice men from the district attorney's office a track record. We're here to listen to some people tell us what happened and to see if the accusations against the accused can stand up under the tough test of your judgment.

"As far as you are concerned—the judge will support me in this—none of the facts are in. That's why we're here. To listen to the facts and come to the kind of fair conclusion you'd want if your sixteen-year-old was in trouble over something he did or didn't do."

Thomassy, hands in pockets, walked thoughtfully over to Mr. Cantor's table, then turned to the jury: "Ladies and gentlemen, you are here to promote justice. Your sworn duty is to remember only one thing—before and during and after a trial—that a man, or boy, is innocent until he's proven guilty beyond a reasonable doubt."

Cantor kept his face rigidly expressionless. He wished Thomassy would move farther away from him.

"At the close of this trial," continued Thomassy, "I'm going to ask his Honor—I'm not going to have to ask him, I'm sure he'll do it anyway. In his charge, his Honor is going to remind you that this boy on trial here stands clothed in the presumption of innocence. It is his constitutional right to be considered innocent throughout this trial. But it's not just his right. It's your right." Thomassy made sure his gaze took in everyone. "The presumption of innocence protects every single person in this courtroom."

Some spectator started to applaud, then remembered where he was, even before the judge's gavel came down.

The first witness called by the prosecution was the young intern, Dr. Karp. Thomassy quickly checked the haircuts of the male jury members. Karp's longish hair was a minus for him. His M.D. was a plus. The two probably canceled each other out in the jury's eyes. Their reaction would depend on how the testimony went.

Cantor had the record show that Dr. Karp had attended the patient, Edward Japhet, had examined him frequently in the hospital, had studied the tests performed in the hospital, and could testify as to the nature, degree, and medical consequences of the injury. Dr. Karp seemed restless with the routine questions.

Cantor then asked, "Would you describe the patient's injuries as serious?" and Karp looked interested at the first question that couldn't be answered yes or no.

"Well," he said, "any injury can be potentially serious."

Cantor anticipated a possible objection by the judge or Thomassy by quickly asking, "We are here not to speculate about generalities but to hear facts relevant to this set of injuries and no other."

*Good boy,* thought the judge.

Karp thought a minute. "Yes, the injuries were serious."

"Would you describe them for us to the best of your recollection?"

"Can I refer to the medical records?"

"Your Honor, Dr. Karp has the patient's records from Phelps Memorial. Can they be marked as the People's Exhibit A?"

After the formalities, Karp gave a precise medical description of the injuries to Ed Japhet's throat. When he had finished, Cantor said, "Doctor, People's Exhibit A refers to a facial injury inflicted by a chain. Would you describe that injury as more serious or less serious than the throat injuries?"

"From a medical point of view," said Karp, "the wound on the face is healing well, scabbing over well. Of course, if it had been an inch higher, the eye would probably have suffered irreversible—"

"Objection!"

"Sustained, Mr. Thomassy. Dr. Karp, the jury concerns itself only with what happened, not with what might have happened."

"I understand," said Dr. Karp.

Cantor continued. "From your experience, doctor, can you at this stage tell whether the facial injury will result in permanent disfigurement, and if so, to what extent?"

"It's awfully hard to say. The scars on his psyche are likely to have more effect than any scar on his face."

Judge Brumbacher saw Thomassy getting to his feet and thought he'd intervene before the objection. "Dr. Karp," he asked, "you are not a psychiatrist, are you?"

"No, your Honor."

"If psychic injuries are not your specialty, would you please confine yourself to physical aspects of the injury. Mr. Cantor, will you rephrase your question?"

"Dr. Karp, from your experience, can you tell whether the facial injury will result in permanent disfigurement?"

"Nobody can." Karp sensed the Judge's displeasure. "I mean, I can't. Okay?" he asked Cantor.

Cantor was satisfied. He had gotten the facial injury on the record, and the jury would remember Dr. Karp's remarks, whatever the objections.

"The prosecution has finished its examination of this witness, your Honor."

Judge Brumbacher asked, "Would counsel for the defendant like to cross-examine?"

Thomassy nodded and approached the stand, glad he had done his homework.

"Dr. Karp, would you say that the patient might have died from his injuries?"

"You mean the throat injuries?"

"Could he have died from the contusions, abrasions, and other injuries upon his body exclusive of the internal injuries to the throat?"

"No," said Karp.

"Then please answer about the throat injuries. From your examination of the patient, from your examination of his X-rays and the results of other medical tests administered at the hospital, are you able to say, with reasonable medical certainty, that the throat injuries might have been fatal?"

Karp thought a long time. Finally he said, "No, sir."

"Thank you," said Thomassy, turning away.

As Karp got up to leave, Cantor was up on his feet asking for redirect.

The judge asked Karp to sit again, and reminded him that he was still under oath.

Cantor paused only long enough to make sure his voice would be controlled. "Doctor, was the patient admitted to the intensive-care unit of the hospital?"

"Yes, he was."

"Was he in the intensive-care unit for three full days?"

"Something like that."

"What is the function of the intensive-care unit?"

"Well, it's a small unit for receiving accident and other emergency cases requiring constant vigilance, nurses always in attendance, frequent checks of the patients' pulse, breathing, the blood situation. Also, there's the equipment at hand for resuscitation in case of heart failure, transfusions. The nurses are experienced in closed chest massage and in assisting the resident if the patient has to be opened fast, things like that."

"Do more patients who enter the intensive-care unit die than the hospital population as a whole?"

"I suppose so. A lot of bad auto wrecks end up there, heart attacks, et cetera. I don't have the figures."

"Would you say that people are put into the intensive-care unit instead of some other section of the hospital because they are in danger of their life?"

Dr. Karp fidgeted. "I guess so, but—"

"Would you say that Edward Japhet was put in the—"

Thomassy was on his feet. "Your Honor," he said, "I think the district attorney might let the witness answer the question before asking another."

The judge asked the court stenographer to read back the earlier question and answer. She had gotten the "but."

"But what?" asked the judge of the witness.

"I was going to say that someone with throat injuries of unknown extent or origin might be put into the intensive-care unit until we found out what was wrong with him."

Cantor released his witness to Thomassy, who had only one question.

"Would you say that in your judgment, Edward Japhet, who had a serious but not prospectively fatal injury, was admitted to the intensive-care unit for further diagnostic purposes?"

"I didn't admit him."

"But you examined him afterward?"

"Yes."

"Then answer the question. Was Edward Japhet admitted to intensive care mainly for precautionary diagnostic purposes?"

"Yes."

"Thank you."

Thomassy was relieved. He was sure most of the members of the jury didn't get the import of the exchange, but he felt confident that they were left with the impression that Ed Japhet hadn't been all that badly hurt after all.

The next witness sworn was Miss Murphy, who had come straight from the hospital and looked tough and regal in her starched uniform.

Cantor was about to put his first question to her when he noticed his assistant, Bob Ferlinger, trying to catch his attention. Cantor thought it would be bad to take the jury's attention away from Miss Murphy. Ferlinger hastily scrawled a message.

"Miss Murphy," said Cantor, "I know you've just come off duty and must rush back, and so I'll dispense with the usual form, if his Honor is willing, and ask you: Are you employed at Phelps Memorial Hospital as a senior nurse, and were you in fact in charge of the desk on the floor where Edward Japhet was a patient after he was released from the intensive-care unit? If the answer to all of that can be answered yes or no, please say so."

"Yes. That's all true."

"And were you on duty at the desk at the time that the second assault was committed against Edward Japhet?"

Thomassy stood but said nothing.

Judge Brumbacher took it upon himself to say, "I have a feeling Mr. Thomassy is about to object. I'm not a mind reader, but it seems to me, Mr. Cantor, that your question had an extraordinary number of objectionable features crammed into its few words."

"I'm sorry, your Honor. I was just trying to condense things so that this witness could return to her post."

"We're engaged in a matter of some consequence. An individual's freedom is at stake. I think you'd better take your time."

"Yes, your Honor."

"Proceed."

Cantor's question was formulated in slow motion. "I ask you," he said, realizing he had said nothing, "on the night of Monday, January twenty-fourth, were you on duty?"

The witness referred to her notes with the judge's consent.

"Yes," she said.

"Was that the night an unauthorized person entered the area in your charge and entered the patient's room?"

"Japhet?"

"Yes, Japhet's room."

"I didn't see the person."

Cantor could see that his assistant was extremely anxious to communicate with him. He made his way halfway to the table where Bob Ferlinger sat restlessly.

"How did you learn of the disturbance?"

Bob Ferlinger held his head in his hands.

"Miss Ginsler was carrying a tray of instruments—I saw that," she said, as if realizing the importance of having to testify that she saw something, "and someone came out of the Japhet room and crashed directly into her, upsetting the tray."

"Objection!" said Thomassy.

When he was recognized, Thomassy said, "Your Honor, I suspect the witness meant to report that the *sound* of the tray crashing caught her attention and that she then saw Miss Ginsler—"

"Mr. Thomassy," said the judge sharply. "That's the kind of thing you can develop on cross but not now. I think Mr. Cantor ought to ask the question again, and the witness should confine herself to what she actually saw and heard herself."

Cantor had used the distraction to get close enough to the table to pick up the message from Ferlinger. The paper said, "Ginsler won't testify."

"Please continue," said the judge.

"How did you learn of the disturbance in the patient's room?"

Miss Murphy felt that her professional reputation was suddenly at stake. "I . . ." she said carefully, "heard this crash. I looked up in time to see the instrument tray falling from Miss Ginsler's hands, spilling all over the floor, and this short man who had . . . who presumably had bumped into her rushing into the stairwell door."

Cantor felt desperate. "Would you . . ." He was going to say, "Would you assume that anyone rushing out of a patient's room in that kind of hurry was up to no good," and realized it would never pass.

"What did you actually see?" Cantor asked.

"Where?"

"Anywhere."

Thomassy had to keep himself from laughing out loud.

"Well," said the nurse, "I saw the scattered instruments and Miss Ginsler in a state of bewilderment, and I accompanied another nurse into the Japhet room and saw the cut tube."

Cantor felt a great relief when Thomassy didn't object. "Can you describe the function of the tube?"

"Well, it goes into the patient's nostril, it's taped, actually, to the face above the lip, and the tube goes down the gullet into the stomach, and serves to drain the digestive fluids that accumulate in the patient's stomach while he is being fed intravenously."

"He was that sick?"

Thomassy started to get up.

"Let me rephrase that. Why was the patient being fed intravenously?"

Thomassy was standing. "Your Honor, shouldn't that question have been asked of a doctor?"

Brumbacher said, "The witness may be able to provide us with a competent answer. The jury can judge. Would you answer the question, please?"

"About why he was being fed that way?"

"Yes."

"Because of the throat injury. It was hard for him to swallow food."

Cantor, greatly relieved, said, "Your witness."

Thomassy took his time getting over to Miss Murphy, collecting the attention of each member of the jury.

"Miss Murphy, did you see the tube being cut?"

"Well, I . . ."

"Please answer yes or no."

"No."

"Miss Murphy, to your knowledge, did anyone see the tube being cut? That is, did anyone report to you they saw the tube cut?"

"No. Just that it had been cut."

"So that neither you nor any member of your staff, and to the best of your knowledge, no other person actually saw who cut the tube drain in Mr. Japhet?"

"That's right."

"Did you see the short man well enough to be able to identify him without any doubt whatsoever?"

"No."

"Is there anything, anything at all, that you personally saw or heard that night in the hospital that has any bearing on whether or not the defendant was present in the hospital or attempted to harm Edward Japhet in any way whatsoever or not? Never mind, strike that, no more questions for this witness."

Without so much as a glance at Miss Murphy, Thomassy stalked to his seat, leaving the nurse, mouth ajar, suspended in astonishment.

Cantor pitched his voice so that it would be heard by the judge and Thomassy. If the jury or the spectators heard, he thought, that couldn't be helped. "Your Honor," he said quietly, "I'm sure Mr. Thomassy forgot himself, and that last question was unintentional. . . ." He glanced at Thomassy as if to say it was damn well intentional. "Nevertheless, would it be appropriate for the court to consider instructing the jury on comments stricken from the record?"

Judge Brumbacher beckoned for Thomassy and Cantor to approach the bench.

"Gentlemen," he said, "I am not about to be sucked into delivering a sermon, because what I would say about the conduct of adversary proceedings just might be overheard and misinterpreted as a libel of the legal profession. I am going to instruct the jury."

Judge Brumbacher turned to the ten men and two women in the jury box. "Ladies and gentlemen," he said in a quiet voice, and they all immediately inched forward in their seats and cupped their attention to catch his soft-spoken words. "When a question or an answer is stricken from the record, either by the person speaking, as just happened, or by me, it is as if the question were never asked. Yet you heard it. Therefore, the last question asked by counsel for the defendant should be erased from your minds as well, and not taken into consideration. Thus the record of the last witness, Miss Murphy, will end with the penultimate question, the next-to-last question, and her answer, and that is all. Would the court reporter please read that question and answer?"

The court reporter held up the punched tape coming out of her machine and in a flat voice read, "Question: Did you see the short man well enough to be able to identify him without any doubt whatsoever? Answer: No."

As the judge recessed the trial until the following morning and instructed the jury in the ground rules for their overnight behavior, Thomassy had to forcibly restrain himself from chuckling at how effective that second reading of the crucial question and answer turned out, just as he had planned.

# Chapter 26

THAT EVENING, before dinner in the Japhet home, Mr. Japhet mixed vodka martinis in a pitcher, poured some over ice for himself, and a smaller quantity for his wife, then asked Ed if he would like to sample some.

"I probably won't like the taste," Ed said.

"How will you know until you try?"

"Never mind, Dad. Some other time."

The three of them sat quite far apart from each other, points of a triangle.

"I wish we knew what went on in court today," said Mr. Japhet. "Ed, you do know why we can't be there?"

"No," said Ed.

"I guess the assumption is that we'll both be witnesses further along, and a witness isn't supposed to hear what the other witnesses say."

"Oh?" said Ed.

"According to Mr. Cantor, I'm on call tomorrow. You will come, won't you, Josephine? And, Ed, why don't you drive there with us? I'm sure they've got some place you can stay until you're called."

"I'd just as soon stay here. I've got all that catch-up reading to do for school."

"I'm sure your teachers will make allowances for what happened."

"They'll make allowances because you're my father."

Mr. Japhet recognized the source of the hostility, but that didn't ease the sting.

"How will you get to White Plains if they call? There might not be time enough for me to come and get you."

"I'll think of something. I can always call a cab."

"What's the matter, Ed. You seem depressed."

Ed looked at his father unblinkingly.

"I mean, this isn't a pleasant matter, but I've seldom seen you quite so down."

Mr. Japhet put his martini on the coaster.

"Is there something special?"

"Not really."

Mrs. Japhet put her drink down also and came over to her son's chair. "Ed," she said, touching his cheek, "you seem so far away."

"I'm right here, Mom."

She retreated to her chair, brushed away.

After a silence Mr. Japhet said, "We are due to eat soon, aren't we, Josephine?"

"No rush, Dad."

"I was thinking," said Mr. Japhet, "that Ed and I might go to Vermont for a few days when this is over. Skiing is what I had in mind."

"Neither of us has ever skied, Dad."

"It's time we learned," Mr. Japhet said, forcing enthusiasm into his voice. "We could go on a Friday and come back Sunday night so we wouldn't have to miss any more school, right?"

"Let it alone, Dad."

*Let what alone?* Mr. Japhet had a sudden vision of Ed in his chair moving back rapidly as if seen through the wrong end of a telescope, becoming smaller and smaller in the distance, until he was only a colored dot, and then vanishing completely over the horizon, leaving Josephine and himself in this living room alone, without the one child they had managed to produce, who didn't need them anymore.

"Dad?"

"Yes, Ed?"

"Do I have to be a witness?"

"What do you mean?"

"Do I have to testify?"

"They can subpoena you."

"They can't force me to say anything."

"That would be contempt of court."

"I guess."

"Contempt is a fairly serious offense."

"I thought that other bit in court was pretty offensive, the whole thing."

"This is nothing to joke about."

"I'm not joking."

"All you've got to do is answer the questions you're asked truthfully."

"I don't *have* to do anything."

"I know you wish all this hadn't happened. So do I. But, Ed, now that the processes of justice are in train ..."

Ed laughed. "I'm sorry, Dad, I didn't mean to laugh, but remember when that police car made an illegal turn in front of us on North Highland, and if I hadn't had my seat belt on I would have gone into the windshield, and you reported it to the chief—we found out about the processes of justice, didn't we?"

"Well, if I had been willing to pursue it to the end ..."

"You were willing. They just made it so goddamn difficult it became too much trouble to do anything, right?"

Mr. Japhet said nothing.

"Remember the kid with the knife you chased, and they

told you even if he tried to mug you, if he fell on his knife while you were chasing him, it would have been your fault?"

"What are you getting at?"

"You were quoting the processes of justice at me."

"Ed, all I hope is that somewhere along the line I have taught you how to make the most of your life, that's all."

"That's a joke."

*That's not a joke.* "In what way have I embittered you, Ed?"

"Nothing."

"What do you mean, 'nothing'?"

"Let's drop it."

It was Mrs. Japhet leaning forward in her chair now, afraid to go over to Ed, in dread of being rebuffed again. "Dinner should be ready now."

"Ed, I don't care if you testify or not. It's your decision."

"You are testifying, aren't you?"

"Of course."

"On your hind legs?"

Slapping his face would accomplish nothing. Mr. Japhet, stung, went to wash his hands. He looked at himself in the bathroom mirror, especially at the gray of death in his hair.

During the silence of dinner, with only the clink of silver on dishes and "Please pass . . ." and "Thank you," Ed thought about the nightmare last night in which he and Urek were the only living persons left in the world.

Thomassy looked up Joe Cargill's number and dialed. He tried to remember what Cargill looked like. They had met six or seven years ago in Washington. Cargill called himself an investigator, but he talked like a lawyer. Thomassy suspected he had been one once. Disbarred? A secretary answered.

"This is George Thomassy calling from New York."

"One moment, please."

When the gravelly voice got on, the image of the man came with it, short, plump, watch chain across the vest.

"Thomassy, how're you doing?"

"You remember me?"

"Sure do."

"There's a schoolteacher up here by the name of Terence Japhet, J-A-P-H-E-T, age forty-seven, teaches biology. I'm calling on the off chance he might have applied for a government job or a grant somewhere along the line."

"Xerox is all I can get."

"Xerox is fine. What would it cost?"

"Nothing classified here, say, one-twenty-five."

Thomassy whistled. He was prepared to whistle, whatever the figure.

"Well," said Cargill, "we can round it off at a hundred. How soon?"

"Soonest. Need anything more?"

"Not with an oddball name like Terence Japhet. I'll call collect to say yes or no. It'll come first-class special delivery, plain envelope. No attribution."

"No attribution. What's the charge if we draw a blank?"

"No charge." He asked for Thomassy's phone and address.

Thomassy was startled to get the collect call in less than an hour. "You're on," said Cargill. "It'll mail tomorrow if we get your check by then."

Thomassy laughed. "No credit?"

"Cash and carry. Make the check out to B and G Delicatessen, if you don't mind."

"Wonder what Internal Revenue will think I did in court with a hundred dollars worth of ham."

"It's a Jewish delicatessen. No ham. Just don't get audited."

"Thanks."

"Anytime. I really should have stuck to one-twenty-five."

"What agency?"

"State Department. Turned down, too."

"Beautiful."

"Any time."

Bob Ferlinger said to Cantor, "If we could prove Thomassy got to Ginsler . . ."

Cantor tried to be patient with Ferlinger, who was three years younger. "Look, suppose you're a doctor and a patient comes to you because he's got a cough and his chest hurts and he's running a fever and he's been to his regular doctor who's told him to take aspirin and nothing's happened so he comes to you and you say, 'Did you have an X-ray?' and he says, 'No,' and you get him X-rayed and it turns out he has pneumonia, you don't go urging him to file a malpractice suit against the first doctor. Cranks do that. If Thomassy got to Ginsler, he got to Ginsler. We just work around that. How the hell would you prove it?"

"We subpoena her, we get her on the stand and ask her if Thomassy offered her anything or put the squeeze on her not to testify."

"She'd lie."

"Under oath?"

"If Thomassy got to her, he didn't pay her, he's got something on her. She wouldn't even have to lie. She could plead the fifth."

"I don't like it."

"Bob, Thomassy isn't on trial. Let's get a conviction on the Urek kid. You understand, don't you?"

Ferlinger didn't, but said he did.

"Good," said Cantor. "Now, let's bring Japhet's father in and go over the ground. He's the key. The jury'll identify with him."

"You think so?"

"It's the preparation that counts. I hope he's a quick study. Let's go."

Mr. Japhet was appalled at the idea of rehearsing for his

testimony. Cantor explained how usual it was. Mr. Japhet was surprised at his own naïveté. He had supposed that witnesses testify cold.

"How come you didn't plead that kid guilty to a misdemeanor?" said Cantor to Thomassy when they were arranging their paper on the adjoining counsel tables before the next day's session.

"You heard of Percy Foreman?"

"Sure."

"He's defended more than a thousand murder cases."

"And?"

"Fewer than six percent ever spent a day in jail. Only one got executed."

"I still think you should have had the Urek kid cop a plea."

"They didn't need me for that. They could have hired anybody."

Cantor was nervous about Mr. Japhet's appearance on the stand. During their earlier meeting, intended to prepare him, Cantor had tried to make it clear that as a prosecution witness, Mr. Japhet was on his side, the side of the law, et cetera, but the man seemed to have his mind elsewhere. When Cantor heard that Ed might refuse to testify, he decided not to press the father more and to proceed to trial without the benefit of a proper rehearsal. It might work to his advantage. An extemporaneous recital of the crime might be more effective. In any event, he would begin by putting Mr. Japhet's testimony at the arraignment into the record of the trial.

Cantor was surprised when Judge Brumbacher refused. "Counselor," he said, using the term at Cantor for the first time, "the point of having a witness is for the jury not only to hear the words but to judge, from the witness's manner, the truth of what he is reporting. Previous testimony else-where can be referred to if inconsistencies show up. Do your work, please, for the benefit of the jury."

Cantor, humiliated, turned to the witness.

"Mr. Japhet, will you tell us in your own words what happened on the evening of January twenty-first."

Terence Japhet looked at his wife, sitting among the spectators. He wondered if he could buy a copy of the transcript so that Ed would have a permanent record of what transpired. Probably not.

"Yes," he said. "I drove my son and his friend Lila Hurst to the dance. He refused to let me help him with the suitcases in which he carried his magic equipment." He saw the impatience in Cantor's face. "Yes, yes, I'm coming to that. He was giving a performance for the students. I picked him up afterward. He and I and Miss Hurst were on our way out of the building—I believe it was empty except for the janitor—it was snowing, and we saw four boys sitting in my car. The Urek boy attacked first Miss Hurst and then my son, knocking him to the ground, then falling on him, and choking him. I beat the attacker on his back, trying to get him to let go, and when I pulled his hair hard, he did. He smashed the two suitcases of equipment and then broke the windshield of my car with the tire chain."

"And then what happened?"

"My son seemed to have great difficulty in breathing. I learned once that if there is difficulty in breathing, or bleeding that you can't stop, you have to get to a hospital right away, so I drove as fast as I could, given the snowstorm and the broken windshield."

"Did the defendant attack your son with his bare hands?"

"He had a chain."

"Is that the same chain with which he later smashed the windshield of the car?"

"Yes."

"Did he use that chain against your son?"

"Yes."

"Was Miss Hurst hurt badly?"

"No. Just my son."

"How do you explain this attack against your son?"

Mr. Japhet clenched his hands on the arms of the witness chair. "The United States is now in a state of war."

Judge Brumbacher leaned forward.

"What I mean," said Mr. Japhet, "is that there is open armed conflict between factions in this country, several kinds in many locations, blacks in open and armed revolt, police counter-attacking and even initiating battle, Weathermen, militant students dynamiting and destroying, National Guardsmen and police killing students black and white, and much less publicized, violence in the secondary schools, serious incidents in every part of the country requiring the occasional closing of schools, armed guards in the schools, the centers of cities a no-man's-land—if this is not civil war, we had better change the definition in dictionaries."

Josephine Japhet had never heard her husband talk this way.

The rumbling among the spectators was overwhelmed by Thomassy's standing shout, "Objection! Objection!" and then when the judge turned to him, he said, "Your Honor, we are trying one sixteen-year-old individual, not a nation."

"Mr. Cantor?" asked the judge.

Cantor couldn't think of anything he might say which wouldn't endanger his career. He shook his head.

"Well, now," said Judge Brumbacher, "I'm not so sure that's all irrelevant, though it is out of the ordinary."

"Your Honor," said Mr. Japhet.

"Yes?"

"May I clarify? I don't want my remarks misunderstood."

"Your Honor, I object!" said Thomassy.

"I've noted your objection and will consider it after the clarification. Proceed, Mr. Japhet."

"I'm sorry. I didn't mean to be so emotional. This whole affair has been terribly upsetting. It has a background. The Urek boy has been involved in an extortion racket in the school—"

"Objection!" said Thomassy, striding toward the bench.

"Please take your seat, Mr. Thomassy."

"The defendant is not charged with extortion."

"It can all be stricken, once we've heard it out."

"But the jury—"

"I will instruct the jury, Mr. Thomassy. Continue, Mr. Japhet."

"This country has been saddled with organized extortion for at least four decades, since Prohibition, and during this entire long period, nearly half a century, law enforcement has not been able to deal effectively with this organized extortion, and as a consequence, youngsters in school emulate the condoned rackets of their elders. My son, the worse for him, resisted this extortion by refusing to pay the monthly charge for leaving his locker alone. If he were an adult in business and did the same thing, he would have been attacked, as he was attacked in the school, and that is my explanation, my answer to the question that was asked of me."

"Are you finished?"

"Yes."

Thomassy was standing.

"Mr. Thomassy," said the judge, "if this case is ever appealed to a higher court, it is possible that my ruling will jeopardize the results of this trial, but I consider the question relevant and material. I think the jury can consider the pertinence of the reply, which I am letting stand. Please continue, Mr. Cantor."

"I have no more questions."

As he approached the witness stand, Thomassy was damn glad he had done his homework.

"Mr. Japhet, you took an oath to tell the truth, the whole

truth, and nothing but the truth in this courtroom. Is it your habit to tell the truth under oath?"

"I've never had to be a witness before."

"Please answer the question. Is it your habit to tell the truth if you take an oath?"

"I tell the truth whether or not I am under oath."

"Will you please tell the court the names of the foreign countries you have visited?"

Cantor was quick to object. "Your Honor, this line of questioning is irrelevant."

"Overruled."

"But your Honor—"

"Let us see where it leads. You may proceed, Mr. Thomassy."

"The question was, please name the foreign countries you have visited."

"I've visited England and France several times, Germany once, Italy briefly."

"Is that all?"

"Yes."

"Have you ever visited any other foreign nation at any time?"

"No."

"Now, Mr. Japhet, have you ever at any time visited the Soviet Union?"

"I have not visited the Soviet Union."

"Have you ever visited any part of China?"

Cantor couldn't take it. "Your Honor, is defense counsel trying to imply that the witness is a Red spy or something?"

"Your Honor, will you please instruct the district attorney to sit down?"

Judge Brumbacher nodded for Mr. Cantor to do just that.

"Have you ever visited any part of China?"

"No."

"Have you ever visited Ireland?"

Mr. Japhet moistened his lips.

"Please remember that you are under oath."

"I have never visited Ireland."

Thomassy removed Cargill's Xerox from his briefcase on the counsel table.

"Mr. Japhet, did you ever seek employment with any branch of the federal government?"

"I may have."

"As a matter of fact, you once applied to the Department of State in Washington for employment, did you not?"

"Yes."

"In order to apply for that position, you had to make a written application under oath, sworn to before a notary public, isn't that correct?"

"I don't know."

Thomassy slowly unfolded Cargill's Xerox and put it before Mr. Japhet.

"Would you please tell the court what this document is?"

"It's an application for employment in the Department of State."

"An application, or your application?"

"It's a facsimile copy of an application I made some years ago."

"Would you please read question number twenty-three aloud?"

Thomassy was wondering when Cantor would object, just as Cantor got to his feet. "Your Honor, is defense counsel going to put that paper into evidence?"

"Certainly."

"Have it marked," said the judge.

"I want to question the propriety of the evidence, your Honor. If it's a confidential application for employment in a government agency—"

"May I see that?" said the judge, taking the document from the court reporter.

"I believe," said Thomassy, "your Honor will find no classified markings on the application. Since the witness has already acknowledged the application to be his, may we continue?"

Judge Brumbacher nodded. "I don't want to hold things up. Let's proceed."

Cantor went back to his seat, angry. Thomassy turned his attention to Mr. Japhet again. "I said, would you read question number twenty-three on the facsimile."

"What foreign countries have you visited?"

"And the answer?"

"England, France, Germany, Italy, Ireland."

"Is that your signature at the bottom of the page?"

"Yes."

"And was it sworn to before a notary public under oath?"

"Yes."

"And were you in fact granted employment in the Department of State?"

"It was to be a special assignment during my sabbatical year, not permanent employment."

"Please answer the question, Mr. Japhet. Were you denied employment in the Department of State, temporary or not?"

Mr. Japhet averted his eyes. "Yes."

"Was it because you lied in your application?"

"I was never told."

"You told this court under oath you had never been to Ireland. You told the State Department under oath that you had. On which occasion did you lie under oath?"

"The family is part Irish, I've always wanted to go to Ireland, and so I put it down, I don't know why. It was a silly mistake. It wasn't a serious matter."

"It was serious enough for the State Department to deny you employment, wasn't it?"

Terence looked at Josephine. He had told her that he had withdrawn his application, that he changed his mind. It was all so foolish. He felt his eyes filling and prayed to control it.

"Mr. Japhet, you are a teacher of children by profession?"

"Yes."

"Would you condone cheating on an examination?"

"No."

"Do you therefore apply a double standard, one for yourself and one for your pupils?"

Judge Brumbacher did not want to see a grown man cry. "You do not have to answer that question, Mr. Japhet," he said.

"All right," said Thomassy. "Mr. Japhet, on direct examination you alluded to an extortion racket in the school. Have you ever seen the defendant or anyone else extort money from a student in school?"

"No."

"You heard about it?"

"Yes."

"That is called hearsay, Mr. Japhet."

"Most of human knowledge is hearsay, Mr. Thomassy!"

"Your Honor, we've had enough philosophizing. I move that this last remark and all previous comments by the witness with regard to extortion and war be stricken from the record."

"You asked the question about extortion, Mr. Thomassy. I'm going to let it stand."

"Very well." Thomassy went over to the jury box to get their attention, and then turned his back to the jury and asked the next question across the space between himself and the witness box. "Mr. Japhet, do you consider yourself hostile to the defendant?"

There was a long silence.

Finally he said, "Yes."

Thomassy turned to the jury when he said, "Thank you." He put his hands in his pockets as he came back to the box.

He spoke more quietly now. "Mr. Japhet, if someone pointed a loaded gun at you, would you consider that to be assault with a deadly weapon?"

"I'm afraid I'm not conversant with the meaning of such things, the technical meanings under the law."

"Never mind, we're just interested in what you think as a lay witness."

"Well, that would be assault, yes."

"If you saw someone pull out a switchblade knife and hold it by your son's throat, would you consider that assault with a deadly weapon?"

"Of course."

"Well, what happened that evening after the dance, what more closely describes what happened, an assault with a deadly weapon with intent to harm, or a fight between schoolkids?"

Silence. Then, "It wasn't just a fight between kids."

Thomassy gave Japhet a withering look, then turned to the jury and said "Thank you" again.

"Mr. Japhet, did your son fight back when he was al-legedly attacked?"

"Yes."

"But you didn't say so in your testimony, did you? You gave this jury a one-sided report, did you not? Mr. Japhet, did the defendant actually strike you?"

"No."

"Did you strike the defendant? Did you beat the de-fendant on the back?"

"I said so."

"Did you pull his hair?"

"I said so. My son was in peril of his life!"

"Does your son ever have fist fights with other boys?"

"I don't think so. This is the only one I know of."

"You mean the night of the prom?"

"Yes."

"Thank you, Mr. Japhet."

On redirect, Cantor asked only two questions.

"Did you actually see the defendant strike your son with a chain?"

"Yes."

"Did you at that moment believe your son to be in danger of his life?"

"Yes."

"Thank you."

Judge Brumbacher recessed the court till two P.M.

Mrs. Japhet asked her husband if he wanted to have lunch at Delorio's, a restaurant nearby they had eaten at once or twice before.

"I'd like to go home," he said. "My shirt's soaking."

"You want to see Ed, don't you?"

"Yes."

She put her arm through his. It was a small comfort.

# Chapter 27

ON ARRIVING HOME, Mr. Japhet immediately removed his jacket, undid his tie, and started to unbutton his shirt. They had to make time. Ed was on the hall phone, saying, "They've just come in." He held the phone up over his head and said, "He wants to talk to my mother or my father. Anybody here by that name?"

Terence and Josephine Japhet stared at the upraised receiver.

"You take it," said Mr. Japhet, bolting up the stairs.

Mrs. Japhet heard a few sentences from Mr. Cantor and excused herself. "Terence," she shouted up the stairs, "you'd better talk to him."

"Tell Ed to put a tie on. Who is it?"

"The district attorney."

"I'll take it on the extension. Tell him to wait a minute."

Mr. Japhet was sponging his armpits with a washcloth when Mrs. Japhet came in the bathroom door and said, "He sounds apoplectic." Mr. Japhet dried himself hurriedly and slipped a fresh shirt around his shoulders before picking up the extension. "Sorry," he said.

The delay had obviously given Cantor some moments to compose himself. "I didn't mean to upset your wife," he said, "but I've just been on the phone with Edward for nearly fifteen minutes. Can you bring him down to White Plains by two o'clock, and I'll try to arrange for a meeting in judge's chambers."

"We haven't eaten. What's the problem?"

"I thought you knew."

"Knew what?"

"Your son refuses to testify."

A moment's pause.

"Of course," Cantor continued, "we could subpoena him, but it wouldn't look right."

"We'll be down."

"Come directly to Judge Brumbacher's chambers. Take the elevator to the fourth floor."

"All right."

When he came down the stairs, Ed was waiting for him.

"Josephine, we'll have to bolt milk and something instead of lunch. Ed, we're going down to White Plains."

"I'm not going to change my mind, Dad."

"I'm not going to try to persuade you to do anything you don't want to do."

"You mean that?"

"I mean it."

Ed managed three doughnuts and two glasses of milk in the time it took Mr. Japhet, standing up, to down one glass.

"I don't know how you do that," said Mrs. Japhet.

"Dad," said Ed, "I heard you were terrific this morning."

"Who from?"

There was the merest nuance of a smile on Mrs. Japhet's lips as she watched the two men adjusting their ties.

Judge Brumbacher, Thomassy, Cantor, and the court reporter were in the room when they arrived. The judge said

it was all right for Mrs. Japhet to stay. "This is very informal," he said, as he beckoned them to take seats around the
conference table. "Mr. Cantor and Mr. Thomassy are both
anxious for Edward to testify, for different reasons. I haven't
asked them if they would subpoena him if he refused to
testify voluntarily, but I think I would grant such a subpoena, since Edward is in fact the only eyewitness to what
happened on the second alleged assault in the hospital." He
turned to Ed. "Well?"

The paneled room was imposing. The circle of adult faces
added to Ed's discomfort. His hands, under the table, were
clasped.

"I've thought about it a lot," he said. "I really don't want
to testify."

"Son," said the judge, "I realize you're only recently out of
the hospital. You've had a trying time. Hopefully, these procedures will be short, and then it will all be over. All that is
wanted is for you to tell us under oath what happened on
the night of the school prom and what happened in the
hospital. You can be as brief as you like."

"Your Honor," said Cantor, "the people would be served if
the young man would testify to everything he remembered
about those two occasions in the greatest of detail."

Judge Brumbacher looked annoyed. "I'm trying to help
you get a witness on the stand. Don't complicate matters.
Mr. Thomassy, I assume you will want to cross-examine?"

"Yes."

"Can you keep it simple?"

"Your Honor, I wouldn't want my hands to be tied by
promises made in this room. The boy is going to testify
either voluntarily or under subpoena from the prosecution
or under subpoena from me, and the sooner he realizes that,
the better."

"I'm sorry," Ed said. "I really don't want to cause any
trouble. It's just that I've made up my mind."

Judge Brumbacher came around to Ed's side of the table,

touched the boy's shoulder briefly, realized it was an inappropriately paternal gesture, and walked completely around the table to resume his seat, speaking finally in the softest voice he could summon.

"Young man, may I explain what testimony is? Your father here is a teacher. Well, to testify is to teach, to tell what happened, to give your personal, truthful knowledge of events perhaps known only to you, so that others, the court, the people on the jury, will be able to learn what went on. There's nothing wrong with teaching, is there?"

"No, sir."

"Good. You will testify, then?"

"No, sir."

"Please understand, young man, that if it becomes necessary to subpoena your presence, and you still refuse to testify, I will have no alternative but to declare you to be in contempt of court."

Mrs. Japhet made a sound. The judge held a finger to his lips, waiting for Ed's response.

"Sir, there's no contempt involved, really. I listened to the lawyers in the other court. I don't understand all the legalisms and the objections and all that. I just don't want to play the game."

"Mr. Japhet," said Judge Brumbacher to the father, "would you like to talk to your son privately and explain the seriousness of this matter, that it is not in any sense a game."

"I think he—"

Ed cut his father off. "I know it's serious. I was the one who got hurt."

Judge Brumbacher was losing his patience. "You did cooperate in giving information to the police when they questioned you, it's all in the report, what harm is there in repeating that? It's so much better for the jury to hear what happened from your own mouth so that they can evaluate what you say."

"Sir, it's just that I know what will happen."

"What?"

"Well, one of these men is going to ask me questions in a way to prove that Urek did it, and the other one's going to ask in a way to prove he didn't, or didn't mean it. I *know* he did it, and he meant it. I just don't want to go through this bit. It's got nothing to do with—"

"Mr. and Mrs. Japhet," cut in the judge, "would you both take Edward into the courtroom? I want to discuss this matter with the attorneys."

The judge, Thomassy, and Cantor watched them go out the door. As soon as it closed, Cantor rattled away at the judge, who silenced him with an upraised hand.

"Gentlemen, I'm as upset as you are, though doubtless for different reasons. Cantor, you won't want to put him on now. With his attitude, he'll blow your case. Thomassy, you never wanted him on. I'm sure both of you will accomplish everything you wanted to in your summations. Let's get on with it. You'll have to work around the boy's testimony."

# Chapter 28

CANTOR PREFERRED to have his discussions with Bob Ferlinger out of earshot of other members of the D.A.'s staff. The empty office on the third floor was perfect. It had a plain table and one straight-backed chair, which was fine, because Cantor preferred to stride about while thinking. In the corner near the window there was a filing cabinet, all four drawers missing. The window itself had half a curtain. Where the other half had gone, only the Lord knew; it was missing the first time they met in that office. This was the fourth.

"Okay," said Cantor, closing the door. "You sit, I'll stand."

"Anything you say, O Tall One," said Ferlinger, putting his feet up on the table.

Ferlinger's impertinence bothered Cantor for practical reasons. It didn't hurt his ego. It was just that if he couldn't command the respect of a kid like Ferlinger, how the hell was he going to impress the electorate?

"You can't wait to try a case yourself, can you, cheeky?"

"Anytime you say."

"How about now?"

"What do you mean?"

"Who would *you* call next?"

"I thought we're having the school custodian."

"I mean after him."

Ferlinger removed his legs from the table. Was Cantor serious?

"Well?"

"I'm thinking."

"You're not going to score high marks in a courtroom with intermissions while you're thinking."

"I know who you ought to call if you had the guts."

"Oh?"

"The Scarlatti kid."

"Go on."

"Get him to cop a plea. Something like disorderly conduct. Anything. But get him to tell how Urek did the damage. That's all you'd need. The jury'd eat it up."

"Anything else?"

"Don't you think it's a good idea?"

Cantor laughed. "There's no charge against Scarlatti. Why would he testify against his pal? He'd be dead in school. His gang wouldn't have him, the other kids wouldn't have him, nobody loves a snitcher, he's got nothing to gain. You get an A for 'effort.' Next idea."

A muscle twitched in Ferlinger's cheek, as he looked at his notes. "How about the Japhet kid's girl friend, Lila what's-her-name? She's not related to the victim, she got attacked herself, she's an eyewitness, and she's a pretty girl."

"Why not?" said Cantor.

"Yes, why not?" said Ferlinger confidently.

"I'll tell you why not, you sixth grade moron. On cross-examination it'll turn out she only got her hair pulled, which will help Thomassy establish his point about the whole thing being trivial. You don't want hair-pulling in a felony case. Besides, she's Japhet's girl friend. A juror in his right mind would assume that she would testify against anybody that hurt her boyfriend—it's the loyal feminine thing to do. And have you looked closely at the jury? There's not a handsome face among them. They'd resent her prettiness."

"You mean there's nothing to be gained by calling her?" said Ferlinger.

"Oh, something. Thomassy'd probably beat her up on cross, but we're not going to win this case on Thomassy being the bad guy. Any more ideas?"

"That psychiatrist we got a line on interviewed both of them. We could get him to testify that Urek is perfectly sane and knew exactly what he was doing."

"Yeah."

"Yeah what?"

"Have you ever had a psychiatrist on the stand? No, you haven't had anybody on the stand. That's a can of peas you don't want to open unless you can control it one hundred percent. Most psychiatrists don't think anybody is really personally guilty of anything bad—at least, they make it sound like that to a jury. Any more brilliant ideas?"

"You seem to have thought of everything."

"Yeah."

"Except."

"Except what?"

"How to win this case."

Cantor stretched his arms above his head. He'd have loved to let one of his long arms sweep down across Ferlinger's fat face.

"Don't," said Ferlinger.

"Don't what?"

"Don't take a poke at me without a weapon in your hand. It's essential for a felony conviction."

"Is that a hint?"

"It's two hints. One for you. One for the case. What was it you said you told your wife?"

"I told her we'd get a conviction."

"Are you going to tell her something different tonight?"

"The case isn't over yet. Look, Urek did it, didn't he?"

"Yeah, you, God, and I know it, but we're not on the jury. That's what Thomassy is working on, convincing the jury. You know what he's doing right this minute? He's with Urek in the cell downstairs."

"So what?"

"He's been with him ever since the meeting with Brumbacher. You don't think he needs all that time just to cheer him up?"

"What are you driving at?"

Ferlinger looked at his fingernails as if deciding whether to file them. "I think Thomassy's going to let the kid take the stand."

"He wouldn't dare."

"I'll bet they're rehearsing it right now."

"The son of a bitch wouldn't dare."

"I'll tell you why he would," said Ferlinger, rising. "You're always yapping about the crucial determinant in a case. Well, the crucial determinant in this case is that Thomassy is smarter than you are."

The custodian seemed too old a man to hold down a full-time job. He walked to the stand in an irregular shuffle, and when Cantor nodded for him to sit down, he held his hands down on the chair and lowered himself onto it slowly and seemingly with pain. His face was deeply lined, and his hair, which was brown and gray, was in a strange crew cut, shaved to a stubble around the sides, the two inches on top pointing straight up.

"Please state your name," said Cantor, all gentleness.

"Felix Gómez."

The stenographer asked him to spell the name. The janitor shook his head. He couldn't spell it.

"Just put it down phonetically right now," said Judge

Brumbacher. "We'll get the spelling from his employment records later."

"Sir," said Cantor to the old man, "are you the janitor at Ossining High School?"

"Custodian," said the old man with dignity.

"How long have you been custodian?"

The old man shrugged his shoulders. "Five years, ten years, something like that."

Cantor looked at the judge. Brumbacher indicated he should let it pass.

"What happened on the night of the dance, after the dance?"

"Lots of clean-up in the morning."

"No, what happened that night?"

"Like we talk about in your office?"

Cantor's blush was visible. "Yes."

"I hear shout, yell, noise. I get flashlight, I go to front door, snowing cold outside, I see trouble, I call police."

"Can you identify any of the people you saw that night out there?"

"You mean, the people out front?"

"Yes."

"Sure. I see Mr. Japhet, schoolteacher, and him." He pointed to Urek at the defense table. "He did it."

"He did what?"

"He choke the kid, why else police get him, why else he here?"

Thomassy stood to object.

Judge Brumbacher leaned over toward the witness. "Mr. Gómez, did you see anyone besides Mr. Japhet out there in front of the school that night?"

"Girl."

"Can you identify the girl?" asked the judge.

"Just girl."

Cantor, anxious to keep the line of questioning in his own

hands, asked, "Did you see the defendant, Urek, in front of the school?"

"He break windows."

"When?"

"Lots of times."

"Did he break windows that night?"

"I think no."

"Did you see Urek in front of the school when you came out with your flashlight?"

"Lots of snow, bad snow."

Cantor's voice rose. "Did you see Urek?"

The janitor paused, his hands crossed in front of his chest. "I think," he said finally.

"You think what, sir?"

The janitor smiled at being called "sir" again. "I think I see." He pointed to Urek.

"Thank you," said Cantor.

The old man got up to leave, but Cantor motioned him back down.

"Your witness," said Cantor.

Thomassy looked, for a moment, as if he might waive cross-examination. Then he approached the stand. He came very close to the janitor.

"Who are you?" asked Gómez. Everyone in the courtroom laughed. Even the judge had a hard time stifling a guffaw.

Thomassy smiled. "I'm the defense counsel, Mr. Gómez. I have a few questions to ask you."

"I already answer."

"These are different questions."

"I guess okay." He began to like being the center of so much attention.

"Do you drink whiskey on the job?"

"What you mean, I never drink whiskey."

"Please answer the question yes or no."

"I answer truth, like I swore."

"What, in truth, do you drink, besides water?"

Gómez smiled weakly. "Thunderbird."

"For the edification of the jury," said Thomassy, returning to his table and withdrawing a bottle from the suitcase underneath, "is this what you drink?" He brought the bottle over to within twelve inches of the witness's face. Gómez instinctively reached for the bottle, which Thomassy withdrew, to the sound of laughter.

Brumbacher rapped his gavel.

"Did you have any of this to drink on the day of the prom?"

"I guess."

"Don't you know?"

"I guess because I have some every day." Gómez looked embarrassed, wondering whether he had made a mistake.

Quickly Thomassy asked, "Do you have a gallon every day?"

Gómez was furious. "No, never, maybe one, two bottles most."

"Only one bottle in the morning?"

"Half."

"And?"

Cantor interrupted angrily. "Will the judge remind defense counsel that 'and' is not a question?"

"Thank you," said Thomassy to Cantor. "Mr. Gómez, do you have the other half with lunch?"

"Sure."

"Mr. Gómez, do you have another bottle in the afternoon, every afternoon?"

"Students never see me. In the basement. By myself! I swear!"

"Do you have another half with dinner?"

Cantor had not sat down. "Would defense counsel like me to produce an adding machine?"

"Now, your Honor, that wasn't called for," said Thomassy. "I am merely trying to establish the obvious, that the witness is a chronic alcoholic whose consumption of wine is prodigious and who probably consumed nearly a gallon by the time the events of that evening transpired."

"Lies!" yelled Gómez, standing. "You try lose me my job! Lies!"

"I have no further questions," said Thomassy, leaving Gómez grasping the railing, his eyes like weak searchlights peering into every part of the room to find a friendly face.

Judge Brumbacher asked the sheriff's deputy to help the witness from the room.

Cantor asked for a meeting at the bench. In hushed tones, glaring at Thomassy, he told the judge, "Your Honor, I am appalled by Mr. Thomassy's treatment of the last witness."

"You are a young man," said Brumbacher. "I am usually appalled by the processes of justice."

"But, your Honor, it isn't necessary—"

Brumbacher was stern. "This is an adversary system. Counselor, we're waiting for you to call your next witness."

Cantor, his head turned, addressed himself to the stenographer only. "The prosecution rests," he said.

Thomassy immediately came in with, "Your Honor, I move to dismiss on the grounds that the People have failed to—"

The judge cut him off. He dismissed the jury. It seemed to take a long time to get them out of the courtroom. Then, as Thomassy started to repeat his motion to dismiss, Judge Brumbacher cut in. "Yes, yes, your motion is noted, and decision is reserved. However, Mr. Thomassy, I will dismiss, and withdraw from the consideration of the jury, the count related to the incident at Phelps Memorial, because"—he lowered his voice so that only the two lawyers could hear him—"the People haven't proved Urek was in that room at the hospital. Thomassy, you know he was there, I know he was there, he knows he was there, but the jury doesn't know, and Cantor can't prove it to them."

The judge impatiently ordered the jury brought back in.

As they were taking their seats, he said to Thomassy, "Let's finish soon if we can. Will you call your first witness."

"Your Honor," said Thomassy, his voice now raised so that the jury could hear him, "I will call the defendant, Stanley Urek, to testify in his own behalf."

That night, at dinner, Judge Brumbacher said to his wife, "Irene, I've been thinking of New Mexico."

"What happened today?"

"I don't see why I shouldn't think of retiring."

"What will you do?"

"I don't know." The judge sighed. "I guess that's the point."

Ed got Lila on the phone at last. "Urek's going to testify tomorrow," he said.

"I heard. It's all over town."

"Are you going?"

"I can't cut school."

"Lila?"

"Yes?"

"You know, I didn't testify."

"I heard that, too. I admired that."

"My father was absolutely great in court."

"I heard."

"I hope we see each other again soon."

"Thanks for calling, Ed. Good luck."

He wondered for a long time afterward whether she meant anything special by that.

The following morning, when the three Japhets came into court together, they sat down in the last row. Then Ed noticed Mr. and Mrs. Urek just two places down. He nudged his father. They moved as inobtrusively as possible to the other side of the courtroom and slid into seats against the far wall.

Ed watched as if it were a play. The court attendant, a woman in a blue uniform, sonorously intoned, "Hear ye, hear ye, hear ye, this County Court Party Two of the County of Westchester is now in session, Honorable Wilton Brumbacher, County Judge, presiding. All persons having business with this Honorable Court come forward and give attention and they shall be heard. Please stand."

The black-robed judge entered, and at once the two lawyers were conferring with him at the bench. Then Ed saw Urek, his hair slicked down, wearing a suit and tie, take the witness chair and raise his right hand, his left atop a Bible, and say, "I do."

Thomassy looked like a man who had had a great night's sleep. He bristled with controlled energy and smiled at everyone, including Cantor and Ferlinger. He put out his left hand, then his right, then brought them together as he turned to Urek with the first question.

"Have you been a student at Ossining High School for the last two years?"

"Yes, sir."

"Have you ever been failed in any course?"

"No, sir."

"Have you ever owned or driven a motorcycle?"

"No, sir."

"Have you ever smoked marihuana?"

It was Judge Brumbacher who stopped the proceeding. "Mr. Thomassy, a witness testifying under oath is not immune to charges arising out of his testimony. An affirmative answer to the question you have just asked might be incriminating. Does the witness understand that?"

"I don't want to speak for the witness, your Honor." He turned to Urek. "Do you know that using marihuana is illegal?"

"Yes, sir."

"Have you ever used it?"

"No, sir."

"Have you ever used, bought, or sold LSD, heroin, amphetamines, or barbiturates?"

"No, sir."

"How did you get the scar on your face?"

"I fell off my bike."

Cantor raised himself to his full height, objecting. "Your Honor, the jury is here to evaluate facts, and I just don't see where the present line of questioning is helpful in determining the guilt of the defendant."

"Your Honor," said Thomassy, "I think the district attorney meant to say the guilt or innocence of the defendant. The point, of course, is that the questions directly relevant to the charges have to be seen by the jury in context, and in this case the context is the character and background of the accused. It is common to suppose that a scar on the face or body of a black man or someone belonging to some other ethnic groups might be the result of a knife fight or some similar form of violence." Thomassy read the face of the Negro woman in the jury box. He had made his point successfully. "I am, your Honor, clarifying the origin of a prominent scar on the defendant's face in order to eliminate the unfortunate but common substitution of prejudice for objective judgment. May I continue?"

Brumbacher nodded. Cantor remained on his feet.

"Did you have something to add, Mr. Cantor, or will you wait your turn?"

Cantor sat down.

"Did you buy a ticket to the prom?"

"Yes, sir."

"Did you go with several friends?"

"Yes, sir."

"Were the friends you went with all students at Ossining High School?"

"Yes, sir."

"Did you dance?"

"No, sir."

"Would you explain that?"

"I don't dance."

"Well, don't be embarrassed, neither do I."

There was a friendly chuckle among the spectators. *Son of a bitch*, thought Cantor, busily scratching notes.

"Did you watch the magic show that night?"

"Yes, sir."

"Did you enjoy it?"

"Yes, sir."

"Did you have a fight later that evening?"

Urek paused only a split second. "Yes, sir."

"What caused that fight? Just take your time and explain it in your own words."

"It was snowing, see?"

"Yes, go on."

"After the prom, me and my friends were waiting for a lift in front of the building. It was very cold, see? There was only this one car left, so we refuged in it."

"You what?"

"Oh. We took refuge in it so's we wouldn't freeze while we were waiting. We didn't figure whatever adult owned the car would mind. We weren't driving it anywhere, just sitting."

"Did anyone object to your sitting in the car?"

"Yes, sir."

"Who?"

"Mr. Japhet."

"Did you ever have Mr. Japhet as a teacher?"

"Yes, sir."

"Did Mr. Japhet seem to recognize you?"

"Yes, sir. He said to get out of the car."

"Was there any other car you could have used for refuge while you were waiting?"

"No."

"Why didn't you go back into the building while you were waiting?"

"Well, we didn't know which of our fathers was coming for sure, and we didn't want to miss, see? If our ride came and didn't see no one, it might have left, figuring we already got a ride, and we'd be stuck there."

"Was Mr. Japhet alone when he ordered you out of his car?"

"No, there was his son, the one that did the magic show, and the girl he was smooching until Mr. Japhet came."

"How did you react when you were ordered out of your shelter?"

"I was mad, but I was gonna help him with the suitcases anyway. They was carrying these two suitcases, see, and I figured if I helped them with the suitcases, maybe they would offer us a ride if our ride didn't come by then."

"Then what happened?"

"Mr. Japhet said to put the suitcases down."

"And then?"

"The girl called me a Polack."

"Have you ever been called that before?"

"No. Besides, I'm not Polish, I'm a Slovak."

"What did you do?"

"I pulled her hair."

"What else?"

"Maybe I twisted her arm some."

"Are you sorry you did that?"

"Sure, but she didn't say she was sorry she called me what she called me."

"Then what happened?"

"Well, the Japhet kid grabbed me. I wasn't going to let him grab me in front of my friends without doing something about it, so I hit him, and that's how the fight started."

Mr. Japhet put his hand on Ed's arm. Ed had put his head down on his crossed arms on the back of the bench in front of him.

"Then what happened? Take your time."

"Mr. Japhet jumped me."

"Had you hit Mr. Japhet?"

"I never hit a teacher in my life."

"What did Mr. Japhet do?"

"He beat me with his fists, and he pulled my hair."

"Did you hit him back?"

"No, sir."

"Did you intend to kill Ed Japhet?"

Urek didn't answer.

Thomassy repeated the question. "Did you intend to kill Ed Japhet?"

"I never intended to kill nobody ever in my life, I swear!"

"Did you have a chain?"

"Yes, sir."

"Where did you get the chain?"

"I found it outside the school."

"What did you do with the chain?"

Urek looked down.

"It's better to tell everything. What did you do with the chain?"

"I hit the windshield of the car—he wouldn't let us stay out of the snow!"

"Did you break the windshield?"

"It broke. I didn't think it would, but it did."

"Are you sorry you broke the windshield?"

"It's insured."

"Are you sorry you broke the windshield?"

"Yes, sir."

"If the insurance had a deductible, would you be willing to pay the deductible?"

"Yes, sir, I promise."

"Did you go to the Ossining High School prom for the purpose of doing harm to Edward Japhet?"

"No, sir."

"You swear to that?"

"I swear it's the truth."

"Your witness," said Thomassy.

Cantor's first question was, "Did you ever kill an animal?"

In a second Thomassy was on his feet and striding toward the bench, his face full of fury. "Your Honor, there was nothing in direct examination about harming animals. The subject of this trial is, did the defendant harm a human being, and I have already asked that question, but if Mr. Cantor is hard of hearing, he's perfectly free to ask the question again."

Judge Brumbacher, who had had some misgivings about letting young Japhet get away without testifying, now felt that his tolerance should bathe the other side. He said to Cantor, "I think you should confine your questioning to matters raised on direct examination."

Thomassy, satisfied, sat down.

Cantor shifted gears, and began again.

"The chain you said you found, did you find it on top of the snow, or underneath the snow?"

Urek did not reply.

"Will your Honor please direct the witness to answer the question?"

"I'm only supposed to answer him yes or no," said Urek pleadingly.

"Did you find the chain on top of the snow?"

"No."

"Did you find it underneath the snow?"

"I just found it."

"Where?"

"Where it was lying."

"Did you hit Ed Japhet with the chain?"

"I hit him with my hand."

"Was the chain in your hand at the time?"

"I don't remember."

"Do you remember choking Ed Japhet?"

"No."

"How do you account for the severe throat injuries he got?"

"We were fighting."

"How do you account—"

"Objection! The witness is not a physician."

"Objection sustained."

"If Mr. Japhet hadn't pounded your back and pulled you by your hair, would you have gone on choking Ed Japhet until he was dead?"

Thomassy didn't have to object. Judge Brumbacher cautioned Cantor, "Would the attorney for the People please try to ask questions the witness can answer?"

"Did you charge students twenty-five cents a month for protection of their lockers at the school?"

"I'm sorry," interjected Thomassy, "but that subject was not covered on direct examination."

"Your Honor," said Cantor, "direct testimony has attempted to paint the defendant as a young man who never did anything wrong in his life, and I'm entitled to go into this."

Judge Brumbacher called both attorneys to the bench. "Mr. Cantor can pursue the question if he is attacking the credibility of the witness. Objection overruled."

Thomassy closed his eyes to let a moment of time pass. He hoped Urek would not be caught in a lie.

Cantor repeated the question. "Did you charge students twenty-five cents a month for protection of their lockers at the school?"

Urek looked over at Thomassy. He thought he saw the barest nod.

"Yes, sir," said Urek.

"Was this a duty assigned to you by the school?"

"No, sir."

"You set yourself up in business on your own?"

Thomassy objected.

"Sustained," said the judge. "Please rephrase."

"Let's just strike it," said Cantor, then asked, "What happened if any student refused to subscribe to your protection service?"

"They all paid."

"All?" shot in Cantor.

Urek looked at Thomassy, but couldn't detect a signal. "Japhet didn't pay."

"Did you threaten Japhet for not paying, did you say that something would happen to him or his belongings if he didn't pay?"

"No, sir, I never threatened nobody."

The judge was getting impatient with Cantor. "Could we please get back to the night of the alleged offense? The present line of questioning isn't going to get us finished today."

Cantor began to feel a sense of deep despair. "You said on the night of the prom that you got into Mr. Japhet's car because you were waiting to get a ride home, is that correct?"

"Yes."

"Did you ever get your ride home from the prom?"

"We walked."

"Wasn't that what you intended to do in the first place?"

"In the snow?"

"Was it your father that was supposed to come pick you up?"

"One of them was supposed to, I don't remember which. They sometimes forget."

"If I got every one of your parents to the witness stand and asked them if they were supposed to pick you up that night—"

"Mr. Cantor," said the judge, "I cautioned you earlier."

"I withdraw the question. Your Honor, frankly, I'm feeling terribly frustrated. The eyewitnesses, the Japhet boy, his girl friend Lila Hurst, the nurse Ginsler, these are all people who should have testified or been made to testify . . ."

"Mr. Cantor," said Brumbacher quietly to the two lawyers, "one cannot retry cases from a different vantage point, except on appeal. Hindsight is of value to us all, and I do understand your present frustrations, but may I tell you that out of my long experience, the most telling effect on the jury is the organization of the testimony in the summations, and you have your summations before you. Each case cannot be argued to perfection. Do the best that you can by the rules that govern."

Cantor tried one last question.

"I remind you that you are under oath and that you must tell the truth on pain of perjury. That means that if you lie to the court, you can be sent to jail for lying, whatever the outcome of the present charges. Now, did you attack Edward Japhet after the prom and cause him great bodily harm, yes or no?"

"Don't answer that question!" shouted Thomassy; then, with every eye on him, said, "I'm sorry I shouted, your Honor, but if the defendant had answered the question as asked, I would have had to argue for a mistrial, and I'm sure we all want to avoid that. If a witness knowingly lies, the court can consider perjury charges. Mr. Cantor made it seem as if there's some kind of automatic jail sentence. This is no way to threaten a sixteen-year-old witness who feels himself guiltless to the point of being willing to put himself on the witness stand and testify under oath. If Mr. Cantor wants some help in framing a question . . ."

"I don't need help," said Cantor. "I'd also like to avoid hindrance, your Honor."

"Proceed."

"Did you attack Edward Japhet after the prom and cause him great bodily harm, answer yes or no?"

Urek closed his eyes.

"Did you attack Edward Japhet after the prom, yes or no?"

"No," said Urek.

"No more questions," said Cantor, hating whatever Ferlinger would say to him as soon as they were alone.

"The defense rests," said Thomassy.

Judge Brumbacher instructed them both that summations would begin promptly at two P.M.

# Chapter 29

THE JAPHETS walked over to Howard Johnson's for their lunch, which began in silence.

The clam chowder came. By the time his mother and father had finished theirs, Ed had had only a spoonful or two. Still, they said nothing.

Finally, when the fried clams were before them, Ed said, "You know, the tricks I do, it's all psychology."

They looked up, puzzled.

"What I mean is, the hand isn't quicker than the eye. It's just that people want to be fooled. You help them by misdirecting their attention. They don't notice what you're really doing, because they don't want to. Most people could figure out most tricks if they really tried. Anyway, I've made up my mind."

"About what?"

"I'm going to give the tricks I still have to the Salvation Army or something."

"Why don't you take time to think it over carefully?" said his mother.

Ed picked away at the clams. "I have, Mom. Don't look

like that. Magic is nothing compared to what we saw today."

"You're upset," said his mother.

"Oh, Mom, you always think that. Dad, answer one question honestly. Who's worse, Thomassy or Urek?"

Neither Mr. nor Mrs. Japhet said anything.

"I thought Thomassy was the real star of this thing. I kind of admire the way he works. The only thing I really worry about is what happens if Urek gets off. You'll have to hire a bodyguard for me, Dad," he said, trying to laugh, "or move somewhere else."

"Let's not even think of that," said Mrs. Japhet. "The facts are so clear."

"Women," said Mr. Japhet, "live by hope."

"The facts have very little to do with it, right, Dad?"

Mr. Japhet sounded tired. "Josephine?"

"You're about to deliver a lecture."

"Not really. I was just thinking how glad I am I teach biology and not social studies."

"Ed," said Mrs. Japhet, "your father is prepared for you to be a cynic at sixteen."

Ed said nothing.

Thomassy went over to the jury box to begin his summation.

"I wonder if you and I couldn't talk this thing out," he said, aware that the judge could barely hear him and many of the spectators probably could not. He didn't mind if everyone but the jury had to strain to hear him.

"My own background is in civil liberties. I wouldn't have taken on this case if I didn't think our laws were served by defending people where there is the slightest smidgen of doubt about what went on.

"I sympathize with you. You've heard a lot of confusing things. Let's try to unsnarl what's happened. Let's see what's been proved.

"First off, I don't want to hear any more about what went

on in any school locker room. Nothing that ever went on in any locker room is on trial here.

"Now, what about the prosecution's eyewitnesses? There's the father, Mr. Japhet. I can understand his being in a blind rage if his kid is getting beaten in a fight. I can even understand his attacking young Urek, but that doesn't make him a good witness. You heard him. He lied under oath. And that wasn't even to protect his son's interests. Here he has testified as a highly interested party. Maybe you'd do the same for your son. Maybe not.

"Okay, who else is an eyewitness? The prosecution comes up with the janitor, an old man. I feel sorry for him. He drinks all the time. He was drinking all day before these events happened. He doesn't even know if he's been at his present job for five or ten years. Imagine that? Not very reliable, I'd say.

"Who else? The doctor. On recross he admitted that Edward Japhet was admitted to the intensive-care unit for diagnostic purposes.

"Who else?

"No one else.

"Let's talk a minute about this so-called deadly weapon. That's important, because the only thing—I repeat, the only thing—that brought this case into this courtroom rather than being heard as a simple misdemeanor by a lower court is the allegation that a deadly weapon was used. Well, what did the boy supposedly do with the bicycle chain? Did he wrap it around Japhet's throat? Nobody said so. Did he lower it down Japhet's throat? Nobody said so. Yet Japhet's throat is where the injuries were. You see how easy it is to be confused about such things. In actual fact, the chain was used in the destruction of property worth about a hundred and seventy-five dollars, most of which is covered by insurance, and I ask you, are you going to convict someone of a felony, a major crime, and send him to jail over a bit of property destruction like that?"

Thomassy moved to the other side of the jury box, followed by a turn in every head in the room.

"We don't like kids to fight. But they always have. We can't send every kid who gets in a fight to jail, can we?

"Now, in our courts we don't usually go into the question of age. It's a politeness we have. After all, if a woman is accused of something or other, you don't want her to be punished twice, first by revealing her age. Age usually doesn't matter all that much. But during the course of this trial, the district attorney's man here has tried to make sixteen sound like sixty. Those of you who are parents know that no sixteen-year-old is a mature adult, that in fact when a boy is sixteen he still doesn't have all his parts in place, because he's still in the process of not only growing, but growing up. The defendant, Urek, is not your son, but he's somebody else's son, and while you are not responsible for his actions the way you might feel if he were your son, you are responsible for keeping an adult perspective on what happened between these two sixteen-year-olds.

"There's been a lot of talk here about whether or not the injuries to the Japhet boy were serious. Well, if they were really all that serious, would the Japhet boy be sitting in this courtroom right now, as he is, right there, along the wall? He looks normal to me. He certainly wasn't brought in here on a stretcher. What's done is done, but I have a question about what wasn't done. He was an eyewitness. Why did he not testify? Stanley Urek wasn't afraid to testify. Why did the Japhet boy refuse to testify to the truth, the whole truth, and nothing but the truth? Yet now he sits in this courtroom, not to tell us what happened—oh, no, he sits there to enjoy his revenge!

"Well, that is not in his power, it is in your power. Which brings me to the crucial point. The charge is that the defendant did knowingly and willfully assault the Japhet boy with a deadly instrument with the intent of using such weapon. All of that has had to be proved *to your sole satisfaction beyond a reasonable doubt.*

"The judge will undoubtedly talk to you about reasonable doubt. I think he'd say the same thing I would. If you have any doubt, any reasonable reason for not being one hundred percent sure that the defendant is guilty of the charge as it is worded, the only conclusion you can come to is that this sixteen-year-old boy is not guilty, any more than a child of yours or mine could be if he was involved in similar circumstances.

"Furthermore, under the protections of our system, each of the twelve of you bears an equal responsibility for this boy's fate. You can talk to each other in the jury room, you can try to persuade each other, but vote your own judgment. Vote your own conscience. Don't go along with the others for the sake of harmony. If any one of you is convinced that there's reasonable doubt"—his eyes took in each member of the jury, one at a time—"I know you'll honor your own convictions and nobody else's. You've all got to agree, or there's no verdict, the judge will tell you that.

"Frankly, I don't think you're going to send a sixteen-year-old boy to start a career of crime in a reformatory or a jail because of a fist fight."

Thomassy hated the rules that gave the district attorney the last word. When Cantor got up to give his summation, Thomassy thought he looked angry. That was a good sign. He'd lost his cool.

But when Cantor began to speak, he exuded bounce and confidence. He had changed his tie and put on a dark blue one with a fleur-de-lis design that had always brought him good luck.

"Ladies and gentlemen," Cantor began, "the respected counsel for the defendant has tried ably to minimize this whole affair and make it look like we've all been wasting our time and the county's money on this case. I remind you the

People set out to prove that Stanislaus Urek did willfully commit the crime of first-degree assault upon the persons of Edward Japhet, Lila Hurst, and Mr. Terence Japhet, a schoolteacher, and that he did so with intent to inflict serious physical injury with a dangerous weapon and with depraved indifference to human life. I remind you that the People set out to prove that Stanislaus Urek did so without any justification or provocation, and I believe that the People have so proved beyond a reasonable doubt."

"Your Honor," said Thomassy, "I move for mistrial."

"Now, wait a minute," said Cantor, storming up to the bench; "it is most unusual, your Honor, for counsel to interrupt a summation and—"

"The district attorney," said Thomassy, "has given the jury his own opinion of the case, and this is clear ground for a mistrial, which—"

"Mr. Thomassy, Mr. Cantor," said the judge, looking as if he was about to stand in anger. "We are not going to send the jury out for a mistrial motion on those grounds, and I hope not on any grounds before the summation is finished. We are spending the People's money deliberating here, and I want this case concluded with dispatch."

Judge Brumbacher knew he was flirting with reversible error by shutting Thomassy up, but he took the risk, determined to get the case to the jury that afternoon. He told Cantor, "The court suggests that you refrain from inadvertent reference to your own opinions."

"Yes, your Honor."

"Proceed."

"Well," said Cantor to the jury, as if to stress that the exchange, which meant nothing to them, really was a strike in his favor, "I'm glad we can go on. Let's look at what the eyewitnesses had to tell us.

"Dr. Karp made it clear that the injuries to Edward Japhet's throat were serious. The charge says 'intent to commit serious injury,' and Dr. Karp did so testify. Mr.

Japhet testified to the willful and unprovoked nature of the attack, and made it absolutely clear that a dangerous instrument was used. The first blow struck was with a chain, a chain capable of smashing a car's windshield with a single blow. But it wasn't a windshield it was aimed at first, but" —he pointed directly at Ed sitting back among the spectators—"that boy's face. Look at it. Do we have to wait a year or more to see if the disfigurement is permanent to determine if the injury was serious? The law is designed to protect society from the intentions of people who commit such injuries.

"Stanislaus Urek tried to choke Edward Japhet to death, and Edward Japhet was saved by his father's timely intervention. That was the testimony. The fact that a respected teacher may have fibbed on an employment application long ago—I ask you who hasn't done some such thing somewhere in his life—the fact that he did or did not get to see Ireland doesn't discredit his testimony as to what happened at Ossining High School the night of January twenty-first, does it? It doesn't discredit his testimony, any more than the custodian's drinking habits discredit his.

"He may have seen it double, but he saw enough to run and phone the police. He saw an assault being perpetrated, and that's what we're here to find out.

"What kind of individual are we dealing with here? Does he learn from experience? This defendant—who's involved with a Mafia-like extortion racket in the high school—will not be held back by moral scruple or the police or the law from committing crime after crime after crime. He must be taken off the streets. He must be put away in a correctional institution. If not, I have a great fear.

"I fear for this nation. We hear a lot of nonsense pro and con about law and order. Divorce those terms from the political rhetoric, and what you have is this: the United States is a government of law, not of decree. If we follow the defense counsel and shut our eyes time after time after time to the breaking of the law, we will pay for it dearly. The opposite of living under laws legislated by our representatives is a state in which power alone governs, and might rules. We call that the law of the jungle.

"As we close this case of the People of the State of New York against Stanislaus Urek, I want to say that the interests of the people, which I represent, are indeed your interests, and it is the people of this county who want you to find the defendant, as charged, guilty of assault in the first degree."

A few people in the courtroom began to applaud, and the judge had to gavel them to silence. *Not bad,* thought Brumbacher. *The tall boy did okay.*

"Come on," said Ed to Mr. Japhet, "let's not sit here." But no one was allowed to leave the courtroom while the judge was charging the jury.

Judge Brumbacher's instructions to the jury were meticulous. He defined first-, second-, and third-degree assault, and explained reasonable doubt. The jury was out for less than forty minutes, and returned with a verdict of not guilty.

# Chapter 30

WHEN CANTOR let himself in with the key, his wife looked up from her newspaper.

"You lost," she said. "Thomassy is really good, isn't he?"

Cantor, who had wanted to be President, slapped his wife's face.

Nobody talked about the case in school, not to Ed, anyway. He waited twenty minutes so he could get a ride home with his father. They walked in silence to the car.

Ed flung his strapped books on the seat between them. Mr. Japhet threw the large envelope full of exam papers on the rear seat. He pumped the gas pedal twice. Urek hunched down on the floor behind the seat, held his breath until the ignition caught.

Mr. Japhet let out a long sigh. Ed looked sideways at his father's slack face. "Rough day?"

"It's not the day."

Near their house, they both caught sight of Frank Tennent scraping his front walk with a shovel. Frank waved. They waved back.

Mr. Japhet decided to park at the curb. "I'll be going out later," he said.

He slid out of the seat, slammed the door, then said to Ed, who was just getting out the other side, "Take my exam envelope, will you?"

Ed reached for the large envelope on the back seat. As he did, Urek bolted up from his crouch and grabbed for Ed's throat.

From the sidewalk, Mr. Japhet saw. He couldn't believe, but he saw.

He ran back to the car, throwing the door open. Urek, roaring, had not been able to get a good grip on Ed's throat. Ed was fending him off with an arm, rearing back, slipping from his grasp, then scrambling out the far side of the car, with Urek getting out on the same side and catching Ed by the shoulder just as they were coming around the hood of the car, and Mr. Japhet screamed, "Stop it!"

Frank Tennent was watching from his driveway fifty feet away. "Help!" said Mr. Japhet. "Help us!" Frank put his shovel down and went inside his house.

Mr. Japhet went toward Urek.

"Don't, Dad."

Just as Ed spoke, Urek's arm spun him around. Urek's left fist went for his face. Ed tried to block it with his right arm, not expecting it to work; it worked. Then suddenly Urek plunged at him, his fists hammering, hitting, hurting, Ed trying to remember Mr. Fumoko's advice.

Ed's hands stiffened, ready to chop.

Urek saw.

"Fight fair, you son of a bitch," Urek bellowed, his left fist again striking Ed's upraised arm. Suddenly Urek's right fist came up from below, slamming into Ed's belly, and as Ed instinctively reached down to the pain, Urek's left hit him on the side of the head, dizzying, and then the right fist smashed into his mouth, Mr. Japhet saying, "Oh, no," and then stumbling up the steps into the house, the door open, yelling, "Josephine!" and with no answer, going to the phone and telling the operator, "Quickly, the police!"

Ed stepped back to touch his mouth. Teeth felt loose to his tongue. The tips of his fingers came away red.

Then Urek lunged, butting him with his head. As Ed tried backing away, Urek, puffing hard, came at him with both hands, as if to choke him again.

"You're crazy," blurted Ed.

Suddenly the back of Urek's hand caught his face again, where his mouth hurt, and Ed tried to back off, but Urek's foot was behind him. Ed lost his balance but didn't fall, then suddenly realized that Urek had got his hands around his neck and was squeezing like the other time. Ed knew he mustn't give up. He kicked at Urek's shins, missed, then remembered what to do, and bringing both hands up hard in the middle, between Urek's outstretched arms, he instantly broke Urek's grasp. *Take advantage of surprise.* Ed's open right hand, with as much force as he had ever summoned in his life, chopped down hard on the bridge of Urek's bent nose. Something clearly cracked.

Urek held his face in surprise, then dropped oddly to his knees. He gestured as if he wanted to pull something out of the inside of his head. His eyes weren't focusing. Suddenly Urek vomited blood; a great gush retched, and then a strange trickle of redder blood oozed from his nostrils. A tableau halted, stopped time; then a terrible, sky-cracking shriek from Urek, falling over and writhing, his eyes rolling upward in his head. Ed wanted to stomp on Urek's head in rage, heard his father scream, "Stop!" from the steps.

They both stared down at Stanislaus Urek scrunched in the snow. The mouth fell open to let blood pour.

Frank Tennent came running over. "I saw," he said, "I saw he karate-chopped him."

The police car came fast, skidding to a dead stop just short of the Japhet car. Two cops got out.

The first knelt beside Urek on the ground. He looked up at his partner.

The second cop said, "Where's your phone?" then, "Never mind," and called the ambulance from the police car.

Urek seemed to be having a barely perceptible convulsion. There was nothing to bandage. Nothing to do.

Dr. Karp got out from the seat beside the driver of the ambulance. The driver pulled the vehicle across the road and backed up toward the Japhet driveway, between their car and the police car, blocking the street.

Karp recognized Ed. Then he dropped to his knees without a word and felt gingerly around Urek's nose, put his ear to Urek's chest, then nodded to the driver, who brought out a stretcher. The policeman helped Karp and the driver lift Urek. Something suddenly made Karp look closer. He put his hand on the boy's wrist, then dropped it.

They were all obviously waiting for him to say something, so Karp said, "The bone penetrated the brain, I think."

"Please get him to the hospital fast," said Mr. Japhet.

Karp saw that the shaking man hadn't understood. "This kid's dead."

The two policemen were standing next to Ed. Mr. Japhet said, "He hit Ed first."

"What's your name?" said one of the policemen to Ed.

"What's his name?" said the other policeman, pointing to the form on the stretcher.

Ed didn't answer. It was a dream.

"How old is your boy?" said the policeman.

"Sixteen," whispered Mr. Japhet.

"Sixteen is manslaughter."

"It was self-defense," said Mr. Japhet.

"Sure," said the cop, taking Ed by the elbow toward the patrol car.

"It's cold out here. We'll fill out the forms at the station house."

"I'll have to tell my wife."

"Can you get a lift from the hospital to the station house, doctor?" asked the policeman.

Karp nodded.

"Dad!" said Ed.

Mr. Japhet went inside to phone Thomassy.